MASTERS OF WAR

Heat choked the *Mad Cat*'s cockpit. Alaric struggled to keep his 'Mech on its feet, and managed it by sinking into a crouch. He shifted the feet and started to come back up, but the engine shut down, freezing the 'Mech as if just about to pounce on the Falcon.

Alaric closed his eyes for a moment. To have your 'Mech shut down on the battlefield was the product of taking foolish risks. He accepted that, just as he accepted victory as a confirmation of having made the proper choices. It was not that he didn't believe he could be wrong; he just knew that any error that did not get him killed generated a tale that made him more of an enigma.

The trick is to avoid making the same error twice. He smiled. *Predictability will kill you faster than mistakes.*

Before he attempted to restart his 'Mech, he glanced out the cockpit. His troops had downed the other odd Falcon 'Mech and were mopping up the remains of the Falcon force. Then they would move on to Ogstrenburg and raze it.

To punish the Falcons.

Alaric nodded once, then began the ignition sequence. He would beat them to the city and lay waste to it. *And the stories they will tell of this battle will be grand.*

MECH WARRIOR™
DARK AGE

MASTERS OF WAR

A BATTLETECH™ NOVEL

Michael A. Stackpole

A ROC BOOK

ROC
Published by New American Library, a division of
Penguin Group (USA) Inc., 375 Hudson Street,
New York, New York 10014, USA
Penguin Group (Canada), 90 Eglinton Avenue East, Suite 700, Toronto,
Ontario M4P 2Y3, Canada (a division of Pearson Penguin Canada Inc.)
Penguin Books Ltd., 80 Strand, London WC2R 0RL, England
Penguin Ireland, 25 St. Stephen's Green, Dublin 2,
Ireland (a division of Penguin Books Ltd.)
Penguin Group (Australia), 250 Camberwell Road, Camberwell, Victoria 3124,
Australia (a division of Pearson Australia Group Pty. Ltd.)
Penguin Books India Pvt. Ltd., 11 Community Centre, Panchsheel Park,
New Delhi - 110 017, India
Penguin Group (NZ), 67 Apollo Drive, Mairangi Bay,
Auckland 1311, New Zealand (a division of Pearson New Zealand Ltd.)
Penguin Books (South Africa) (Pty.) Ltd., 24 Sturdee Avenue,
Rosebank, Johannesburg 2196, South Africa

Penguin Books Ltd., Registered Offices:
80 Strand, London WC2R 0RL, England

First published by Roc, an imprint of New American Library,
a division of Penguin Group (USA) Inc.

First Printing, April 2007
10 9 8 7 6 5 4 3 2 1

Copyright © WizKids, Inc., 2007
All rights reserved

To Brian Pulido

Today screenplays and film festivals, tomorrow the world!
All in five hours a week.

ACKNOWLEDGMENTS

Sharon Turner Mulvihill gets a huge helping of thanks for her patience. From the start this project seemed snakebit, but there she was with the snake-bite kit. Loren Coleman, Randall Bills, and Kevin Killiany helped out greatly as well. Without Howard Morhaim—my brilliant agent—this project would never have happened. And thanks to Kassie Klaybourne for keeping me sane.

1

Alaric Wolf walked through the star field displayed in the holotank like a god striding through reality. The measured step, the narrowing of his cerulean eyes: Though no one was watching him, and though he was not sure gods even existed, he comported himself as one. Always aware, always projecting a larger-than-life image of himself, he dared not let down his guard.

He studied the various worlds. As he reached out with long, slender fingers to touch a planet, a window full of information would open. The forces of nature had created the worlds, and though man had been spread through the stars for more than a millennia, many of the worlds were barely tamed. Man had blunted their wild essence in a few places, and yet those victories could easily be reversed.

The tenuous nature of man's dominion over the universe could not be denied.

As he studied the worlds he considered a debate

that had raged since before man left Terra. While science had, over the years, provided some answers, it fell to every man to decide for himself which was more important: his nature, or the way he had been nurtured? Genes or training, technology or some innate aspect of man that could not be quantified, which was most vital to supremacy?

The Clans—who designed their own society—chose nature as paramount. Children were born of unions created by scientists, literally bred for war. They prized faster reflexes and greater stamina, they selected for presence of mind and a predatory love of war. Even the nurturing process and the series of trials a Clansman endured before he was considered worthy of entering the breeding program imposed a Darwinian selection process. Combat would weed out the weak, so only the strong would survive and reproduce.

Had he been alive when the Clans invaded the Inner Sphere, Alaric was certain he easily would have accepted their genetic superiority as truth. Even granting that Clan technology had outstripped that of the Inner Sphere, the Clans' initial series of victories could not be ascribed to that alone. The Clans had blown through opposition, virtually unstoppable. Their superiority could not be denied.

He paused before a glowing golden world burning in the holotank, but did not reach for it. Tukayyid. There the forces of the Inner Sphere had met the Clans in open warfare, and stopped them. The Inner Sphere had learned much about the Clan way of fighting, and had allowed the Clans to overreach through arrogance. Defeat at Tukayyid had ended the great invasion and stopped the drive to Terra.

Alaric smiled, turning to look at Terra, that blue ball at the heart of the display. Terra had been the birthplace of humanity, and had become a grand prize. Whichever Clan took it would become the ilClan—

the greatest Clan of all—and their leader would be supreme. There would be no doubting him, his bloodline, or his leadership capabilities. He would transcend humanity and become a god.

He laughed lightly, ignoring the hollow echoes that came back to him. The Clans had been stopped in their drive on Terra, suggesting to some that their superiority was an illusion. Then the Inner Sphere struck deep into Clan space and destroyed a Clan. They exterminated the Smoke Jaguars, managing with a task force to do to a Clan what only the whole of the Clans had ever managed to achieve. Then they invaded Strana Mechty, the Clan homeworld, and buried once and for all the notion of Clan superiority.

Many Clansmen had never recovered from that blow. Their solace was to turn inward and fight each other, as if to declare the Inner Sphere warriors unworthy as foes. This was folly, of course, because ignoring the Inner Sphere and heaping contempt upon their warriors did nothing to destroy them.

Others reacted differently. Vlad Ward, the man Alaric had hoped was his genefather, had challenged the Inner Sphere. He knew their weakness. Though they were capable of waging war, they hated it. They considered it a weakness to resort to war, though their history showed an affinity for and constant reliance upon war. In threatening them, he'd carried away Katrina Steiner, Alaric's genemother; giving Alaric life and Katrina a legacy she'd otherwise have been denied.

Though her blood coursed through his veins, it was the nurturing that made him different. She'd not been overprotective, just maternally cunning in how she had him trained. She did insist on little things, like his calling her "Mother," even though the term had little currency among the Clans. She did not curb his headstrong nature as much as channel it. She gave him breathing room that allowed him to make decisions rationally. The heat of battle might demand instantaneous action, but proper planning minimized those situations—which was to his advantage across the board.

More importantly, his mother had showed him something to which many Clansmen remained blind: that appearance, when unchallenged, becomes reality. If one acts to discourage challenges—if the bluff is never called—then people must accept as real what has been presented to them. Given a choice between realizing they are stupid enough to be deceived, or believing they are truly in the presence of greatness, rare is the individual who will choose to think badly of himself.

He pressed his hands together in an attitude of prayer. *First you let them think they are smart. Then you destroy them.* His mother was a master of political manipulation and, save for one flaw, would never have come to the Clans. Among the Clans she had limited avenues of self-expression, so spent a great deal of time preparing and perfecting him as an instrument of vengeance upon her enemies. Her enemies, as it turned out, were the people of the Inner Sphere and her hatred for them knew no bounds.

Especially so in the case of my genefather.

Alaric's stomach knotted. He fought the pain, refusing to give any outward sign of discomfort. The knowledge of his father's identity was still new to him, still raw. He'd grown up thinking his genefather was a proper Clansman—perhaps even Vlad. Vlad possessed every virtue a Clansman was meant to possess: strength, cunning, intelligence, courage and a calculated ruthlessness that destroyed weakness wherever it might be found.

Believing Vlad was his genefather gave Alaric a sanctuary when his mother's meddling seemed too much. He recognized it as the orphan fantasy, that someday his *true* genefather would come and take him to greater glory. His mother's obsession with the glory she had known and lost in the Inner Sphere made the fantasy all the more seductive.

He had endured her control over his life and kept his resentment to himself. Whereas others tested out of their sibkos as soon as they could, becoming warriors and proving their worth to Clan Wolf, she held him back. She told him to bide his time, to watch and wait; but passive predatory practices were at odds with the Clan ethos. As much as he resented it, he could see the advantages her strategy won for him.

And when he was unleashed, he channeled his pent-up frustrations into his battles. He tested late, but destroyed his foes. It was not enough that they conceded his superiority when they saw he had maneuvered them into an untenable position; they had to know pain—so they'd not think of challenging him later.

Memory is a tricky thing. We forget pain, but scars are there every day to remind us of our weakness.

Alaric had hoped that the nature of his victories would bring forward his true father. Acknowledgment would gain him nothing, and many were the Clansmen who had been bred from stock left behind by warriors who had died gloriously. Still, he wanted a legacy, a Clan legacy, and was certain one waited for him.

Then he learned his father's identity, and learned of his father's death. The fact that Alaric had survived and thrived within the Clans was cold comfort for learning that he was of pure Inner Sphere stock. It was true there had been warriors from the Inner Sphere who had joined the Clans and even had risen to high rank among them, but this was by far the exception, and Alaric did not like being a statistical anomaly.

Not that his bloodline was anything to be ashamed

of, even if only examined along the maternal line. Katrina Steiner and Hanse Davion had both been great warriors and greater leaders of their nations. Their progeny—Victor Steiner-Davion—had eclipsed both of them, proving the worth of the line in the area of martial skill. The Inner Sphere had its own rather dynamic testing program, and countless were the moldering bodies of would-be rulers littering Inner Sphere worlds. Alaric yet had cousins and half siblings who lived and ruled within the Inner Sphere.

As a youth studying the history of the Clan invasion, Alaric had been fascinated with his uncle Victor—though he learned quickly never to mention him around his mother. Had Victor been of the Clans, he would assuredly have served as a role model for Alaric. Victor had been physically small, yet fought with a ferocity that had enabled him to successfully lead the coalition that had repeatedly thwarted the Clans. Victor had led the task force that had attacked the Clan homeworld, and his victory had secured a future for the Inner Sphere.

In Victor, Alaric found much to admire, save for two incidences in the man's life. When Victor returned from Strana Mechty, he discovered that Katrina had usurped his realm from the regent he had left behind to rule in his stead. He stood at the head of an army that would gladly have followed him and deposed her, but he declined to fight her. Given the choice between waging a war and leaving his people subject to a tyrant—and Alaric was under no illusions about what sort of ruler his mother had been—Victor turned from bloodshed.

And then, later, when Devlin Stone and his revolution started the drive to create one unified nation within the Inner Sphere, Victor endorsed the plan. It was another move toward peace and away from war. It was a move away from man's base nature; and as much as Victor and others tried to nurture peace, the effort always failed.

Alaric again studied Terra and thought about when he traveled there with his mother for Victor's funeral. He'd found the world beautiful. The caress of soft breezes, the verdant plant life, the gentle and unceasing rustle of waves on beaches—this world called to him, though generations of his people had been raised far from it. It was the cradle of humanity, and even the most cursory study of it revealed so much about the forces that shaped mankind.

He recalled visiting museums and wandering through displays showing the evolution of mankind. Alaric was certain others viewed the extinct life-forms with a sense of nostalgia or loss, but he drew from them a greater lesson. Neanderthal had coexisted with modern man for several millennia, yet ultimately had succumbed to modern man's more violent tendencies. Animals that had vanished had been hunted to death: the mammoth, giant sloths, flightless birds; the list was endless. And while others saw those extinctions as a warning against a profligate disregard for the sanctity of life, Alaric just took it as confirmation of man's true nature.

I think, therefore I am. He knew the philosophical concept, and could see the logic in it, but it seemed too limited. It was not enough for him to know he existed. *Others* had to know he existed. *I can cause others to die, therefore they know I exist.*

That was how people had known his genefather existed. His mother, though she hid it well beneath a veil of hatred for his genefather, also defined the man that way. He was the one who could have killed her. Even his passing had not lessened this sense—she clearly feared he would somehow reach out from the grave and destroy her.

And Alaric knew that because he was the man's

son, someday she could come to fear him as she had his father.

But she won't act against me because she believes the illusion, too. Alaric lifted his head, straightening his spine. He had learned well from his mother, and as he read and studied his father, he discovered a lesson that Katrina never learned, but that his genefather clearly had. It was a lesson so basic as to be accepted as military wisdom, yet few people ever understood the true nature of the axiom.

Know your foe. There wasn't a military leader who had avoided gross defeat when he ignored that tidbit. Embracing it had led to countless victories. From the first hunter who ever stalked game, through Vlad Ward and Devlin Stone, the warrior who studied his enemy for weaknesses—and then exploited them—knew victory.

His mother was indeed very good at spotting and exploiting weakness, but she concentrated on specific enemies. Her hatred for Victor had kept her focused on him, which led her to make mistakes that ultimately resulted in her defeat. In combat that sort of focus was known as a lack of situational awareness and it often proved to be a fatal flaw.

His father, however, had possessed more vision than Katrina. The man had somehow realized that his foe was human nature itself. While he might focus, from time to time, on a particular individual, Alaric's study of him suggested he was always studying mankind as a whole. People might think of themselves as unique, but the simple fact was that aside from minor and cosmetic differences, the vast majority of people unthinkingly followed in the footsteps of others. If one figured out the general tendencies for humanity, shaping strategies to deal with them as a group became almost simple.

For Alaric this meant fostering and directing the

sense that he was something special. At his mother's urging he had never showed weakness—and never had mercy been a trait ascribed to him. He was known to be smart, and never let others see how hard he worked to gain knowledge. He'd spot their assumptions about him, then act counter to those assumptions. He cultivated an air of mystery and superiority because if anyone decided to know him as their enemy, Alaric would be one huge paradox centered on his implacable nature and aggressive mien.

Men may fear me, and that's all to the good. Their inability to understand me will spawn much fear, and in those too stupid to be afraid, it will create confusion.

Over and above that, Alaric acknowledged one more truth he'd taken from his genefather. While he thought the man had made certain disastrous choices, Alaric understood how his genefather had made those choices. He had truly known his foe.

It was himself.

And so, like his father, Alaric needed to know himself. He could cultivate a legend. He could even appear as a god to others. Mankind had not so sufficiently evolved that the sense of peace one found in superstition had vanished—but without knowing himself and his own weaknesses, he would always be in jeopardy of failing himself. He might even, as his mother had through her loathing of her brother, sabotage his own future.

This he would not allow himself to do.

Through nurturing he was a creature of the Clans and the Inner Sphere. Through his nature he was heir to the Inner Sphere. He meant to lead Clan Wolf in the conquest of Terra, then to assume the thrones to which his blood entitled him. It was a bold proposition for his future, but one that would not remain beyond his grasp forever.

Know your foe. Know thyself. Alaric's eyes tightened. *You are Victor Steiner-Davion's son. You must learn what that means and embrace it.*

Alaric smiled as a klaxon began to wail deep within the bowels of the ship. *You are called now to war. Go and fulfill your true nature.*

2

The Jade Falcons, for reasons known only to them—
and reasons utterly incomprehensible to Alaric—
allowed his force to land uncontested. Some in his
command suggested their recent civil war had dissi-
pated their forces to such an extent that they couldn't
contest the landing. They might even have been interested in capturing his DropShips—an absurd notion,
to be certain, but the Falcons had always dreamed
well beyond their grasp of reality.

And reality was the reason the Wolves had come
to Koniz. During their Trial of Possession for the
Khanship of their Clan—what his mother dismissed as
a civil war—the Falcons had dared raid Wolf worlds
for supplies. Such transgressions could not go unpun-
ished, and this was a point Alaric had stressed to his
subordinates. Despite his emphasis, however, he was
certain that few of his troops truly understood the
import of his words.

Alaric waited with a Star of heavy 'Mechs in a small

wooded vale fifteen kilometers south of the town of Ogstrenburg. The Falcons had established their headquarters there and had suggested the plains to the south as a suitable battlefield. In fact, the plains were part of the local watershed, so the ground was soft. Had he landed his command in what appeared to be the most convenient place, they would have been attacking up a rise on slow terrain.

Instead of accepting the Falcon invitation, he landed beyond the southern plains and sent three Stars of light and medium 'Mechs up and over the wooded hills. They made quite a show of coming through the woods and even torched several tall trees to mark their passing. When they reached the plains, they hesitated and began to pick out a firm path through the soft ground. This had them moving in three columns toward the Jade Falcon position.

It also gave his Star plenty of time to get into position. Alaric shifted his shoulders, resetting his heavy neurohelmet on the shoulders of his cooling vest. As oppressive as its weight and confinement could be, he relished the sensation. Others might feel it to be a burden, especially while waiting, but he translated the weight into the potential for glory. In combat it would be as nothing—forgotten even—and the aching muscles in the aftermath would be a sign of survival.

He smiled within the confines of his helmet. He'd had his helmet's faceplate mirrored, and his helmet painted with the snarling visage of a wolf. He refused to remove it until combat was finished, allowing no one to see what few emotions escaped his control to be displayed on his face. He was always implacable; the helmet transformed him into an avatar of war.

He watched the *Mad Cat*'s displays. The primary showed his systems to be green and functional, from the long-range missile launchers to the extended-range lasers in both of the 'Mech's arms. The *Mad Cat*, with its birdlike legs, forward-thrusting cylindrical torso and weapons pods where other 'Mechs had hands, was one of the most alien-looking 'Mechs. He chose it specifically for that reason since it made it even easier to disguise his humanity.

The secondary monitor carried the feed from a holocamera wielded by an elemental team stationed high on the hills overlooking the battlefield. His trio of Stars, with the medium 'Mechs in the middle and slightly ahead of the others, advanced within range of the Jade Falcons. Everything that could be wrong with the Wolf formation was. The wings had no contact with the center. They were traveling in columns and were bunched too closely to offer each other much support. If the Jade Falcons waited as long as they should to cut loose, they'd smash his troops. If they struck as he would have in their position, none of the Wolf 'Mechs would make it off the battlefield.

But they won't strike as I would. They are Falcons and a garrison force. Their foolishness will betray them.

The Falcons had deployed themselves on the reverse slope of the hills, hiding from direct-attack weapons like autocannons and energy beams. From their position they could launch long-range missiles at the Wolves with impunity. They should have done so when the Wolves had just begun to mount the slope. Alaric's 'Mechs would have to slow on the uphill climb, making them easier targets to hit.

The Falcons should have waited longer to attack. *If they were not Falcons, they might have.*

Hundreds of missile contrails arced through the sky. Explosions lit the battlefield. At least half the missiles missed their targets, sowing fire between the wings. Those that did hit 'Mechs shattered armor. One *Ryoken* staggered, then fell on its back as the missile barrage ripped away an arm.

What at one moment had been a meadow filled with

long green grasses became a pockmarked landscape. Smoke rose from craters, and hunks of turf hung from the 'Mechs that were still moving. None of his Wolves had been destroyed, though all had taken damage. Their advance had been stopped, and as the downed *Ryoken* struggled to its feet, the rearmost Wolf elements turned to run. The left wing broke to the west, with the center quickly following through muddy terrain. The right wing cut east on a course that would have allowed them to flank the Falcon position, but only if the Falcons were stupid enough to have left it open.

And despite what he might think of the Falcons, Alaric would not allow as how they might be that deluded about their own competence. *No battle has ever been won by assuming the enemy is stupid.*

Alaric raised his 'Mech's left arm, signaling the others in his Star to be ready. He could have tight-beamed a command, but he didn't want to risk detection. Moreover, a silent signal carried more import with it. He was concentrating so much he didn't want to waste words.

The Star of light 'Mechs moved east along the base of the hills, then curled back toward the south just past the edge of the Jade Falcon position. Boiling out from around the hills and coming up over the top, two Jade Falcon Stars gave chase. Lasers, red and green, flashed past the retreating Wolves, burning black swaths through the grasses.

The Wolves, flying toward the woods, did not shoot back. The pilots knew their only salvation lay in reaching cover. The Falcons, on the other hand, knew glory awaited them for bringing down their enemies. Once they'd crushed that flank, they could turn and catch the others.

Alaric dropped his 'Mech's arm, then hit the triggers on his joysticks. The *Mad Cat* rocked back as long-range missiles arced up and away. A wave of heat washed up through the cockpit, warming his flesh but having no effect on his spirit. The battle had been joined. *They will be punished.*

Two hundred LRMs reached out from the vale to pepper the battlefield. A *Fenris* led the Falcon advance and caught the first wave of missiles. Fiery explosions rippled up the 'Mech's body. Crushed armor flew away in scales. The 'Mech spun and dropped to its knees, and then the *Cougar* racing out of the smoke smashed into it. The *Fenris* flopped facedown and the *Cougar*, shedding armor from its legs, stumbled to the ground.

Per their plan, the heavy 'Mechs launched a second salvo that wreathed the Jade Falcons with fire. The Wolves' light 'Mechs turned east and north again, using the smoke and confusion to flank the Falcons. A pair of *Uller*s pumped shots from their gauss rifles into the Falcon ranks, following the silvery balls with a storm of red laser darts. Though the light 'Mechs kept moving at speed, the Falcons had clustered so closely together that it was all but impossible to miss a target.

Over to the west, the fleeing Wolves also turned and came hard at the Falcons' western flank. Beams flashed as the 'Mechs raced up the slope toward the Falcons. Alaric suspected the Falcon commander had led the chase to the east, abandoning the position to a lesser officer who now found himself overwhelmed as light and medium 'Mechs overran his position.

His day is just going to get worse.

Alaric stalked his 'Mech from the vale. He moved quickly, but not hastily. Those following him spread out in good order, launching more missiles as they came. Alaric did not, but instead swept his crosshairs over the battlefield. He targeted the struggling *Cougar* and stabbed two green beams from his large lasers into its right leg. What little armor remained there vaporized beneath the infernal caress. Myomers snapped and the ferro-titanium bones melted. The *Cougar* sagged to the right, the 'Mech's weight burying its right arm in the soft ground.

The *Cougar*'s pilot, as bold as she was foolish, thrust her 'Mech's left arm at his *Mad Cat*. The large laser pulsed out a stream of energy bolts that peppered his 'Mech's right thigh. Armor melted and the monitor image shifted color from green to yellow to warn him of the damage. Alaric rode with the shift in balance caused by the loss of armor, then paused and deliberately took aim on the 'Mech's cockpit.

Twin beams converged, making ferro-ceramic armor and flesh stream into a fiery puddle in the meadow.

The Falcon force broke, but one Star captain had the presence of mind to keep his unit together. They dashed east, blasting through the light 'Mechs harrying them. The light 'Mechs wheeled to give chase, but did not follow so closely that they could be ambushed. They'd keep the fleeing Falcons away long enough for Alaric to crush the Falcon center.

More missiles and lasers destroyed the remains of the Falcon pursuit force. The fighting at the crest of the hill had become fierce, with short-range missiles corkscrewing into targets, and red, green and blue energy beams lighting the landscape. Alaric's Star rushed across the torn, muddy meadow and up the hill, with Alaric himself anchoring the right flank.

Alaric focused, aware of but unconcerned for those Wolves fighting beside him. The Falcons had allowed themselves to be pushed out of the redoubt and his light 'Mechs had already slipped into the trenches. This afforded them cover while the retreating Falcons had none. This hardly left them defenseless, however; a pair of curiously inhuman looking 'Mechs descended on silvery plasma jets to interpose themselves between the fleeing 'Mechs and their pursuit.

A cold thrill trickled through Alaric's guts. He'd not seen the like of these 'Mechs before. Their clawed feet sank talons into the ground and the triple claws on the hands snapped open and shut reflexively. The triangular head gave the 'Mech a raptorial look, and odd, winglike appendages sprouted from the shoulders.

Finally, I get to see their Jade Hawks *in battle. Were they worth being kept secret?*

Flights of short-range missiles shot from their breasts, ripping apart a *Ryoken.* The paired small lasers slung beneath each forearm spat out darts of coherent light, melting armor. Their weird appearance and the fierceness of their assault made the Wolves pause. As the retreating Falcons regrouped to lay down covering fire for their allies, the two heavy 'Mechs crouched before launching themselves into the air.

I can't let that happen. The world and the cacophony of battle fell away. Time slowed. Alaric swung his crosshairs around to cover one of the Falcons. His *Mad Cat* twisted at the waist to keep him on target while his 'Mech traveled to the northeast. As his target ignited his plasma jets, Alaric pulled the trigger and pumped kilojoules of energy into the enemy *Jade Hawk.*

Heavy green beams slashed scars over the right thigh and breast, narrowly missing one of the SRM launchers. His medium lasers hit the right arm, peeling away armor. The pulse lasers stippled that same arm, disintegrating all but the last of its armor.

A cyclone of heat filled the *Mad Cat*'s cockpit. Sweat slicked every inch of Alaric's exposed flesh. Lights flashed, warning of excessive heat and degrading the 'Mech's capabilities accordingly. His 'Mech slowed and the crosshairs tracked sluggishly. Another salvo like that and his 'Mech might even shut down, which was not something conducive to his life or legend.

But neither is allowing my command to be slaughtered.

One of the Falcons dropped another of his light 'Mechs as it soared high and to the west, instantly placing itself in a flanking position against the Wolves. The 'Mech Alaric attacked had likewise intended to flee in that direction, but the loss of armor radically shifted the war machine's center of balance. The jump jets lit up, but the right shoulder rose faster than the left. The 'Mech arced east, not west, and the pilot wrestled it to the ground, somehow managing to keep it on its feet.

Alaric swiveled the *Mad Cat* at the waist, brought his crosshairs on target, and when a gold dot glowed at their heart, he hit his triggers again. The various lasers blasted energy into the *Jade Hawk*, scattering it over the 'Mech's torso and right arm. The large laser's green beam melted through the thin veneer of armor that remained on that limb. A pulse laser filled the arm with scarlet energy needles, exploding one of the small lasers. The right claw snapped open and locked as myomer fibers burned.

The *Jade Hawk* shot back. Short-range missiles pounded the *Mad Cat*. Explosions cratered armor all over the 'Mech. One hammered the cockpit, spalling armor fragments that nicked Alaric's legs and arms. He hissed, more in annoyance than pain, then fought with his 'Mech as the heat sensors pushed into the red zone.

As much as he wanted to shoot again, to do so would guarantee a total failure of his 'Mech's systems. The gyroscopes lost synchronization for a moment, starting the 'Mech on a lurch to the right. Alaric punched a foot down on a pedal and wrenched the 'Mech back upright. The left leg dragged, gouging a deep furrow in the ground.

It could be a grave.

The Jade Falcon stepped forward, closing with him. The left claw reached out, aiming for the cockpit. Alaric imagined it punching through the armor, plucking him from his command couch and crushing him. It would have been a novel way to die, falling prey to the claw of a 'Mech he'd never seen before. But it would have been equally ignominious, so he rejected the idea.

For just a heartbeat he imagined what his foe was feeling. The *Mad Cat* had to be glowing white hot on a secondary monitor in that cockpit. The Falcon was certain the Wolf pilot was helpless. Indeed, he was barely able to keep the 'Mech upright. And with its array of short-range missiles, the Falcon 'Mech was much better suited to infighting than the *Mad Cat*.

For that moment he savored what his enemy was feeling, that piquant taste of victory of one man over another.

But I am not a man. I am meant to be a god.

The *Mad Cat* thrust both weapons pods at the Falcon. The large and medium lasers flashed, and pulse laser darts leaped from the *Mad Cat*'s torso. Armor melted, running like wax to congeal again in rivulets below black scars. One emerald beam caught the Falcon in the center of its chest, passing just beneath the point of its triangular head.

A secondary explosion shook the 'Mech. It stumbled drunkenly, black smoke pouring from the hole. Its outstretched claw gave the impression it had intended to steady itself by grabbing the *Mad Cat*, but it missed entirely. It drifted to the left, then twisted at the waist. Missiles shot from it, most missing the

Mad Cat—and those that hit scattering but not penetrating armor.

Then the Falcon went down, crashing heavily onto its side. An oblong panel on the head burst outward, and the pilot ejected. She rode a jet of flame past Alaric's 'Mech and down to the battlefield, where Wolf elementals would later hunt her down and kill her.

Heat choked the *Mad Cat*'s cockpit. Alaric struggled to keep his 'Mech on its feet, and managed it by sinking into a crouch. He shifted the feet and started to come back up, but the engine shut down, freezing the 'Mech as if just about to pounce on the Falcon.

Alaric closed his eyes for a moment. To have your 'Mech shut down on the battlefield was the product of taking foolish risks. He accepted that, just as he accepted victory as a confirmation of having made the proper choices. It was not that he didn't believe he could be wrong; he just knew that any error that did not get him killed generated a tale that made him more of an enigma.

The trick is to avoid making the same error twice. He smiled. *Predictability will kill you faster than mistakes.*

Before he attempted to restart his 'Mech, he glanced out the cockpit. His troops had downed the other odd Falcon 'Mech and were mopping up the remains of the Falcon force. Then they would move on to Ogstrenburg and raze it.

To punish the Falcons.

Alaric nodded once, then began the ignition sequence. He would beat them to the city and lay waste to it. *And the stories they will tell of this battle will be grand.*

3

Anastasia Kerensky smiled as the man waiting in the briefing room fidgeted. She'd studied him as he came into the hotel and as Ian Murchison escorted him to the room. Small and bookish, the man radiated irritation. The look he gave her as she entered the room conveyed his belief that time was money, and that her tardiness would cost her.

"I am pleased to meet you, Baron Saville. I hope Dr. Murchison has made you feel at home."

Saville raked his thinning hair into place. "I am not accustomed to being kept waiting, Colonel Kerensky. I've come with a serious offer. If you don't want your Wolf Hunters employed . . ."

She raised a hand and kept the smile on her face. Slipping past Ian, she moved to the head of the table, forcing Saville to turn in her direction. "If you insist on giving vent to petty feelings, I can assure you that the Wolf Hunters have no interest in working for you or those you represent." She kept her voice even, but full of the edge that had cowed warriors far tougher than Saville ever dreamed of being.

The words had an effect, though not the wholly desired one. "You'll find me to be as professional as you are, Colonel." The man nodded once, sharply. "And I do appreciate your coming here to Castor to meet with me."

"How is it that you came to negotiate with us?"

The man's brown eyes narrowed. "I beg your pardon?"

She let her smile fade into a bemused grin. "I've had time to research you and your situation. You hail from La Blon and have a rather successful global communications and entertainment business there. You make a great deal of money, but you have not nearly enough to pay us what we'll demand. In fact, in the last four months you've made inquiries with a number of other mercenary units, small ones, to protect La Blon. More specifically, to protect your holdings on La Blon. Your offer to us suggested a wider mission. This would require liaisons on other worlds, and a greater pool of money than you possess."

Anastasia had expected her comment to spark ire or to intimidate, but she got neither result. Instead Saville seemed to relax. *Perhaps there is even more here than I expect.*

"Very good, Colonel. You've done your recon. Others have learned some of what you have, but no one as completely. This is why I think you are exactly what we need." Saville leaned back in his chair and scraped a hand over his clean-shaven jaw.

If he'd had more in the way of a chin, Anastasia might have thought more of him. "Your backers?"

"Their identities will be revealed in due time, Colonel. You'll likely puzzle them out yourself." He glanced around the room. "Your subordinates may even be listening to us and researching what was Prefecture Nine as we speak."

Ian's brows arched upward. "Goodness, you think we're spying on you!"

Saville laughed. "Hardly, Doctor. I'm just supposing you would do what I would do in your position. Let's not kid each other, shall we? The Wolf Hunters are good, but hardly what the Steel Wolves were. You're in a process of transition and reformation, which can be difficult. We have resources and needs that are compatible with you achieving your goal."

Anastasia shook her head. "You presume a great deal if you believe you know our goal."

"Hardly, Colonel. You know that I am a communications mogul. Knowledge is power. Information is more valuable than gold."

Ian straightened. "There's not a fact in the world that's ever stopped a laser."

"True, but bad information will kill someone just as easily as a laser." The small man shrugged. "There is a need for an elite fighting unit. You may see heavy duty. You may see no duty at all. I don't know which, but I have to assume the former. This is why I've asked to meet with you."

"Go on."

"Thank you, Colonel. I'll come right to the point. The Jade Falcons have made incursions into our prefecture. We've heard rumors that they're involved in a civil war. It has not yet slopped over into the prefecture, but we expect it could. Your primary mission would be defensive. You would be tasked with making certain they take no more worlds. As The Republic has retreated into its shell, we will get no help from them."

"Nor do you think you require it." Anastasia nodded slowly. "You said our primary mission is defensive. And our secondary mission?"

"That would depend on how bold you are, Colonel." The small man smiled easily. "It may come as no surprise to you that those of us in the Ninth have a growing sense of unity. We would not be averse to having the worlds now in Falcon possession returned to us. Many very wealthy people fled those worlds, and have almost limitless resources available for the effort of liberating them again."

"Defending a world, Baron Saville, is much easier than conquering one." Anastasia tapped a finger against the tabletop. "The Clans will bargain, so we can set terms to be in our favor for the battle. If we go on the attack, we surrender that advantage to them. That means we would have to come in hotter and harder than they could ever imagine."

"I'm heartened, Colonel, that you didn't say taking worlds would be impossible."

"It is for us, right now."

"But we can make it easier."

The man's comment caught her off guard, but she covered her reaction. "Do you really think you can?"

He nodded confidently. "I, too, have done my research. You scattered the Steel Wolves. You jettisoned the warriors who were not up to your standards. I'll confess that you sent away many who, in data files, seemed quite competent. Even so, the elite core remains. My belief would be that you intend to hone their skills until, as you suggested, they can hit hotter and harder than imagined. Do I understand your situation correctly?"

Anastasia gave him a reluctant nod. Saville understood her situation to the limitations of his ability to understand the whole Clan culture. Anastasia had been raised as a Wolf. She had been trained and tested over and over again to become the best warrior it was possible to be. Some of her compatriots believed that meant doing everything according to regulations, precepts and wisdom laid down for ages.

Anastasia knew it required something more. A study of the history of warfare showed its constant evolution. At one time, masses of warriors hidden behind huge shields and wielding long spears had been the dominant force. They were replaced by more mobile infantry, and they were supplanted by the power of cavalry. Centuries later, warriors with rifles and bayonets reigned supreme. As weapons became more deadly, tactics evolved, and what once might have been accepted wisdom was shown to be folly in a new age.

The evolution always occurred after a period of stagnation. Anastasia felt warfare was moving into such a period, which provided an opportunity. She could guide the next stage of the evolution. She could become the master of warfare, leaving no enemy to stand against her.

And leaving no goal unattainable.

Saville knitted his fingers together. "I'm glad to see we have the same sense of things, Colonel. My associates and I have made offers to other units, but we've also been recruiting mercenaries and militiamen. Our intent is to cull from them the very best warriors, under the guise of forming our own corporate units—not unlike the model of Bannson's Raiders. We would hope for a different level of success, however, and that success would be your success. It would be simple for us to fold our units in with yours, or for you to cherry-pick our best warriors."

"That's an interesting proposition, Baron."

"It can be made more so." He spread his hands apart. "As I said before, knowledge is power, and lack thereof can leave some powerless. We have at our disposal the means of obfuscating the identities and records of those we make available to you. As I understand the bidding process, your enemies would be privy to records in order to make their bids. These troops would appear only to be as good as you wish them to be on paper, with no duplicity on your part."

"What an interesting idea." Anastasia caught the look on Ian's face, but didn't change her expression. "You'll find us to be very expensive, even if we never move from our defensive posture."

"That goes without saying. We'd like you and your people on La Blon within the month. We can begin the process of negotiating a contract as you head into the system. You'll find us realistic in what we offer. The price may be lower than you would like, but we won't charge you for the things we can supply freely. We have no desire to cripple you through a company-store mentality."

"La Blon is doable, yes." Anastasia folded her arms across her chest. "I look forward to seeing you again, Baron, on La Blon."

If it surprised the man to be dismissed so quickly, he gave no sign. "Very good, Colonel. A fruitful result of our business shall be to our mutual benefit. I anticipate nothing less." He stood, then bowed his head to Ian. "Farewell to you, too, Doctor."

Anastasia nodded, then glanced at Ian. "A moment, Ian."

Murchison nodded, then walked Saville to the door. He shook the man's hand, then closed the door behind him. Before he said anything, he checked the table and chair for listening devices, then smiled sheepishly at Anastasia.

"Sorry. I thought he protested too much about spying."

"I will, of course, have our quarters swept just in case." Anastasia stared after the baron. "Your assessment of his character?"

Murchison frowned. "Something about him I don't

like. He comes in sounding like a patriot, but there is something more there. Your impressions?"

"He's a merchant. You can smell it on him. He thinks in terms of profit and loss. He's as bad as a commander who sees troops as numbers." She pulled the chair out and sat at the head of the table. "His offer is quite lucrative."

"Now who's sounding like a merchant?"

Anastasia laughed. "I'm a realist, Ian. You know what is at stake here."

The man appropriated Saville's seat. "Your goal is to make us Wolf. You want us to be the pinnacle of what it is to be a warrior, and, not coincidentally, give me all the work I can handle. I'm not sure I see how the baron's offer will bring you closer to the first goal, but my hands will be full."

"Ever the optimist, Ian. Merchant though he is, Baron Saville did see some things clearly." She leaned forward and tucked a lock of red hair behind her ear. "It's probably because he's a merchant that he sees some things others do not. An organization is made up of people. They have to be melded into a team, and in what we do, there is a terrible penalty paid for failure.

"Nearly a century ago, when the Clans invaded the Inner Sphere, they assumed that they had the best equipment and the best people available. Initially it seemed as if this was true, but the people of the Inner Sphere learned and adapted. What had been an over-whelming advantage quickly faded. Moreover, people from the Inner Sphere proved themselves capable of competing with Clansmen on their own terms."

"Phelan Kell."

"Among others." Anastasia's expression sharpened. "I know we can train warriors, and that we will have to train them, but I need the best of the best. I will make them better."

"I know you can, but that will require combat. You're accepting a position where we will be watchdogs."

"That will never happen, Ian. Saville or his masters will find a way to put us into battle." She smiled. "How much have you studied evolution?"

Murchison blinked. "I know it, believe in it. What, in particular, are you referring to?"

She laughed lightly. "In the evolutionary sciences the prevailing view is a theory called *punctuated equilibrium*. It states that a species might evolve quickly in isolation, and then spread out to achieve dominance when conditions outside its haven were ripe for doing so. If you look at the history of warfare, this is certainly true. The phalanx arose in Greece. The French learned how to wield cannon to their greatest effect, and the Germans mastered the same lesson for the machine gun."

Murchison nodded. "And the Clans developed in isolation from the Inner Sphere."

"Precisely. La Blon will give us a chance to adapt and evolve in peace. We will gather the most elite warriors available, meld them into a unit that fights cohesively, and be prepared for whatever we face."

"But will you be able to make outsiders into Wolves?"

His question gave her pause. So far, she had operated under the assumption that any warriors she took in would subordinate themselves to her and her ways. She would make them Wolf Hunters. Whether or not that would make them Wolves was something she'd not considered.

And that's because I think of the Wolf Hunters as being more *than Wolves.*

She considered whether she was being naive, then rejected that idea.

"It's an interesting question."

Murchison rested his elbows on the table. "It's one thing to bring people into a unit. Another to train them, but yet another to create the sense of belonging that is part of being Wolf. You're not recruiting them—you're *converting* them. Being Wolf is like a religion."

"No." She shook her head. "Religions, for all the comfort they offer people, ask them to look beyond themselves. They offer their lives to a deity. They take direction from a deity. They ask a deity for boons, all of which is fine provided you agree to a central supposition."

"And that is?"

"That God exists."

Murchison blinked. "But . . ."

"Just consider that He doesn't, or that He does, but doesn't interfere with human affairs." She sat back and pressed her hands together, fingertip to fingertip. "All those prayers asking for the strength to do something a person doesn't feel he can do by himself go unanswered. The deeds done as a result of those prayers still happen, which means the person always had that power within himself. Looking outside, when all you need is inside, is the critical element. More importantly, I can't have people praying for salvation when I need them thinking about their jobs."

"So you will convert them to being Wolf?"

"You may have hit upon a process, yes."

Murchison smiled. "And you're the goddess of the Wolf Hunters?"

"I may not grant salvation, Doctor, but I'll consign plenty of people to perdition." Anastasia smiled carefully. "I don't require being worshipped, just obeyed. The Hunters will believe in themselves, their training and me. That will be enough to win against all we face."

4

**Domain, Clan Wolf Occupation Zone
30 November 3136**

Had it been possible, Alaric would have delayed the meeting with his mother yet further. It was a game they'd played through the years. Alaric had gotten only slightly better at it, coming up with excuses for why he could not meet with her immediately. This time he had delayed by citing the exhaustion he felt from his return to Domain.

She accepted his excuse initially, graciously even, then set to work. Within a day he'd been given medical leave and assigned to a recovery facility that just happened to be the clinic where she spent a great deal of time and even more money. A helicopter had ferried him from his base to the mountain chateau.

As much as he wanted to be elsewhere, Alaric admired the towering mountains—some soaring nearly eight kilometers. Knife-edged, they stabbed into the skies. Winds whipped snow from the peaks, as if some invisible grindstone were sharpening them and snow was stone dust. The jagged mountains shredded clouds, and sunlight reflected blindingly from the snowfields.

The first time he'd seen the mountains, nearly ten years earlier, he'd resolved to climb them. He'd made the mistake of mentioning this to his mother, and she forbade it. Alaric considered defying her, but she had a Star of elementals enforce her order. He had no doubt more elementals lurked below, for just as he would never lose his desire to conquer those heights, she would never forget his desire and defiance.

Katrina Steiner. He'd first heard of her before he ever knew she was his mother. She had been the stuff of legend then, the woman who had defied Victor Davion—her brother and the conqueror of the Clans. She'd stolen his realm from him, but only temporarily. And when he'd defeated her and bound her over for trial, Vlad Ward of the Wolves traded peace for her.

Back then, when he was little, he had admired Vlad and secretly wondered what power this woman had over him. One day, quite by accident, he'd caught a glimpse of her. Tall and slender, with white-blond hair and icy blue eyes, she was the most beautiful woman he'd ever seen. He'd been too young to realize her flawless beauty was as much due to Clan medical technology as it was genetics; but it was also more than physical. The way she moved and the air of confidence she wore drew him. She burned with life and ambition.

The whine of the helicopter's rotors shifted pitch as the aircraft struggled up through the thinner air. For just a moment Alaric wished it would crash. He knew he'd not die in such an accident—that was not possible. The snowpack would cushion the craft's impact. While he had no desire to have to walk to the chateau, the crash would give his mother pause, and *that* he wanted.

She might realize, for a heartbeat, that the universe did not have her at its center.

Very soon after his first glimpse of her, Katrina began to take an interest in him. It was nothing special at first. She needed members of a sibko for a presentation, or he was included in a group sent to work on her estate as part of their training. She found ways to reward these small services. He became a frequent visitor—not so frequent that it impeded his studies—but often enough that he occasionally missed a critical exercise. Her interest in his life delayed his progress, and this rankled.

Alaric's eyes narrowed, as much against the snow's glare as the memory of the first time she'd summoned him alone to visit her. He'd refused an invitation to visit with others. His refusal had been polite, but when he arrived ire twisted her face and fury burned in her eyes. Fear had coiled in his guts and though he massed as much as she did at that point, Alaric did not doubt she easily could kill him.

Even with just a glance.

He shivered and discovered he was clutching the arms of his seat.

The copilot looked back at him and smiled. "Do not worry, Star Colonel, we will get you to the clinic in one piece."

"I am certain you will. Thank you," Alaric replied automatically, betraying none of the surprise running riot in his head. *Star* Colonel? It would be an unearned promotion, but one he coveted. It was one he might even have won had his mother allowed him to train and test on a normal schedule.

He smiled. She knew him better than to imagine he would be grateful, so he wouldn't be. He would accept it without comment. The promotion was, after all, just a gateway to further challenges. *What has she gotten me into now?*

The helicopter began its descent. A swirling curtain of snow shrouded it, then rolled out like smoke. The aircraft settled slowly, sinking to its belly in the snow. Before the pilots had begun to shut down the engines, Alaric had released the buckle on his safety harness and crouched by the passenger hatch.

The pilot hit a switch and the hatch cracked open. Snow scoured Alaric's face. He shielded his eyes with a hand; then ducking his head, he stepped from the helicopter. The crust beneath the dusting of powdery snow held until he reached the edge of the helipad, and then he stepped onto a walkway and quickly entered an icy tunnel.

Five elementals waited for him just inside the doors. They greeted him silently, and then one went to fetch his luggage. The other four surrounded him and led him deeper into the complex. He'd visited often enough to know the route to Katrina's suite; but they were not there to guide him.

They are coursing *me, as hounds would course prey toward the hunter.*

He shook his head. He considered voicing a question, but he knew he'd get no answer, so why bother? The elementals must have found their service to his mother degrading. How could they tolerate being denied the glory of warfare to act as her dogs?

Up and up they traveled, climbing as close as he would ever get to the mountains' pinnacles, until they reached the clinic's penthouse suite. No elevator serviced that level—Katrina reveled in walking and claimed exercise kept her young. Alaric assumed it was something more; given the history of Inner Sphere rulers who had died falling down stairs, he wondered if she weren't tempting fate. Every time she negotiated the stairs without incident, she could take it as an affirmation that God or fate had endorsed her continued life and the success of her plans.

He smiled, certain he'd hit on the truth of it. He wondered if she realized this, or if this confirmation spoke only to her subconscious. He decided it had to be subconscious, for as politically brilliant as she was, she sometimes failed to think far enough ahead. She'd been content, for example, to steal her brother's realm without having him killed. She wanted him to suffer, of this Alaric had no doubt, and wanted to lord her victory over him. The problem was, her desire to savor victory left a path open for him to return and defeat her.

And that is a valuable lesson. He smiled. Not the lesson of her leaving herself vulnerable when savoring victory. He never intended to let her see him as the sort of rival that needed to be defeated. No, the valuable lesson was in remembering that enemies are not truly defeated until they are dead.

Alaric arrived in his mother's foyer. The elementals split into pairs. One warded the stairs to prevent his escape, and the other stood guard at either side of the frosted-glass panels leading into the suite. Alaric took up his appointed position and lifted his head, but refrained from raking his fingers through his tousled blond hair.

The panels slid back. The brilliance of the snow-fields poured through the suite's glass wall, filling the room and blinding him. He squinted—involuntarily, despite thinking himself prepared—but did not shield his eyes. He stood stock-still, slowly letting a smile twist his lips. He tugged at the hem of his jacket, as if nervous, and waited for her to beckon him to enter.

Katrina Steiner stood at the far wall, at first a slender silhouette. She affected a casual pose, as if she were lost in studying the mountains soaring above the clinic. She turned her head slightly to the left, peering back over her shoulder. Her hair, so blond it could have been a mantle of snow itself, reached almost to her waist. She'd not plaited it because she liked him to do that for her. It was something that bonded him to her, and one part of the ritual they would engage in.

She turned fluidly, smiling easily, raising a hand toward him. Her voice betrayed none of her years, but filled the white room with warmth belied by its austerity. Her gown, made of white silk, had been belted with links of gold that matched a necklace and bracelet. The links on all three had been shaped in the form of a running wolf.

"My dear Alaric, do come in. I was hoping that was your helicopter."

"I am sorry to keep you waiting." He stepped into the room and the glass panels slid shut behind him. "I hope you did not worry."

She slowly blinked her blue eyes. "Can a mother ever stop worrying?"

"I would not know."

"Of course not." She held a hand up, her delicate fingers capped by long white nails. "You must remember I was not raised among the Clans, so I see motherhood in a more traditional fashion. My mother never stopped worrying about her children, and I shall never stop worrying about you. That's why I had you brought here. If you are ill, I shall tend to you myself."

"Fatigue is not an illness, Mother." He almost hesitated before adding that title. She expected it, and would bristle when he did not use it. Yet while she noted the difference in his upbringing and her own, she somehow failed to understand that her insistence he call her Mother did not draw them closer. It distanced them. The Clans raised their children in sibkos—cadres of children who trained and tested together. They were the products of genetic matching by the scientist caste: There were no connections between parents and their offspring.

To make me call you Mother just reminds me how different we are, and how little you understand me.

"A mother knows many things, Alaric, more than you might expect." She gestured toward a white leather couch. "Don't stand there. Sit. Relax. That is what you are here for."

No, I am here for whatever you desire. "You are most kind."

"I am proud of you, Alaric. Because of your action on Koniz I received word you were promoted to Star colonel. This is splendid news, though there are difficulties ahead that you will have to deal with."

Alaric seated himself, shivering at the leather's coolness. "Such as?"

Katrina's smile wavered for a moment. "I don't know."

Alaric's stomach tightened. Perhaps for the first time ever, he'd heard doubt in her voice. She genuinely didn't know what was going on, and that worried her. *Despite that, she has engineered things such that I shall be in the middle of whatever is happening.*

Katrina glided to the white leather chair opposite him, but did not sit. "Do you know either Star Colonel Bjorn or Donovan?"

He frowned. "One is two years my senior, the other a year behind me. Both will be candidates for a Bloodname. I have seen neither of them fight, but they tested out highly and have fought off Falcon supply raids. Why do you ask?"

"I had a communication from Khan Seth Ward. He asked after you. He said he had heard good things of you—things that rivaled the stories told of Bjorn and Donovan." She clasped her hands together and rested her chin on them. "He suggested the three of you might well represent the future of the Wolves."

Alaric covered his nose and mouth with his hands and stared blankly past his fingertips. Though the

Wards had been progressive as khans, Seth Ward certainly had to know of his parentage and had no reason to celebrate it as a product of Clan breeding programs. Bjorn and Donovan, on the other hand, had been genetically crafted down through generations. He and they were polar opposites; for the khan to mention them as she reported he had was remarkable.

He lowered his hands. "What do you make of this, Mother?"

She blinked, surprised a second time. He had never before solicited her advice. This had never stopped her from offering it, of course, or chiding him for failing to abide by it. He found her surprise refreshing, though also a bit frightening.

"I am of several minds, Alaric." She slowly lowered herself into her chair. "Since the invasion, the Clans have polarized. Once the myth of invincibility was shattered with the death of the Smoke Jaguars, the Clans have been free to seek their own identities. The Wolves are among those who have remained the most pure—at least this is true of those who remained with the Clans. I have to suppose he sees something in you that suggests long-term success."

"But why mention me with the others?" Alaric's frown deepened. "We are nothing alike."

Her eyes flashed. "Perhaps that is the key. It could be that while traditional Clan values are what may win the future, it could take more unorthodox approaches to things to succeed. Recall, if you will, that Phelan Kell was born of the Inner Sphere, and you share blood with him through my maternal side."

And my paternal side as well.

"It well could be as you say, Mother. The next logical step would be testing."

Katrina nodded carefully. "Hence your promotion."

Alaric's head came up. "You did not arrange it?"

"I had not yet thought to. It *is* premature, especially

for one who took unnecessary risks against the Falcons. You could have been killed."

"But I was not. There is no Falcon who could kill me."

"You're probably right there." She smiled coldly. "Your Steiner blood does not make you invincible, but death works hard to claim us."

He nodded. His mind flashed to rumors of Katrina having arranged for her mother's murder, the murder of a cousin, even the murder of Victor Davion's lover, Omi Kurita. *How many of her kinsmen has she claimed?* His eyes narrowed. *Did she finally get my father?*

Alaric stood. "One thing is obvious: Whatever the khan's plans, I will be pitted against Bjorn and Donovan. I may rest here, but I will work as well."

Katrina smiled. "I've studied them, you know. I would be pleased to share my thoughts with you."

"And I would be most grateful if you would." Alaric nodded to her. "And in return, if you would allow it, I will braid your hair—in your warrior braid."

"I should like that very much, Alaric." She took his right hand and kissed it. "Then we—warriors together—shall plan a course to victory."

5

Trillian Steiner forced her weariness away and bowed to the archon. "Thank you for seeing me, Archon."

The archon smiled easily and slid from the Lyran throne. Two 'Mechs flanked her, and should have dwarfed her, but the vitality in her light eyes made that impossible. She clasped her hands before her, then spread them, welcoming her envoy.

"Thanks are due you, Trillian. I know this was a confusing mission." The archon's smile lessened slightly. "There was once hope that intrigues were a thing of the past, but they have again become a staple of the Inner Sphere."

Trillian nodded. "I know that, but isn't the mission you sent me on an acceleration of our descent into the chaos of the past?"

The elder Steiner laughed. The sound could easily have risen into hysteria. "You're not seeing the world in the way it is. This is no surprise. You grew up embracing the dream of Devlin Stone. He made you believe peace was possible. It was a noble dream."

"It was one you grew up with, too."

The older woman half closed her eyes. "It was one I wished could come true, but those who raised me were wary. Part of their wariness was bigotry. Devlin Stone had been captured in the Federated Suns. Victor Davion supported him early on, as did his brother, and that spent a great deal of Steiner blood to establish The Republic."

"But Victor was half Steiner."

The archon shook her head. "So it was said. I grew up revering his mother, Melissa, venerating her as if she were a saint. She likely was, to have tolerated Hanse Davion and borne his children. Victor ceased being a Steiner when he had his mother assassinated."

Trillian's eyes widened. "Baseless rumors."

The archon turned, her eyes aflame. "And you know that for a fact?"

"You know as well as I do that there was ample evidence that Katrina had Melissa Steiner killed."

"Of course, Trillian. It couldn't have been trumped-up evidence, could it? I mean, if she slew Melissa, how could Victor have ever given his mother's murderer up to that Wolf? That was the only way he could be sure his secret was safe."

"But Victor gave her over to prevent war with the Wolves."

The archon raised an eyebrow. "Or, perhaps, Katrina went with Vlad to forestall a war. Perhaps she believed Vlad would attack, and agreed to go in silence. Perhaps it was a deal Victor and Vlad struck back on the Clan homeworlds."

Trillian's stomach tightened. "You don't honestly believe what you're saying, do you?"

"Don't think me mad, my dear." The archon smiled, then strolled to a side bar to pour two small glasses of an ice wine. "As I said, intrigues are a staple of the Inner Sphere once again. Rumors and tales that once had little currency have returned to virulent potency. People revive these tales to resurrect old hatreds. There are people on thousands of planets reliving ancient struggles and atrocities. They dwell in fear, and that allows others to manipulate them."

The archon extended one of the tiny glasses to her. "Come, drink with me. I understand you had initial success in your mission, but now I want the details."

Trillian accepted the glass, touched it to the archon's, then sipped. The thick, sweet wine made her smile. Made from grapes that had been allowed to freeze before harvest, the wine tasted of youth and began to set her at ease. *It reminds me of when Stone's peace prevailed.*

"As bidden, I went to Arc-Royal to speak with Patrik Fetladral. He's a very big man, an elemental, with a wide face and firm handshake. He has a scar on his left cheek that makes him a bit more exotic than he would be otherwise. Without it he might be good-looking, but with it he is handsome—though he betrays no knowledge of this. His brown eyes are restless, but he's never distracted, just always thinking. While we engaged in several rounds of talks, he also insisted we spend leisure time together. He plays chess extremely well and is an excellent shot with a bow."

The archon nodded. "But you were better."

"As you knew I would be. He took down a deer. I got a bear. We saw wolves, but they are considered sacred among the exiles."

"So you earned his trust."

"More easily than I've earned yours." Trillian sipped more wine. "I offered him your proposal. He agreed, in principle, but said he would need to make some consultations. He's to let us know by January fifteenth."

"You need not affect that disapproving tone with me, Trillian." The archon smiled, then glanced down. "Just make your accusation."

"Not an accusation, Archon, a question. The Wolves, those here and those who are still with the Clans, are dangerous. Even the enclave Wolves can be lethal. You invite the Clan Wolves into our home. You expect gratitude, as you might expect it from a wolf invited in to warm himself before a fire. Gratitude is not in a wolf's nature. You'll wake up in the middle of the night with his hot breath on your throat."

The archon laughed. "Colorful, Trillian, but you know it's not accurate. The Wolves are dangerous, no doubt about it, but the Wolves-in-Exile have warded the Lyran Commonwealth for decades. They are committed to our survival, and we need them where they are. Things are happening within the Clans that could presage another invasion and I cannot have that border stripped of troops."

"I agree, Archon, but our borders are safe as it is."

"No, they are not." The archon's expression sharpened. "Old hatreds, Trillian. Old wars are reawakening ambitions. The rulers of former Free Worlds League fragments are as hungry as they have ever been. They know of the pressures on our Clan border. Opportunists will be plotting to nibble away at our holdings. I need a force that can punish them. I can and will be training warriors to fulfill that duty, but until I can bring them online, I have little choice but to draw my strength from wherever it is available."

"But there are mercenaries. . . ."

"There *are*, and the best are under contract in the prefectures. As long as this is true, the Marik jackals will believe we are vulnerable."

Trillian thought as she sipped, then lowered her

glass. "You actually want one of them to attack, so you can use the Wolves to punish them and take worlds from them."

The archon set her glass down. "Never think I want war, Trillian. I might never have believed that Stone's peace was possible, but I hoped it would last for my lifetime and then some. The old ambitions to unite the Inner Sphere beneath one First Lord never took root in me, but I will not let my realm be crushed beneath the ambitions of others."

The younger woman opened her arms. "With all due respect, there is only one reason Clan Wolf would come into the Lyran Commonwealth, and that is the prospect of a war in which their warriors could test themselves. That is the Clan way. If they come here and there is no war, how do you think they will react?"

"You're naive, Trillian, if you don't think there will be a threat we can use them against."

"And you, Archon, forget the lessons of history."

The older woman raised an eyebrow. "I'll accept your insolence only because your comment intrigues me. What history am I forgetting?"

"The first Punic War. Rome defeated Carthage and demanded such steep reparations that Carthage could not pay its mercenaries for the war they'd just waged. The Carthaginians had to fight a war against the hired soldiers. How do we pay the Wolves when there is no war?"

The archon returned to the side bar and refilled her glass. "You, my dear, forget a different lesson of history. Do you remember what happened to the Mongols who conquered China?"

"They established a dynasty."

"True, but it was said of ancient China that those who conquer China are conquered by it. Culturally

they were, and so shall the Wolves be conquered."
The archon extended the decanter toward Trillian.
"Look at what has happened to the Wolves-in-Exile."

Trillian shook her head, more to refute the notion
than to refuse the ice wine. "The Wolves-in-Exile
were given a mission that melded them into the Arc-
Royal Theater. It was the mixing of two warrior cul-
tures. Your previous comments tell me you don't believe our Wolves have become lambs."

"Nor do I expect these new Wolves to become
lambs."

"What then?"

"I expect them to become *our* Wolves." The archon
raised her glass in a silent salute. "I don't dream of
being First Lord, but as long as there are those out
there who do, I will do what I must to thwart their
dreams. Surely this is not a vice."

Trillian shook her head. "But neither should it be
mistaken for a virtue."

"A very good point." The archon sipped, then
smiled. "We'll just have to make certain it is a
reality."

6

Verena sighed. It didn't look good at all. She'd been traveling far too long and offloading her *Koshi* had been an ordeal. Myomer fibers in one leg tore so that the leg dragged, striking sparks and scraping a white scar across the ferrocrete.

And now this. The billet assignment had her bunking in a large dorm with her troops. She had her own room—she could see the doorway from where she stood—but packing crates and other debris had been stacked in front of it.

Between her and the doorway lay the dorm and her troops. The rectangular room was filthy, and not just from where the crates had been dragged in. The scrape marks actually carved away the floor grime. The bunks hadn't been made and the yellow tinge of the sheets suggested things hadn't been laundered in a while.

But why should the sheets be clean? The troopers

aren't. They had to be the most sullen and unkempt lot of warriors she'd ever seen. She'd not expected her new command to come up to the standards of the Steel Wolves, but these soldiers looked worse than homeless folks searching garbage containers for meals. *And they definitely smell worse.*

She dropped her duffel bag in the doorway and removed her beret. She folded it and tucked it into her belt at the small of her back. She clasped her fists over it, then looked around at what were now her people. She stood taller than all but a couple, but the bigger ones didn't worry her. They'd grown fat and their eyes were dull.

The only one she found the least bit dangerous was lounging on a bed halfway into the room. Small and slender, with dark hair and eyes, he watched her openly. He wasn't challenging her, just sizing her up. Those who were going to challenge her were shifting around, pretending they didn't feel a flutter of fear at the breadth of her shoulders, or the fact that she wore her blond hair short enough that getting a handful of it would take some doing.

The little one has to be Kennerly. Colonel Bradone had warned her about him. As far as the leader of the mercenaries was concerned, he could do without Kennerly even though the guy was Demon Company's best pilot. "He's a snake, and a venomous one at that. Kill him if you have to."

Weariness washed over her. After she'd been dismissed from the Steel Wolves she was certain she'd find a new position quickly. Other warriors were being snapped up by elite planetary guards and mercenary units, but no one seemed interested in her. Bradone had actually rejected her first application to join the Badgers, then had asked her to come to his headquarters two weeks later. He'd not lied about the horrible position he was offering her, and she took it, even though it was a step up in responsibility from the position she'd had in the Wolves.

You were wrong about me, Anastasia, and I'll prove it.

She cleared her throat. "My name is Captain Verena. I have been assigned to command Demon Company."

"Go away. We don't want you." The speaker, a heavyset woman who was busy braiding greasy red hair, didn't bother to look at Verena as she spoke. "Captain Farras is coming back."

Verena slowly shook her head. "Captain Farras has been bound over for trial on manslaughter charges. He will not be coming back for a long time."

A man levered himself up off his bunk and hooked his thumbs behind his belt buckle, holding back his stomach. "That's where you're wrong. We're fixing to saddle up and go bust him out of the jail in Overton."

"That will not be happening."

The big man lifted an eyebrow. "Who's going to stop us? You?"

"If you force me to, yes." Verena kept her voice even and soft, making them work to hear her. "Of course, I do expect you to force me. That does not worry me. The shape you are all in, the condition of this barracks, the only thing I have to fear here is catching a disease."

Kennerly leaned his head back against the wall. "The dead don't get sick."

"Very true, Kennerly." She hardened her gaze. "This would explain why you all appear somewhat healthy."

The redheaded woman looked up from her braid. "Now, that just doesn't make any sense. We ain't dead. We're the Demons. Bradone might not like us because we're hard-drinking and antisocial, but we're also the best fighters he's got. We've pulled his ass out of the fire in more exercises than anyone can imagine."

Verena nodded. "I know. I have reviewed the exercises. You use unconventional tactics. . . ."

"Hell, we just disobey orders. . . ."

Verena shrugged. "I was giving you the benefit of the doubt. It does not matter. Cowardice is cowardice, and quite obvious."

The Demons looked at her very surprised, so she took a step into their domain. "Cowards. If you were not, you would already be beating on me. Right, Kennerly? They are all just talk. They get wound up, but need a spark. Any warrior worth his sweat already would have thrown a punch."

Kennerly just chuckled.

Verena looked at the big man. "You must be Harkous."

Puffing himself up, he smiled and began to rock back on his heels. "I am indeed—"

Before he could complete whatever comment he was going to make, Verena went for him. Two steps and she launched herself in a flying kick. Both feet landed in his ample gut, snapping his body forward. He flew back, catching his calves on his bunk, dragging it askew. His body slammed into another trooper, a woman whose chin collided with his head. She went down without a whimper, and Harkous landed on her.

Verena landed on Harkous' bunk and bounced up. She got one foot on the floor, then caught the redhead in the face with a roundhouse kick. That dropped her cleanly onto her back. With the two of them down and Kennerly across the room, Verena vaulted back over Harkous' bed and kicked a third trooper in the side of the head. He reeled away, and then the fight was on.

She got her back against a wall and ducked beneath a woman leaping from the side, who landed in a tangle with another trooper. A man tried to tackle Verena, but the wall held her up. She slammed an elbow into his spine, then kneed him in the face. Blood gushed from his shattered nose and he went away.

The next three came as a group, and Verena got poked in the gut with a broomstick. She snatched at it and broke it in half, then used it to parry the next attempt to stab her. The shorter stick brought her assailant closer, so she drove her forehead down into the woman's nose. Verena saw stars, but the woman fell back.

From then on Verena lashed out blindly with fists and feet and the half of the broomstick she'd retained. Several of the Demons went down with a single punch, but two men, the Everett twins, kept coming. They actually seemed to enjoy mixing it up with her—at least until a knee to the groin took one out of the fight, and a blow with the stick half tore an ear off the other and spun him around. He looked at her with wide eyes, one of which she blacked with a punch that knocked him across the room to the foot of Kennerly's bunk.

Verena sniffed, then wiped at her nose. The back of her hand came away bloody. The Demons were all on the floor, some of them groaning, most of them bleeding, save for a couple cowering and Kennerly lounging on his bunk.

She waved him forward. "Come on, it is your turn."

Kennerly shook his head. "Not me, Captain. I've got no problem with you."

"I find myself disinclined to believe that." She pointed around the room with the stick. "They never would have thought about busting Farras out of jail. They never would have taken a step toward organizing such a thing. You thought of it, just as you thought of having them block the door and jump me. Your turn."

Again Kennerly shook his head. His gaze became

sharp, and he met her stare easily. "I have no problem with you, Captain. I understand why you're here and what you hope to accomplish. I'll be interested to see if your experiment works."

"What I have to accomplish? I will make the Demons into a crack unit." Verena tossed the stick aside. "Do you doubt that?"

The man laughed. "No. That you'll accomplish quite simply. They're cows. You've cowed them. You want them to wash and clean and go out on parade, they'll do it. They're small minds. You called them cowards, and proved they *are* cowards. They knew it, and now they know you know it. So they'll toady up to you, all 'Yes, Captain and No, Captain.' This place will be so clean you could perform surgery on the floor and the beds will be so tight you could toss a DropShip on one and it would bounce into orbit."

The Demons who were still awake watched them, and seemed more afraid of Kennerly than they were of her. They nodded with his words, watching and hoping she would accept them. A couple of them who had refrained from fighting were already trying to tidy things up, but they were doing it quietly so no one would notice.

Uneasy, Verena wiped her nose again. "And what about you, Kennerly? Will you toe the line?"

"Oh yes, Captain, of course I will." He gave her a predatory grin. "I will be the best of the best. You'll end up making one of us a lieutenant, and it will be me. You'll find I have organizational skills and can motivate people. You've seen that already. And, let there be no mistake about it, I *want* to be your lieutenant. I want to work closely with you, Captain. I want to be there to see if you accomplish your goal."

She shook her head. "You have already said I will."

"Your goal for the unit, yes." His eyes glowed darkly. "Your goal for yourself, though, Captain, that is the one I want to see if you achieve. I don't think you will. You've already made one misstep, and you will make more."

"What are you talking about?"

"Come now, Captain, do you suppose we don't know who you are? They may not, but I do. I know you were sent away when the Steel Wolves were dissolved. You're an enclave Wolf. You're not good enough to be one of them. If you were any good at all, you wouldn't be here, not with us. Colonel Bradone had rejected your application a priori, not wanting castoffs from the Clan iron wombs in his command. Not prejudice on his part, mind you—he's served with Clanners before. He just knows, we *all* know, that if a Clan warrior is any good, she remains a warrior with her Clan. If she isn't, she teaches. If she can't teach, well, she has to sell her skills. Much like being a prostitute, isn't it?"

Verena's hands tightened into fists. She wanted to pound Kennerly for saying those things, but a voice inside her agreed with him. *Beating him will not invalidate the truth.* Anastasia had seen the truth and sent her away. The only means by which she could change that judgment of her was by proving how good she truly was.

Demon Company would be her salvation.

And Kennerly will be your damnation.

Verena opened her hands. "You read the files I sent to the colonel with my application."

Kennerly nodded solemnly. "I found them most interesting. Educational, really. Unlike the colonel, I've never been around Clanners. And, if you are wondering, I did want you to join us. I hadn't expected Captain Farras would actually kill someone. I just wanted him to get into a fight in Overton so the colonel would bust him down to lieutenant and find someone else to command the Demons. You, in fact. Farras, as your lieutenant, would have led a mutiny. I thought it might be fun to watch."

"You are deprived of that pleasure."

"Oh, but this will be so much more fun." Kennerly opened his arms. "I will be perfect, you know. And now that you know I was thinking of Farras leading a mutiny, you'll have to suspect me of planning the same thing. But I won't. I won't betray their loyalty."

Kennerly rose from his bunk and kicked one of the Everett twins. "Stop holding your groin. It's the most useless part of you. Sew your brother's ear back on. You, Watson, you know what a mop is?"

A slender, rat-faced man slowly rose from behind a bed. "A mop's that thing I used to make your mom happy."

"That's cuz you rode it away thinking it was a pony. Now you'll use it the right way. Clean up the blood."

"Bugger off, Kennerly."

Kennerly's expression hardened and his voice dropped. "Clean. Now."

Watson shivered, but went looking for a mop.

"You see, Captain, they won't like me. They never have. I'm not one of them."

"You are like me, are you?"

"Not at all, Captain." Kennerly drew himself up at attention. "I know what I am. I know my limits. I know what I fear. I know what amuses me. I know how to bend limited minds to my will and how to get what I want. I take my amusement very seriously, and you've just become it."

"And you think I need you?"

He held up a hand. "No. I know you better than you know yourself. Right now you'd like to hit me, just to prove you're tougher than me. But that would just be a physical display of your gross insecurity. Your dismissal from the Steel Wolves is like acid dripping through your soul. It's eating you alive. You are in free fall, and you're grabbing at limbs on the way down. Beating up these losers broke your fall, or delayed it a bit. You now know you're tougher than them. It's a meager validation of your self-worth, but it will suffice, *for a time*. Whipping them into shape will be further proof of your worth. Winning exercises and battles will keep it there. That's what they represent to you."

Verena suppressed a shudder. "And what are you?"

"I remind you that you are an imposter." Kennerly chuckled. "No matter what you do here, you'll never prove to yourself that you're good enough. That validation won't come until Kerensky tells you she was wrong and invites you back. And that is a dream that will never become real."

Verena shook her head. "Believe what you want, but you are wrong."

"No, I am not. You hate that I'm right." Kennerly shrugged. "It really doesn't matter, Captain. You'll do what you must."

"And you?"

"I'll do what I must, too. Farras was too easy to destroy." Kennerly smiled much too eagerly. "I hope your destruction will be much more entertaining."

7

**Domain, Clan Wolf Occupation Zone
15 December 3136**

Alaric successfully hid the surprise he felt—unlike Bjorn and Donovan, who both looked as if they'd just learned they were freebirth. Despite his own racing pulse and the tightness in his chest, he catalogued his rivals' reactions and labeled them *weaknesses*.

The trio of young men had been summoned to Khan Seth Ward's headquarters. Alaric had arrived last. The other two lived nearby, whereas Alaric had remained at the clinic. The summons triggered hours of discussion with Katrina as she coached him through how to act.

She even dismissed his anxiety at the delays their sessions were causing. "If you are first to arrive, you may get points for punctuality, but you do not get to make an entrance. You, Alaric my dear, *must* make an entrance."

And so he had. He wore a dress uniform and was pleased that the wolf-fur trim actually kept him somewhat warm on the journey halfway around the world.

Likewise, the two elementals his mother detached from her retinue were impressive in their dress uniforms, and trailed him from the helicopter back two respectful paces. They then joined the pair of elementals the khan had sent as guides. By the time he entered the conference room, his rivals had been waiting awhile and had availed themselves of refreshments. This meant that when he arrived, they had to hastily set down their cups, brush crumbs from their lips and straighten their jackets.

Advantage, Alaric. Mother would be pleased.

Bjorn shook his hand first, grasping it firmly and pumping it several times past the three that Alaric thought quite sufficient. Tall and blond, Bjorn had a breadth of shoulders that suggested he'd be more at home in elemental armor than a 'Mech's command couch. His grin put Alaric off because it came too easily and revealed poppy seeds caught in the man's teeth.

Donovan, by contrast, would have been utterly unremarkable save for the aquiline nose that dominated his face and suggested mixed blood from Jade Falcon flowed in his veins. His enormous nose set his brown eyes a bit wide in his head, encouraging Alaric to dismiss him as stupid. What saved him from that misjudgment was how the man's eyes darted around, taking in all details. While he did smile when he shook Alaric's hand, the expression came slowly and was calculated, betraying the man's nature.

He thinks, but thinks too much. He overanalyzes. Alaric smiled, understanding that someday, far too late, Donovan would realize his mistake. Bjorn, on the other hand, reacted quickly without sufficient forethought, which made him a good Star commander but a disaster as a strategist.

We are the future of the Wolves. Three futures, two of them dead ends.

Before Alaric was forced into mind-numbing banter with the other two men, the elementals at the door snapped to attention. Alaric executed an about-face and did the same. So when Khan Seth Ward entered the room, his quick reaction time saved him from letting his surprise show on his face. He took joy in his rivals being unable to conceal their reactions, and only regretted their having already set down their cups, for they surely would have dropped them to the floor.

No one would ever accuse Khan Seth Ward of being physically imposing. In fact, he seemed far too slender—mainly because his cooling vest hung half laced and seemed oversized. His regulation boots looked too big for his slender, pale legs, crisscrossed with scars. Acne scars pockmarked his face, and the trace of unshaven beard did little to hide them. His dark hair had thinned, but he did not shave his head, and his brown eyes peered from deep eye sockets, accentuating his skull's death's-head appearance.

Despite his looking so casual, the ease with which he dominated the room put the trio of men to shame. He came in still glistening with sweat from having piloted a 'Mech, simple and eloquent proof that he was a warrior. Warriors were what all of them were supposed to be, yet they had chosen to appear in the finery and pomp of the Clans.

With a simple act of dress he shamed them, stripping them of any sense of self-importance.

The khan looked at Alaric. "I am pleased you were delayed. It gave me more time in the cockpit. One can never have too much."

Alaric bowed his head in acknowledgment; his companions felt the need to respond affirmatively. *He did not ask for comments. It was not a question.*

Seth Ward smiled, his dark eyes sparkling. "I see you have found the refreshments and made yourselves welcome. Good. 'An army travels on its stomach.'"

Bjorn smiled. "The Great Father, Aleksandr Kerensky, said that."

Donovan frowned. "He was quoting Napoleon."

The khan glanced again at Alaric. "Do you wish to eat?"

"I ate on the flight. Slept as well."

"Very good, then we are set to go." The khan turned back to the doorway. "Ah, there you are. Come in and we shall get started."

As his invitation a woman entered the room. Her long black hair showed signs of having been recently released from a braid and hung down over the breast of her cooling vest. Like the khan, she still glowed with perspiration. Alaric put her age at five years older than himself, making her a decade younger than the khan. He found her rather plain, but not wholly unattractive. Her gray eyes contrasted intriguingly with her dark hair and complexion.

"This is Selvina Woods. She is Khan Patrik Fetladral's envoy from the Exiles."

Alaric's mind raced, seeing spheres within spheres. The khan's entrance had reminded them of their true nature. That he had been exercising with one of the Exiles, and that she was attired as he was raised her above them as well. Wordlessly the khan acknowledged her standing as a warrior, which, in turn, elevated the Wolves-in-Exile.

Or was meant to.

This was not easy to achieve for Alaric. He would have thought it impossible, but his surprise at her appearance had opened the hatch to it just a micron or two. Vlad Ward, khan of Clan Wolf and his mother's consort, had opposed the exodus that split the Wolves. He had fought hard to save Clan Wolf from extinction. The stories of his battles were yet legend among the Wolves and marked the depth of passion they felt for their Clan.

His mother had an entirely different take on the Wolves-in-Exile, but she loathed them to the same degree as did Vlad. Phelan Kell had been a distant cousin of hers, son of Morgan Kell, an infamous mercenary leader. When Katrina took the throne of the Lyran Commonwealth and split it apart from the Federated Suns, Morgan defied her. Whenever she told the story, her hand would creep up to massage her throat. Alaric was certain she did not realize she was doing that, and she never spoke of what caused her to feel so threatened still. Regardless, her hatred of the Exiles had been poured into him until it overflowed.

But now, here, Khan Ward offered a different view of the Exiles. He crossed to the sideboard and passed a bottle of water to Selvina before taking one himself. "Please be seated, all of you. You will treat what the envoy says with the same respect you would give words coming from the khan's mouth, *quiaff?*"

Alaric nodded and seated himself at the middle of the conference room's table, halfway between Ward and the envoy. The other two chose seats closer to the khan, but neither dared seat himself in the closest chairs. Bjorn toyed with crumbs from a muffin, while Donovan clasped his hands together and tried to look comfortable.

Selvina set down her bottle. "We have been approached by the archon of the Lyran Commonwealth. Our position in the Commonwealth establishes us as a defensive force against Clan attacks. We are very strong, but our mission restricts our ability to respond to other Commonwealth needs. The Commonwealth has requested that we come to you and offer a mutually beneficial alliance."

Bjorn still played with crumbs, but his eyes weren't tracking what his fingers were doing. The very suggestion that the Wolves, their Exiles and an Inner Sphere nation might unite had blown past his capacity for rational thought. Donovan's eyes had tightened and a vein at his temple pulsed. He started to reach for his cup, then hesitated and folded his hands together again.

Alaric absorbed the information and fended off the negative reaction he heard as a chorus of Vlad and Katrina. Vlad rejected it as a union with inferiors, and the Wolves should hold themselves to the highest standard. Moreover, the request for an alliance revealed weakness. The Wolves should hunt down the source and exploit it. That was a wolf's nature.

Katrina would reject it immediately based on her hatred for the Exiles; but her rejection was not as vehement as Vlad's. In fact, quickly on the heels of it came a question, likewise looking for weakness, but weakness that would allow her to return in glory to the realm she had once ruled. In a glimmer of insight she would see this opportunity as the favor of the gods shining on her. She would return in triumph to the Lyran Commonwealth, victorious against all her enemies.

"The Commonwealth approached us because what they have in mind is similar to our Exodus. They want you to bring Clan Wolf in its entirety to the Lyran Commonwealth. As with our Arc-Royal Theater, they want to position you to be able to defend and attack as necessary." Selvina leaned on her elbows. "The archon's representative was coy, but they are clearly more interested in your taking war to the enemy preemptively than they are in waiting for you to get hit."

Seth Ward leaned back in his chair. "You presume they want to place us on the border with what was once the Free Worlds League?"

"The League's shattered remnants are the only true threat the Commonwealth faces. That border has long been in dispute, and there are rich worlds there. The conquest of any of them would materially benefit the party taking them, grossly shifting the balance of power. The League's confederation is nonexistent, but a successful attack on the Commonwealth could begin to unite their forces or encourage other adventurism."

Donovan shook his head. "Unification out of that chaos is impossible."

Alaric flicked his comment away with a quick gesture. "The same could have been said of the Inner Sphere eight decades ago, but war with the Clans united the worlds in a common cause. The fall of The Republic has caused the old political notions to reappear. We have no reason to believe Marik nationalism could not be quite potent."

Selvina bowed her head. "We agree. Moreover, my Wolves view this as an excellent opportunity for us to heal the rift that sundered us so long ago. The Wolves have always been first among the Clans. Both branches have thrived. While anything approaching a complete reunification would take time, there is no reason we cannot act together in a manner that will benefit both of us and confound our enemies."

A solemn nod from the khan killed Bjorn's intended protest of that point. He realized he'd lost by saying nothing in the previous exchange, but he was unable to read power flows and nuances. This skill Alaric had learned from his mother, and secretly delighted in watching the energy arcing around the room.

Alaric allowed himself a smile. "The suggestion, then, Colonel Woods, is that the remainder of Clan Wolf would uproot itself entirely and move to the Commonwealth."

"Exactly." Selvina nodded. "It is a task of enormous logistical complexity, but we still know how it was done in the past."

The khan smiled. "A move such as this has been

long anticipated in certain circles. We have run simulations. It can be done."

The Exiled Wolf nodded. "We always anticipated you might pursue us. Now we may be united again. We have the Jump- and DropShip assets to help you accomplish this journey. Of course, as with the first Exodus, speed and secrecy will be paramount, and just as much for the Commonwealth's protection as your own."

The vastness of the project and its various implications exploded in Alaric's mind. Pieces of it began to align themselves, but it was Donovan who began to articulate things. His need to verbalize in order to comprehend was another weakness, but at least he was capable of understanding the gravity of the task.

"If Marik forces catch hints of any alliance, they would be forced to attack. This would put us at a disadvantage. While our troops could swing into combat almost immediately, we face the challenge that our noncombatants would be scattered throughout the fleet, in order for us to use transportation assets in combat roles. If we were forced to land sudden influxes of Wolves on worlds in order to free up transportation, that could trigger protests and other problems. It might cause enough trouble that the archon would be deposed and then we would be invaders in a new realm, with no way back out."

Bjorn agreed. "First off, we have to secure our base of operations."

"Exactly. We need to control perception and move with utter secrecy. We will have to be stealthy."

Khan Ward nodded. "Your thoughts, Colonel Alaric?"

"I cannot discount the wisdom of what my peers have said. It is a conundrum, and not an easy one to solve." Alaric nodded toward the Exile. "You have had time to think on this."

"I have, and would gladly make my thoughts known to you. You will, however, find them flawed. I am only able to *project* what your assets and needs might be. Any estimates and suggestions would have to be revised in light of actual figures, and I can easily imagine your reluctance to communicate the same to me. If you did, it would leave you vulnerable whether you agreed to this offer or not."

She smiled. "Therefore, I shall assume any data to be generally correct, but also discounted by a factor of ten to twenty percent."

Donovan and Bjorn nodded, but stopped when the khan shook his head. "The Inner Sphere's intrigues might force such caution, but between Wolves we have no need to suspect treachery. I will give you the information you desire and risk this being some sort of elaborate trap. I am certain you know any war with us would be one of mutual annihilation. Neither of our peoples are given to such wasteful foolishness."

Alaric brought his hands together. "If you will forgive me, Khan Ward, it sounds as if you are considering this proposal seriously."

"Is there a reason I should not?"

"Neg, though the chances of it working well are slim."

The khan smiled. "Fortunately for me, I am not the one who needs to make it work. You three are. I want the three of you to come up with plans to make this work. Each will be judged, one or more of them may be adopted, and you each will play your part, if the plans are implemented. Do you understand this?"

Alaric limited his response to a curt nod.

"Very well. You will be taken to your quarters here and all the necessary data will be made available to you. You will have a staff of three subordinates to work with you, subordinates of my choosing. You will formulate your plans and present them to me in two days."

Two days? Alaric shivered.

Bjorn nodded enthusiastically.

Donovan adopted the curt nod.

Khan Ward stood. "Two days, gentlemen. Two days to secure the future of Clan Wolf."

8

Domain, Clan Wolf Occupation Zone
17 December 3136

Of course their plans are flawed—they are mere mortals. Alaric had known their presentations would be flawed before either man began to speak. Each had duplicated his data and report, making copies available to the khan, the envoy and the other advisers Seth Ward had invited to listen. They studied their datapads, then tipped their heads back and closed their eyes, as if this would somehow allow knowledge to seep into their brains.

Donovan displayed the most nervousness. He flicked the buttons on the datapad, flashing screens forward and back, scrolling down through long streams of data. Alaric did not doubt that the man had equipment lists broken down by the serial numbers of the parts in every 'Mech he intended to use. He'd clearly checked and double-checked all of his figures. He'd be able to project the entire cost of the operation to the nearest billion C-bills, which would delight the Lyrans no end.

Bjorn, on the other hand, just smiled obliviously. He clearly assumed he had the entire operation locked up. He might even have thought of a trick or two— an errant missile will find a target now and again. Ultimately, however, his bliss must come from ignorance, because there was no way he could deal with the overwhelming amount of data created by planning an operation like this.

So, just as Donovan found himself drowning in data, Bjorn blithely skated above it all. Neither man had found the middle ground, but Alaric had. The key was knowing *what* data had to be handled and ignoring the rest. This he had done, and that was why he was superior to his mortal competition.

Bjorn rose first to make his presentation. "Khan Ward, distinguished guests, the charge I was given was to plan a new Exodus from our occupation zone into the Lyran Commonwealth. Our *presumed* destination is the border with the old Free Worlds League."

Alaric raised an eyebrow. *Presumed?* Bjorn's delight with himself clearly stemmed from his belief that he had found a loophole in the planning. He'd not solved the problem they'd been given, he'd found a solution and redefined the problem.

The blond man hit a button on his datapad, and the lights in the amphitheatre dimmed. A holographic representation of the Inner Sphere burned to life, and shading delineated the political realms: blue for the Commonwealth, gray for the Wolves, green for the Jade Falcons and silver for the remains of The Republic. The gray and blue bordered each other, making for an easy transfer of troops and personnel.

"The key problems we face are the need for speed and for secrecy. It was pointed out that if the enemy gets word of what we are doing, they could attack the Commonwealth and political pressures could topple the government. We would be trapped in a foreign nation, no longer welcome, and face an exodus as difficult as that of the Ten Thousand from Persia three millennia ago."

A nice historical reference. I wonder how much time you wasted looking for it.

"A solution suggested itself to me almost immediately." Bjorn's grin grew. "Eighty years ago the Exiles staged an exodus and have offered to help us accomplish ours. My plan is bold and simple. We, for our part, will follow their original plan and blast our way through the Jade Falcons. No one will suspect a thing. We will hurt them enough that they will not pose a threat to the Lyran Commonwealth.

"What this will do, then, is free the Exiles from their duties in the ART. As we come through the Falcons, *they* will leave their homes and head toward the border with the old Free Worlds League. Their passing will cause no alarm and will position them perfectly to deal with the League leftovers. We will come in and take their old positions, and they will travel to the holdings we were to be given. If we need to switch places later, that can be arranged."

As he spoke the star chart changed. A gray shadow fell over some Falcon worlds, and shades of blue shifted within the Commonwealth. At the end of it all, the Commonwealth's blue had a gray tinge, but glowed far more intensely, suggesting vitality.

Though the animation did not impress Alaric, the basic tenets of the plan did. Not that it would work, but at least Bjorn had enough sense to realize that making the journey as short as possible was absolutely paramount. The longer the Wolves were on the move, the more vulnerable they became.

In theory, because a JumpShip could leap thirty or more light-years at a time, any journey could be accomplished without having to land on a planet. The JumpShip would merely arrive in a system, recharge the Kearny-Fuchida jump drive, then leap to another system. Depending on the route chosen, pursuing a force would be impossible and anticipating where they would end up would be doubly so.

Theory, however, gave way to practicality. While JumpShips could operate independent of planet-falls, the personnel and equipment in the DropShips they hauled could not. Just feeding the troops would require reprovisioning. Even if the Clan stripped every last ounce of food, fuel and spare parts off the worlds they were leaving, they would run out of provisions well before they reached their destination.

As the Napoleonic maxim advised, an army travels on its stomach, so either they were going to have to tighten their belts, or find supplies along the way. Bjorn's solution of making the trek short helped a great deal in that department; but it was unrealistic to expect the Exiles to accept an influx of Wolves while their military went far away to fight. And the Exiles would be disinclined to pick up lock, stock and barrel and staff the worlds intended for the Wolves, no matter how logical a solution to the problem that was.

Most importantly, the Jade Falcons were unlikely to accept being blasted through. Their internal struggle might make them appear to be weak, but both sides would certainly unite to oppose the Wolves. The Jade Falcons had fought tooth and talon when the Exiles first made their escape, and there was no reason to assume the Falcons would do less this time.

Even if it is the shortest distance between two points, one should never willingly wander into a minefield.

Donovan rose next to present his plan. At the touch of a button on his datapad, the Inner Sphere map shifted. Individual data windows concerning worlds bordered the whole map, shifting to the center and growing larger as he spoke about each world in turn. Given his nature and the number of the worlds, Alaric guessed the presentation would take only slightly less time than the exodus itself.

"As you can see, the pressing needs for speed and secrecy are the driving factors in my plan as well. I have mapped out several routes to our destinations that I consider optimal. By creating a relay system of JumpShips, we can move our assets very quickly across Commonwealth space and have our troops positioned to counter any Marik strikes. As you will note, I have graphed the speed with which news tends to radiate out from worlds, and I have broken those worlds down into classes. We will be moving through the third class of worlds, the ones that rarely contribute information of value or timeliness to discussions within the Lyran Commonwealth, significantly delaying news of our passage. Secondarily, I have grouped the worlds into networks that map data transmission, and have adjusted our travel routes accordingly.

"This then brings me to a discussion of the merits of our various units and the optimal configurations for their transport priority based on performance estimates, working relationships between personnel, compatibility of equipment on an intraunit basis, interunit basis, and resupply capability of the various worlds where we will be stationed. In all cases I was able to find matchups that provided a minimum eighty percent combat-effective compatibility rating. The one world pushing that envelope on the downside is within striking distance of a highly compatible Marik world, so we might just hit it and take it preemptively."

Donovan then proceeded to take the assembly through his plan, stage by stage, pouring a mind-numbing amount of detail onto the holographic display. He truly *had* covered everything, and even provided statistical variations to account for transport failures and other unforeseen circumstances—though the success of his plan counted on fewer rather than more disasters.

One small detail had escaped him. Bjorn's plan had involved an attack on the Jade Falcons. It was predicated on being able to repeat the success of the first exodus, led by Khan Phelan Ward. Donovan, instead of repeating history, chose to let speed maintain secrecy. If people were able to move on his timetables, the window for discovery and reaction would be tiny.

The problem was, success depended on a *lack of discovery*. A chance raid by a Falcon or Ghost Bear force could reveal everything. That, after all, was the problem with deception: If it didn't work, it was absolutely worthless. Magicians had known that for ages. If you plan to deceive, you must first misdirect. Donovan's plan provided no misdirection, no way to control the minds of the enemy.

Without controlling their minds, you allow them to think independently. That gives them the chance to think of a way to oppose your plans.

Finally Donovan concluded his presentation. Khan Ward rose. "Thank you, Star Colonel Donovan. You have given us a great deal to consider. Though it is a little early, I suggest we break now for lunch, and resume the briefings in the afternoon. Does that meet with your approval, Star Colonel Wolf?"

Alaric stood slowly. "Actually, sir, I would prefer to give my presentation now. I am aware of the hour and will be able to give my presentation without delaying lunch."

Donovan shook his head and tapped the datapad. Bjorn just smiled. The khan's eyes narrowed, but he nodded. "Proceed, Star Colonel."

"As has been noted, speed and secrecy are paramount to this operation. If we cannot move quickly enough, we risk exposure and being preemptively cut off from our objective. The problems we face are simple. Delays will happen. Secrets will be revealed. We have no control over either factor, no matter the depth of our planning. The key to success, then, lies in managing the reaction of others when they learn of our plans, and channeling their reactions into events that are to our benefit."

Alaric tapped his own datapad and the Inner Sphere map appeared. "The most logical routes into the Lyran Commonwealth are obvious and certainly should be used. These will be the routes along which our support personnel will move as quickly as possible. Full employment of our assets in this capacity should allow our noncombatants to reach the designated home-worlds by April of next year, provided we begin moving by the middle of January. This schedule would involve completely stripping these worlds and destroying anything of use to the Ghost Bears or Jade Falcons. This exodus, logistical nightmare that it is, can be accomplished and shall be.

"It is important to remember, however, that we are Wolves. We are warriors first and foremost, not meant to slink through stars silently or retrace steps taken by our ancestors. Ours is the right and duty to blaze new trails. Not only do we know this, but our enemies know this. They know it is the fabric of who we are, and it is playing to their knowledge of who we are that will win the day for us."

He hit a button on the datapad, and the map tightened to show a slice of the Inner Sphere running from the Wolf occupation zone down through the former Republic Prefecture IX. "I propose that we initiate a push into the former Republic and drive toward Terra. We pour down through Prefecture Nine and hit Jade Falcon worlds on the way. We push all the way to the edge of The Republic's core. And I propose we tell everyone exactly what we are doing."

Murmurs sounded, and Donovan's chuckle rose

above them all, but Alaric ignored them. "I propose we tell the Falcons and the Ghost Bears that we are driving for Terra, that we will shatter The Republic's fortress and accomplish what we started out to do nearly a century ago. We are tired of waiting, of having our martial spirit questioned. We are going to prove the might of the Clans once and for all.

"Imagine what our enemies will think. You know they will all believe it. They will marshal forces to get there before us, but entangled as they are in their own affairs, they will be hard pressed to do it. Because we say we are stripping everything for this drive, risking it all, the Falcons and Ghost Bears will also have to flood our occupation zone to fill the void. The Marik pretenders and every other House in the Inner Sphere will have to make preparations for the event of our success, calculating what it will mean to them."

Alaric smiled slowly. "We will not need to hide what we are doing. We will be in charge of our enemies' perception. They will see what we want them to see. They will react against what they believe we are doing. They will be in no position to stop us. By the time they learn our true plans, if they ever do, it will be too late.

"It will be too late because we are Wolves. We are warriors. They fear us. All of them, and with good reason. Our courage and audacity will leave them gasping and reacting, not planning and anticipating. They will allow us our victory simply because they cannot conceive of a way to stop us."

Khan Ward leaned forward in his chair. "This is interesting, Star Colonel Alaric. I only have one problem with it."

"Sir?"

The khan raised an eyebrow. "If we tell our enemies that we are driving for Terra, we will be lying to them. Is this not beneath us?"

"We would not be lying, sir." Alaric lifted his chin. "I set a challenge, sir. I bid for the right to take Terra."

The khan frowned. "Our enemies would see through so thin a deception."

"It is no deception. If we make it to Nusakan, we can make it to Terra."

"And I would bid against you, saying the ability to reach Nusakan is insufficient evidence of success in taking Terra."

"Yes, sir."

"It is a bold plan, and one not without merit. If I accepted your plan and your challenge, you know you would have rivals in its execution." The khan glanced at Bjorn and Donovan. "They may not possess your audacity, Alaric, but they are not to be discounted. Neither are the troops you would face."

"I am aware of that, sir." *But they are mere mortals.* "I have the utmost respect for them and our enemies. I simply believe that they leave themselves open to manipulation that benefits our cause."

Seth Ward smiled slowly. "Oh, I have no doubt they will believe we are headed to Terra. And I am equally certain they will slip into the vacuum we leave behind. With luck, the Falcons and Ghost Bears will even clash over worlds and do each other great harm.

"My only real question is this. Will we do ourselves even greater harm following your plan? Have you an answer for me on that, Star Colonel?"

"We are Wolves, my Khan. We are the masters of war. It is our element. No true harm can come to us when we are engaged in it."

9

Overton Conference Center
Overton, Baxter
Former Prefecture IX, Republic of the Sphere
3 January 3137

Verena stood at the back of the presentation hall, happily anonymous in the darkness. Delegations from all over Prefecture IX had come to Baxter to plan for the defense against the Wolves. Mercenary leaders and commanders of planetary garrisons all expressed disbelief at the Wolves' audacity at announcing their plans. Though the warriors had come to plan, many clearly thought they were wasting their time.

Verena knew they weren't, but that was not for her to say. Colonel Bradone represented the Badgers while she and the other Badgers acted as hosts for visiting dignitaries. The hosting duties mostly fell to the battalion's other companies. The Demons, though they *had* improved in the last two weeks, were hardly presentable. Fortunately, they were still combat-worthy, which would be the most telling thing in the new year.

General Artor Bingham of the Skondia Lancers mounted the steps to the stage and took his place behind the podium. "Ladies and gentlemen, you've all had the briefing materials and a chance to study them on your way here. We are in a unique and, I am sad to say, challenging position. You were all hired to hold off marauders, and well suited to that task. Now we face a hammer, and the blow will fall on you."

Not a hammer, a stake driven by a hammer—a hammer hefted by a 'Mech.

Bingham kept his voice warm and remained composed, his shock of white hair granting him an air of dignity. "Many of you are serving on your homeworlds with local garrisons. We also have many mercenary units here, some storied, some new. For all of us the fight to come will be difficult and we can really expect no succor. The Republic remains silent in the face of our requests for help. Likewise the Lyran Commonwealth and the other prefectures. They all appear to be shoring up their borders to prevent the invasion from spreading, but they see no benefit in helping stop the invaders here. As one of them put it, 'Stopping a flood is impossible, but channeling it is altogether doable.'

"So far, the most cogent suggestion I've heard is to evacuate everyone and let the Wolves race through to Terra. There are moments—moments in which I feel we are being abandoned—when this sounds like a good idea. If I believed they'd pass through us on their way to Terra—taking nothing, harming nothing—I'd give them the coordinates of pirate points and lend them JumpShips. I resist taking that path because I have no desire to give Skondia over to invaders. I would avoid fighting the Wolves, but I don't think that is possible, so we need to organize our defenses as best we can."

A woman rose, but Verena couldn't make out who

she was. "Do you think opposition is practical, General? Your briefing material indicates that the Wolves are coming with every piece of military equipment they have. It's a complete mobilization of their armed forces. It's not raids we're facing, or their contests for the possession of a world, it's a tidal wave of men and machines."

Somehow the woman managed to keep panic out of her voice, but only just. Being raised in the Clan culture gave Verena a very clear window on how things would go. The Wolves would arrive in a system, request information on the defenses, and challenge the defenders for possession of the planet. The Wolf warriors would bid among themselves to see who could take the world with the most efficient mix of troops, so they would try to match their foes as closely as possible. An easy victory conferred no honor on a Clan commander unless his tactical planning turned it into a rout.

General Bingham nodded. "That's a very good question. How can we be expected to stop a Clan onslaught? We have one simple advantage—they have limited supplies. By plunging headlong into their assault, they distance themselves from factories and re-supply. We need to disperse our troops, force the Wolves to move and expend supplies. We need to draw out the battles, shift and move. We must establish hidden caches of supplies so we can continue fighting. We have to slow them down, bog them down, so they will quit."

Another woman stood, and though Verena only saw her in silhouette, the simple movement of rising to her feet identified her. Verena knew her before she spoke, and as her words filled the hall, Verena's cheeks began to burn.

"Anastasia Kerensky of the Wolf Hunters. Your suggestion has a problem, General. You have correctly analyzed the weakness in the Wolf plan, but you have failed to see the other side of it. The delaying tactic to run them out of supplies worked very well for Precentor Martial Focht in the battle of Tukayyid, but that was because he bargained hard and forced the Clans into a compromising position. The Clans were constrained to bargain hard because they were being compared to other Clans, and were positioning themselves for ascendancy in Clan politics.

"Here, however, we have a more desperate situation. Because they cannot easily resupply themselves from an industrial base, they need to take an industrial base. This means they cannot afford to lose any worlds. While individual Wolf commanders will bid hard against each other for the honor of taking a world, they will not be so foolish as to underbid the forces needed to take it."

Verena shook her head. There was no faulting Anastasia's logic. The Wolves *were* trapped into taking every world they attacked. They had put themselves in a position of following Sun-tzu's ancient dictum to identify your target, hit it, and get out. Do not wage war without material gain, and do not wage it for a long time.

"Thank you, Colonel Kerensky. You have succinctly articulated the key difficulty we are facing. My advisers and I have come up with a strategy that we hope will answer this. We are initiating a doctrine of segmentation. The idea is that when challenged to defend a planet, we specify which zones we will defend, and with what troops. If we defeat the Wolves in one district, we will be safe there. They will challenge us elsewhere, but the process will protract the war."

Various leaders murmured appreciation for that plan, but Anastasia shook her head. "That might work, General, but segmentation stands outside Clan tradition. If they came in and challenged you for the possession of a continent, you could put your plan into effect. When they challenge for a planet, however, they are under no obligation to reduce their bid. In fact, most would assume your ploy to be one prompted by cowardice, steeped in deception."

The older man's head came up, but he did not voice any anger. "Do you have a suggestion that will help us?"

The Wolf Hunters' leader nodded solemnly. "Your core assertions are correct. The Wolves are going to need to hit and hold worlds to resupply themselves. If we look at Prefecture Nine, we can identify worlds by the supplies they offer. Some are meager pickings, some are rather abundant. Skondia, for example, is a treasure trove, Baxter less so. Corridan Four is so poor I would bypass it, if I were them."

"You would suggest then, Colonel, that we heavily defend the rich worlds and let the others go?" General Bingham frowned. "It strikes me that even our most heavily defended worlds would fall prey to a well-bid onslaught."

"Without a doubt, sir, but you are making a couple of assumptions that are utterly unwarranted. First off, your plan to disperse supplies is a very good one. It will allow our troops time to move and strike. It will not give the Wolves the swift victories they need. It *will* tie them down, and even frustrate them. That is the first step in how we defeat them."

"And the second step?"

Anastasia looked around and Verena could feel control of the briefing shift. Here she was, leader of a new mercenary unit no larger than the Badgers, and yet men and women were listening to her as if she were Devlin Stone himself. Part of it was that the situation was so dire they'd gravitate toward anyone who said she had a viable solution. Over and above that, however, Anastasia possessed a presence, a confidence that made people believe her even before she revealed the depth of her planning.

"The second step is simple. Look at who we have here. We have planetary garrisons that will be defending their worlds. We have corporate militias that will defend property. We have mercenaries who will prosecute their assignments. Right now we anticipate that we will all hold firm on our worlds—and if we do that, we will all be pounded into ferroceramic splinters.

"But do not look at us as separate units, look at us as a collection. If we truly defend Prefecture Nine, we can stop the Wolves. We delay them as much as we are able when they fight to possess the world. Then, once they have it, we challenge them for possession. We force them to defend. We force them to eat up more time and waste more resources, preventing them from taking whatever supplies we leave behind. They may take worlds, but they will not benefit from them."

The simple logic of Anastasia's plan was lost on no one. Once the Wolves had attacked a world the defenders would have a wealth of information about them. The frontline troops would likely be lifted off the planet to attack another world, while garrison troops would replace them. A successful counterattack would require the frontline troops to return and take the planet again. Depending on how the defenders maneuvered, worlds would change hands constantly, or the Wolves would be forced to tie up far too many troops holding their worlds.

And once outsiders see how we have bottled them up, they will come help us. Victory has many fathers, but defeat is an orphan. If we succeed, when we succeed, all sorts of possibilities open up.

Verena shivered. The plan was simple, incredibly simple. It was just an extrapolation of Bingham's plan.

If delaying them on one planet would work, delaying them multiple times on that planet would work better. The Wolves would expect everyone to fall back before them, to be brushed aside by that tidal wave of men and 'Mechs, but this would be striking back. It made perfect sense, obvious sense.

And yet I missed it. She frowned. *Why is that?*

General Bingham swiped a hand over his jaw. "There's a great deal of logic to your plan. I doubt the Wolves would expect us to be stripping planets of their defenses to strike back and contest conquered worlds."

Anastasia opened her arms. "Once you make the enemy dance to the tune you call, you are one step closer to victory. But do not misunderstand me. The Wolves initially will be taken by surprise, but they will adapt. The fighting will be fierce. Every unit represented here will have its mettle severely tested. I daresay that whether we are successful or not, half of us here may not be alive this time next year. Most of the dead will never get the chance to be buried on worlds they call home. That is not a problem for me, but it may well be for your troops.

"I would make one other point, and it is one that must be taken most seriously by every commander here. Our units will have to be divided into two groups. For better or worse, some will be hammers, the others will be anvils. Anvils will defend worlds and suffer a furious beating. Their job, at the very least, is to slow the Wolves, test them, learn their weaknesses and report that information to the hammers."

The mercenary leaned forward on the back of the chair in front of her. "Units with no planetary assault skills will be anvils. This is not going to be a venue where assault skills can be learned on the fly. No leader can be offended or feel slighted because his unit is not nominated for liberating a world. If we let ego dictate our actions, we will die one and all."

Bingham's white brows arrowed together. "And who will make the determinations of capabilities?"

Even though Anastasia could only be seen in silhouette, Verena could feel her smiling. "I will take that responsibility. In fact, I demand that job. I know the Wolves. I know their ways. I know we can frustrate them."

"Frustrating is not *defeating*, Colonel Kerensky."

"You are correct, General. If anyone stands here and tells you they can guarantee defeat for our enemies, you know you are listening to an idiot—one who will likely get himself and his troops killed quickly." She folded her arms. "I offer the opportunity to win. Collectively we will have to make the most of it."

"Do you actually hate her, Captain, or deceive yourself into thinking that your desire to *be her* is really hatred?"

Verena's head snapped around. "Oh, I hate her, Kennerly, hate her with a passion."

"If that's true, you're more of a fool than I thought." Kennerly drew up a chair at Verena's table at the rear of the Officers' Club.

"I do not recall inviting you to sit."

"You didn't, but you don't want to be alone." He sipped the lager he'd brought with him. "Has she even noticed you?"

"It is not my place to distract the commanding officers." Verena stared across the room to where Anastasia sat with Colonel Bradone and General Bingham. Part of her wanted to wander over as casually as possible to say hello, but the knot in her gut wouldn't let her get to her feet.

"You're disappointing me, Captain. Don't you think

it would be better for you to renew acquaintances now, rather than risk her failing to acknowledge you tomorrow when the Badgers pass for review? Wouldn't that be embarrassing, to have her not recognize you as you stand before your troops?"

"You actually think she would not recognize me?"

Kennerly's eyes slitted. "No. You are absolutely correct, Captain. She would recognize you. She knows you're here. She's studied all the unit rosters, their skills and capabilities. You're not alone in being a castoff from her Steel Wolves. She does know you're here, but the question is, will she let others know she knows you?"

Verena felt her shoulders knot up. "Why wouldn't she?"

"Ah, you used a contraction. Your Clan sangfroid melts. You would have to tell me why she'd not want to be associated with you. Did you embarrass her that much when you served under her?"

"No, no, I did not." Verena turned and glared at her subordinate. "That is all history, old history. It does not matter."

"But of course it does, Captain." Kennerly smiled. "Until you know why she let you go, and until you prove to yourself that she was wrong, you'll never rest. While we're fighting the Clans, you'll be fighting yourself. And the thing of it is, *we* can win. But you? Pfft."

"You better hope I can win, Kennerly." Verena gave him a hard stare. "When I fight my battle, you will be in the thick of things with me. If I do not win, it will be bad for all of us, and none of us will survive."

10

Alaric checked the restraining straps on his command couch, then snugged them tight. He double-checked the *Mad Cat*'s weaponry and ran some diagnostics. He'd changed the 'Mech's weaponry configuration for the assault on Yed Posterior, removing the long-range missiles and adding heat sinks so the trouble he'd had on Koniz wouldn't be repeated. Moreover, shifting to energy weapons cut supply problems, though he didn't anticipate being on the world very long.

He'd been gratified that Khan Ward chose his plan as the organizational document for the exodus. Donovan's meticulous planning was put into place to deal with logistical organization. Very quickly the invasion took shape and Alaric had looked forward to bidding against his rivals for the honor of picking which worlds they would invade. Since they had come up with the plans, the khan made it clear they would receive primacy of placement.

I should have expected a trap. He knew that *trap* was perhaps harsh, but he certainly felt trapped. The first three worlds to be hit were Yed Posterior, Corridan IV and Baxter. Baxter was prime among them because it had been settled the longest, had plenty of light industry, a thriving agricultural system and enough political turmoil to fracture defending forces. When he'd begun his planning, Baxter was the target he'd studied and earmarked as his goal.

Khan Ward had other ideas. Instead of allowing the three of them to bid for their targets, the khan assigned them. Alaric had taken great delight in Donovan's being handed Corridan IV, since the planet's chemistry made it a poisoned pit that was highly dependent on trade with other worlds. While the concentrations of heavy metals and rare earths did make it very useful in the manufacture of electronics components, the supplies it could provide would be of only tangential use to the invasion.

Bjorn's being awarded the Baxter assignment had surprised Alaric. The Baxter operation would require planning well beyond Bjorn's abilities. There was no doubt that any unit Bjorn chose to lead would fight well and hard, but Baxter wasn't going to be lightly defended. The person invading it had to think in terms of *campaign*, not battle.

The same had to be said of Yed Posterior, a cloud-shrouded water world whose meager landmass consisted of archipelagoes. The world was self-sufficient and produced a lot of exportable protein through aquaculture. Between that and water, the world would be useful, but the hideous storms for which the planet was famous and having the population spread throughout chains of islands ensured that it would be difficult to maintain control of the world.

To exacerbate matters, Khan Ward then bid for Clan Wolf against each of the commanders. If their bid on the number of troops they would use was not what the khan thought was appropriately efficient, he would assign the operation to another Star colonel. Alaric hated bidding against the khan because he had no advantage. Another of his peers he could have read and bluffed, but the khan did not fall prey to such psychological maneuvering.

It is because he knows I would bid going all by myself with a spoon if that was what it took. My bluff has been called even before it was offered.

Yed Posterior boasted a militia that was supposed to consist of two infantry companies, one company of mobile artillery and two lances of light and medium 'Mechs—all industrial refits. Alaric was confident of defeating them—even without a spoon. He ended up bidding two 'Mech Stars and two elemental Stars, but chose to employ only one of the 'Mech Stars. He had no intention of calling down reinforcements, but instinct told him that having them available would be useful.

The distant echoes of an explosion rumbled in his 'Mech's cockpit. He keyed his radio. "What was that?"

The *Romulus'* captain replied, "We are coming down in a storm and just got hit by lightning. A short-range missile launched and exploded close by. Nothing to be worried about."

"Keep me informed."

"As ordered."

A lightning strike and an explosion—two ill omens, though Alaric had no desire to believe in such things. They fit, however, with the rather jaunty attitude of the militia commander when Alaric had declared his Trial of Possession for the world. The man had cheerfully told him what they would be defending with. "All we have, and reinforcements if we can find them."

Alaric countered with his force description and got, "Bring 'em all. Enjoy your stay. Happy hunting." That was not the response he'd expected, and as his DropShip burned in toward Henderton on the big island of Belleisle, it preyed on his mind. Granted the defender had an advantage in that he knew the terrain better and had trained on it, but the Wolves were superior warriors and they piloted superior equipment.

It was the "happy hunting" comment that rankled the most. Alaric's plans hinged on his bringing the militia to combat quickly, hammering them hard and winning the trial. Once he had done that, garrison troops could come in, the world could be raided, and he'd move on to Marfik or La Blon. Hunting down the militia would take time he didn't have and didn't want to spend.

The radio crackled. "Ten minutes to touchdown, Star Colonel. Scanners are negative for enemy contact in your landing zones. Storm interference is causing problems, so I do not know how accurate those scans really are."

"Understood. Thank you." Alaric punched a button that relayed the arrival data to the rest of his troops, and then he switched his radio to the tactical frequency.

"We may not see them now, but they *are* waiting for us. They believe they have a chance against us, but we know they do not. Remember your operational directives. Innovation and initiative tempered by discipline is what this fight demands." He reached up and snapped his neurohelmet's mirrored faceplate in place. "We are Wolves. We will hunt. We will win."

Rain slashed in sheets over his cockpit canopy. Alaric had kicked his holographic display over to infrared, but all it showed was water drenching a landscape of palm trees and giant ferns. Oversized fungus abounded, spotting the landscape and clinging to buildings as ivy might on other worlds. Though he'd entered the industrial outskirts of Henderton, the planet's abundant plant life all but hid factories deep in a rain forest.

Lightning exploded, splitting the night with argent fire. For a half second the flash illuminated the blade of a forestry 'Mech ducking behind a warehouse. Alaric swung his crosshairs onto it and hit the triggers on his joysticks.

The particle projection cannons in his 'Mech's claws spat artificial lightning. Jagged blue-white beams sizzled through the night. The beams' hellish power would be enough to melt the militia 'Mech's arm clean off, or decapitate it. But to do that, the beams had to hit, and they didn't.

On any other world they'd have blown through the warehouse's wall, but not here. Yed Posterior's climate forced engineers to plan against natural lightning strikes—and on this planet, they made a PPC's beam seem like a static spark. The PPCs did melt some stone, but energy played through a lattice in the mortar, draining into the planet.

Alaric ground his teeth. This was *not* how his invasion was supposed to be going. He'd landed unopposed and marched directly on Henderton. The city had been built in the crater of an extinct volcano, where a collapsed wall to the west gave the city an excellent port facility. The volcano's walls had been holed and tunnels built that would accommodate a 'Mech's passage, but there was no way Alaric would let his troops get trapped there. Instead he'd taken the 'Mechs along the coast and into the industrial district. Once through that he could secure the ports and their warehouses. When his elementals captured the nearby spaceport, DropShips could begin the looting.

The militia was using unconventional means for defense. As the Wolves approached by the coastal route, the defenders detonated charges high up on the crater's walls, triggering landslides. The cascade of rocks did score some armor and killed two elementals, but primarily served to slow the invaders' advance. A point of elementals scaled the heights and eliminated some of the defenders, but reported that the crater walls were honeycombed with tunnels.

As if to confirm the full import of that report, shoulder-launched short-range missiles would periodically spiral down. Again, more of an annoyance than a real threat, they simply forced the Wolves to keep their eyes open. Attack could come from any quarter.

And it did, most unexpectedly. Two 'Mechs that had been fitted out for marine salvage work rose from the ocean depths while his 'Mech Star was strung out on a causeway. They launched flights of LRMs that hammered a *Puma* and all but tore off one leg. It still limped along, and his 'Mechs had blazed away in response with their PPCs, but the militia 'Mechs had melted away in a froth of bubbles.

And then had commenced the hunting game in the industrial district. Alaric glanced at his secondary monitor. His 'Mechs had established a cordon and were moving point to point to clear the area. The elementals infiltrated the factories and reported sporadic fighting. The most annoying part of those battles was that the people they fought appeared to be private security forces and untrained civilians, not the militia.

And yet there is one 'Mech in here somewhere. He shook his head. The forestry 'Mech didn't have much by way of weaponry—just a big chain saw and a jury-rigged medium pulse laser. The hybrid 'Mech could grind away on his *Mad Cat* with both for a long time before doing any serious damage. The problem was that it was able to elude the cordon, and yet allowed itself to be seen. It was drawing him on, but into what he had no idea.

Off to the east lightning flashed and something exploded.

"I'm hit. I'm hi—" The frantic radio call died abruptly.

Alaric's monitor showed the *Puma* had gone red. "Star Commander Zuzanna, report on the *Puma*. What happened?"

The staccato sound of machine-gun fire prefaced her report. "Partisans used a cable to ground a lightning rod on the *Puma*. When that last bolt hit, the surge must have shut down his engines. Derek is moving in the cockpit."

"Cover the *Puma*. All units, make certain you are clear of entanglements. Star Commander Raynald, I need your Point with me."

Without waiting for the elementals to join him, Alaric pivoted right and fired both PPCs at a scrolling metal door in the side of a warehouse. A wave of heat washed up through the cockpit as the door flashed from red to white and evaporated. Alaric sent the *Mad Cat* into the warehouse, ducking low on the bird legs to keep his profile small.

"What have we here?"

He swept his crosshairs over the forestry 'Mech's torso and hit the firing triggers. A volley of red energy darts scattered themselves over the militia 'Mech's arms, head and chest. Armor dripped and the wounds glowed hotly around the edges.

Then the 'Mech disappeared.

"*Stravag* dogs." Alaric pounded a fist against the arm of his command couch. "I should have seen it."

He marched his 'Mech forward cautiously, shifting around to the right, while keeping his crosshairs focused on the square opening where the forestry 'Mech had vanished. He crept closer and closer, finally rising up to the 'Mech's full height. He thrust both claws toward the hole, but saw nothing save a ferrocrete slab rising flush with the warehouse floor.

It all made perfect sense. The storms on Yed Posterior were a nuisance, and the residents had taken the logical precautions. They could easily have built roads up the side of the volcano and down through natural passes, but tunnels were storm-proof. Within the industrial district it only made sense for there to be a series of tunnels that would allow 'Mechs and other vehicles like forklifts to move from one place to another without having to worry about the weather.

They will make us enter their tunnels to root them out. Happy hunting, indeed. It was a mark against him that he had not anticipated this. There had to be lifts in every warehouse and factory, with the elevators operated through a coded transmission. That meant he needed to find the codes—a fruitless effort because the militia would just have them changed—or had to tunnel his way in. That would be the most effective way to approach things, but would pin down his forces and give the enemy the ability to hit them.

And while it might be the most effective way to deal with things, it would also take the most time. It was time he did not want to spend, but he really had no choice.

Anger spiked in his chest and his hands curled into fists. *How dare they defy me?* Even as that question echoed inside his head, he had two answers. The first, practical, was that of course they had to defy him. He was attacking their home. Only cowards would refuse to defend it, and it looked as if more than just the militia was willing to undertake the defense.

The second answer ran deeper. He saw himself rising out from the cockpit of his 'Mech, his awareness soaring through the factory roof. His feet rested firmly on the ground and as he raised his head, it brushed the underside of the clouds, inviting lighting to wreathe him. He could feel its tingle as it ran over his body. He reached out and caught a fistful of it and hurled it toward the center of the city.

They defy me as mortals have always foolishly defied the gods. Their resistance was a test of *him*, not of the Clans. Alaric knew very well the ancient dictum that no plan survived contact with the enemy. He had expected to deal with things quickly. The world and its defenses had surprised him and caused problems; but were the problems insurmountable?

Of course not.

Alaric smiled. No doubt the militia leaders were pleased with themselves. They'd surprised the Wolves with their tactics. They were able to move with impunity on their world and the invaders could not. The militia could elude them and draw things out, costing him time, denying him conquest of the world.

But the failure of a plan to survive contact with the enemy cut both ways. They had their plan, and it was predicated on a pattern that Alaric would change. His declared goal was possession of the world; in reality, all he wanted was possession of its resources.

And, for all their pluck and ingenuity, they could not deny him access to the resources. It might take him time to eliminate the militia and take the world, but he could take his loot immediately. Moreover, he would do things they would not anticipate, since they believed he intended to remain on Yed Posterior.

But I do not. Alaric smiled slowly. *They will pay for their defiance, I shall see to that. They have invited the wrath of the gods, and they shall see how terrible it can be.*

11

Baxter's dual moons hung high and full in the sky with nary a cloud to obscure them. Verena studied the landscape, from the open fields below her position up to the hills that ringed the valley she overlooked. A gentle breeze teased golden grasses, and just for a moment she relaxed.

What a beautiful day.

Kennerly's voice crackled through the speakers in her headset. "Beautiful day to die, isn't it?"

"Either you read minds, Lieutenant, or you have a soul."

"Neither, Captain. That thought is just the *common* thought. I knew you'd be thinking it."

"And what were you thinking?"

"It's an even better day to be killing someone."

"Oh, I think we will be getting to do plenty of that." At least that was her hope, though Verena knew it was unlikely. The strategy that Anastasia had outlined and everyone had accepted spoke against any pitched battles. It was to be a war of hit and fade, snipe and run. The whole idea was to bleed the Wolves.

She understood and accepted that wisdom. Sun-tzu advocated hitting the enemy where he was weak, and to appear strong where you are yourself weak. She knew all the classics of military doctrine, and had taken to poring through Hackworth's *Vietnam Primer* to study how he advocated fighting an insurgency so she could counter those tactics.

But will it do any good? The Demons had been placed in the Emerald Basin Planetary Park to secure the Badgers' escape route from South Allshot. From the moment the Clans had appeared in the Baxter system, South Allshot had been a prime target. The manufacturing facility there produced miles of my-omer fibers every month, and the main plant was surrounded by factories for 'Mech subassembly and refitting. Last month's production had been shipped off-planet already or hidden in caches, and key manufacturing components had been disabled in the plants, but it would not take long for the Clans to make them operational again.

The trick was for the Badgers to contest control of the factories without causing too much damage. *The old Solomonic solution of splitting the baby will not do.* Back when the Republic of the Sphere was whole, a scorched-earth policy would have made sense, because The Republic's resources would have been devoted to bringing things back to normal as quickly as possible for every planet it protected. Without that sort of support, rebuilding the industry could take forever.

The Badgers didn't contest the landing at the Allshot spaceport off to the east, but instead were fighting a retreat out of the industrial zone. They hoped for two things. The first was being able to draw the

Wolves into an ambush in the park. The second was making them believe they'd beaten the Badgers badly enough that they would not mount further operations. That would free them up to hit supply convoys heading from the industrial zone to the spaceport. As the Clans were forced to devote more forces to protecting their convoys, the Badgers could go after the factories again.

It all made perfect sense, and Verena was prepared to play her part. The battalion's Animal Company, under Colonel Bradone's command, was already engaged in the hit-and-run battle through the factory district. The Beasts had been stationed north near the capital of Overton and had prepped defenses that would slow the Clans down a lot. She'd hoped her Demons would be given that job, but Bradone chose to keep them close, citing her experience with the Steel Wolves as the reason.

There were two ways she could have read that, and neither was good. The first was that Bradone didn't trust the Demons despite the way they had begun to straighten up. The second, which she considered worse, was that he didn't trust her. It could have been that since she was untested he wasn't sure how she would handle things.

Then again, maybe he thinks my being part of Clan Wolf makes me sympathetic to the invaders. He would not have been the only person to think that. While everyone understood that the Wolves-in-Exile and Clan Wolf had been split for decades, their doctrines and practices were similar enough that from an outsider's point of view, it was hard to tell them apart. More than one military leader had wondered if Anastasia Kerensky was leading them into some sort of elaborate trap.

She shook her head to banish that thought and again studied the fields before her. She punched up her tactical plots so they overlaid themselves on the holographic display. She'd plotted a safe zone through which the Animals could move. She expected them to come fast. The whole company consisted of two light and one medium 'Mech lances, so they should be able to outdistance their Clan pursuit. Once they entered the safe zone, she'd direct her 'Mech lance's fire at the lead Clan elements. That would slow them; then they'd move to flank her.

And when they do that, wham!

Verena nodded solemnly. "This will work."

Kennerly chuckled dryly. "See the gold grasses?"

"What of them?"

"In under a minute they'll be gone. It'll just be dirty craters and fire."

"Just as long as there are Wolves in the bottoms of those holes, who cares?"

A light flashed on her console and she punched the corresponding button. "Demon leader, go ahead."

"Animal leader, we're incoming. Be ready, they're coming fast."

"Acknowledged, out." Verena cut her radio over to the Demons' tactical frequency. "Incoming, get ready. As we planned it."

She swallowed hard and felt perspiration rise on her flesh. Her heart began to pound, and not as it had before when she was in combat. That had been excitement. She had been a Wolf and a Wolf looked forward to combat. She'd been sent away, stripped of her identity, made into a mercenary who had been accepted into a company because they needed someone fast.

Damn it, Kennerly, get out of my head! She wanted to rub at her eyes, but her neurohelmet's faceplate was in the way. Kennerly was wrong. The only thing she had to prove was how good a shot she was. She already knew she was a warrior. She knew precisely how good, too, because she'd tested out well enough to become a line trooper.

The voice of her self-doubt, which had weeks ago begun sounding like Kennerly's voice, tried to whisper more horrible things, but she forced herself to focus. She checked all of her monitors. Her *Koshi* was green. The fields of fire had been laid out perfectly. Her people were in position and would follow her orders. If they did everything they were supposed to, they'd get out of it fine and the Clans would be hurting.

But no plan survives. . . .

Verena swung her crosshairs up. Something moved at the far edge of the basin. It came up over the rim and hopped oddly on its way down into the valley. *Flea. That's One Lance.* A second *Flea* appeared, followed by a *Commando.*

Where's the Mercury?

Animal Company's first lance poured into the basin without the *Mercury.* After that came Two Lance. A *Commando* led two *Mongooses,* and Lieutenant Carter came up last in her *Hermes.* All four of the 'Mechs looked worse for the wear, with armor hanging in tatters. Benson's *Commando* had taken the most damage. Its right arm was frozen pointing at the ground, with tattered myomer fibers flapping from a hole at the shoulder.

Three Lance, the medium-class-weight command lance, came last, with Colonel Bradone bringing up the rear in his *Vindicator.* The black, humanoid 'Mech had once been painted with golden stripes, befitting the unit's totem animal. The battle had blistered paint and soot stained the gold decorations. The PPC that replaced the 'Mech's right forearm had been melted away. Armor had flaked and melted all over, giving Verena a clear view of the 'Mech's internal structures. She wondered for a half second what could have done that much damage, but as Bradone's 'Mech started down into the basin, his pursuer crested the hill. It walked on bird legs, its cylindrical body thrust forward. Both arms ended in thick weapons pods. Its talons gouged through the turf as if the pilot wished to anchor it there. It stood a giant above fleeing villagers, and then took a step forward.

Bradone slowed his 'Mech, then turned. The pulse laser on the *Vindicator*'s head flashed, lacing red darts over the Clan 'Mech's right claw. Armor rained down in fiery drops that started the grasses burning.

The Clan *Mad Cat* stabbed both weapons pods forward. Artificial lightning crackled. Both argent beams hit the *Vindicator* square in the chest. Armor evaporated and secondary explosions spat out structural members. Missiles poured out, cascading down, bouncing off the *Vindicator*'s legs.

Bradone's 'Mech reeled backward. Grasses and dirt flew as the 'Mech left its feet. It fell back, slamming down hard. Verena felt the vibration when it hit. She watched, waited—her held breath burned her lungs. *Get out of there!*

The Clanner took another step into the basin. A claw came up and took careful aim.

"Fire *now!*" Verena spitted the *Mad Cat* on her crosshairs, and the dot at their junction flashed gold. She hit the trigger. The twin medium lasers in her 'Mech's left arm lanced out at the Clanner. One missed low, but the other carved a black scar across its ankle. Kennerly's PPC ripped a beam across the aiming claw, and two more PPCs from her lance's *Panther*s scored leg armor.

As surprised as the Clan pilot might have been, he didn't shift his aim. His PPC flashed a beam that struck the *Vindicator* in the chin. It ripped up over the canopy and fire exploded from within. The spherical head sagged like a rotting grapefruit, but a command couch burst upward and soared into the air.

"He's free!" Sheila Carter's voice cut through on the tactical channel. "Two Lance on me. Open fire lanes, Verena. We'll get the colonel."

"Negative, Lieutenant. Demons, lay down your fire, *now*." Verena shifted her aim as two more Clan 'Mechs skylined themselves on the far hills. "Animals, keep with your escape lanes."

Verena's two artillery lances complied with her orders. The missile carriers and hovercraft launched multiple volleys of long-range missiles that filled the sky with contrails. The missiles swept over the far hills, sowing them with a harvest of blazing explosions. Clan 'Mechs vanished in clouds of smoke and fire—though Verena knew better than to imagine she'd done more than scratch armor.

"Carter, move!"

The *Hermes* had stopped and was turning toward the spot where Bradone's command couch was going to land. Unlike the missiles, which had flown smoothly, the chair's path had been erratic, and only one of the two parachutes deployed.

He can't be alive, and won't be when he hits at that speed. Verena shook her head. The couch fired as the cockpit melted. He couldn't have survived.

"I have to get him."

"He is dead."

"Shut up. You don't know him. He's alive!"

Kennerly's voice cut into the frequency. "Carter, get back here, or my next PPC beam runs right up your butt."

"Kennerly, he's alive."

"Three. Two."

"Kennerly, shoot the damned Clanner." Verena snapped off two laser shots at the *Mad Cat*. "Carter, he is dead. You do not want to join him."

"But—"

"Get back here. We need you. Now!"

Another volley of missiles crashed down, this one scattering along the inside of the basin's lip. Several caught the *Mad Cat*, shattering armor. Smoke and dust covered the Clan 'Mech, though it still glowed hot when Verena shifted to infrared.

Savrashi! He is white-hot. The pilot had to have been constantly firing his PPCs and everything else as he pursued the Badgers. Another shot or two and his 'Mech would shut down. *And then we could take him apart.*

Almost before she knew what she was doing, she made her *Koshi* take a step forward. *No, wait!*

"Badgers, we withdraw as planned. Animals, form up at point delta. We cover you, you cover us." Verena glanced over as the *Hermes* retreated in the wake of the other 'Mechs. "Carter, how much pursuit did you have?"

"One lance. That one guy, he just kept coming. He was fast and shot well."

"He is backing off now." Verena glanced at her tactical monitor. "One last volley, Demons. Then we pull out. This did not go quite as planned, but it could have been much worse."

Verena sat against one of the mine walls clutching a hot cup of coffee. The Badgers had pulled back into a chain of mines that had been converted into shelters back when the people of Baxter were preparing against the original Clan invasion. Knowledge of the caves and tunnels was hardly a secret, but they were located far enough from South Allshot that the Clanners would have ample warning if the Badgers emerged to attack them.

Kennerly walked over and sat beside her. "Mechs are being refitted. We'll be fully operational in three days. We've gotten communication from Major Peres up in Overton. He's confirmed your command of both companies pending his appointment of a captain to run the Animals."

She looked at him. "You did not volunteer?"

"No, and I told him picking Carter would be a mistake. I think he'll send Abbie Dannik down. Until then, you're it." Kennerly smiled at her, but she knew it wasn't a sign of friendly feelings.

"Say whatever it is you want to say, Kennerly."

"Not say, Captain. I want to ask you a question."

"What's that?"

The man's eyes glinted coldly. "Why didn't you go for him?"

"Who?" She set her coffee down. "The Clanner?"

"He was almost shut down. If you'd emerged and challenged him, he would have responded. He would have cooked himself, and that would have ended a big threat. You could have proved something."

"Yeah, I could have proved how stupid I was."

"Easier to tell yourself that would have been stupid than it is to believe you're a coward, isn't it?"

Verena gave him a level stare. "You saw what I saw. Why did you refrain?"

"I was under orders, Captain." Kennerly gave her a short salute. " 'Mine is not to wonder why . . . ' "

"That is crap. Answer me straight, Kennerly. I have seen you shoot. If you had gone after him, you could have hurt him, maybe even killed him. You knew we would cover him with missiles. You could have been the big hero." She opened her arms. "This unit would have been yours."

"Which is exactly why I didn't do it." He shook his head. "I don't want this unit. As long as you have it, the pressure grows. I think you'll crack, and it will be sooner rather than later."

"Why is that?"

"Because I believe that tonight, or tomorrow night, you'll begin to wonder if Bradone really *is* dead. You'll be able to think about what the Clans are doing to him even now. What information they'll get, what secrets they'll learn. See, everything has changed, and now figuring it all out is on your shoulders."

Verena just stared at him, then through him, watching that command couch arc through the air. *He is dead. No one could have survived that.*

"You are a sociopath, Kennerly, do you know that?"

"I'm sure I am, Captain." The man smiled as he stood. "Pleasant dreams."

12

Alaric's eyes burned and his shoulders ached. He was fairly certain he'd never be dry again, and almost as certain he'd never sleep. The Yedders had proved persistent and resourceful, but he believed the battle against them had finally turned the corner.

The first thing he'd done was to call in his reinforcements. That did cost him some prestige, but it also gave the Yedders more to consider. With the extra lance in tow, he abandoned the factory district and secured the spaceport. Once he'd done that, he called down multiple DropShips and began looting the planet.

He went about it in a very systematic fashion. He and his troops would pounce on a warehouse complex, strip it as quickly as possible of everything they could move, and ferry it back to the spaceport. Once the cargo was loaded, they would push on and raid another warehouse.

To distract the Yedders from what he was doing, he staged other minor raids. His troops hit the world's planning office to get a map of the tunnels. He had computer technicians wage a covert war with the Yed militia to crack the codes that operated the lifts and gates to the tunnels. He even had elementals commandeer equipment to dig tunnels of his own. This latter effort resulted in some running gun battles through the basements, sewers and streets of Henderton, with the Yedders getting the worst of it.

A logical choice would have been to break into the tunnels and start hunting, but that would just have encouraged the Yedders to wire the tunnels with explosives. Alaric and his people might get in, but their chances of getting out would be minimal. Moreover, the Yedders could just evacuate the maze and let the Clanners wander around until they starved. Going into the tunnels would work only if the militia's 'Mechs were known to be there.

His raids were not without danger, but by the time the militia figured out what he was doing, he'd already taken precautions to limit the effectiveness of any counterstrikes. Moving the spoils from the warehouses to the spaceport provided the enemy with the best chances to attack, so Alaric and his people just made that process as difficult as possible.

To do this, they demolished the city for two blocks on either side of the main route. Everything was leveled, from stores and apartments to civic buildings. The buildings might have been built to withstand lightning strikes, but battering by a 'Mech could put a dent in almost any structure. In addition to giving the Clanners clear fields of fire, their action sowed great fear among the populace and sealed up uncounted tunnel entrances.

After they finished looting a warehouse they would bring it down, too. They continued this process, inexorably working toward the sea. It seemed very clear there would be no stopping them.

Some did try, but their efforts were ineffective. Regardless, Alaric instituted a practice of razing any building from which a shot was fired at his troops. Aside from that, however, he left the locals alone. The message was clear: Let us pillage your planet, we'll let you live.

While he *was* pleased with the assets he was pulling off the planet, the fact that Yed Posterior hadn't yet been pacified was not making him happy. It didn't help at all when he learned from his reinforcements that Donovan had secured Corridan IV in half a day, and managed to do that without damaging the industry or suffering a single loss among his troops.

When heading in to Corridan, Donovan announced he'd be grounding at one specific location. It *was* a good landing site, but the most direct route between it and the capital city presented several points where the opposition could ambush him. The leader of the Corridan militia had written a book about military strategy, which Donovan read. In studying the maps of the area, he picked out the most logical location for the man to stage an ambush. Instead of landing where he had intended, Donovan's troops performed a combat drop on the militia's position and broke them almost immediately.

Donovan, Alaric had been told, already had pulled his line troops, had garrisoned the world and was back with the fleet planning his next assault.

And I am stuck here on Rainworld.

Every six hours the Yedders added to his frustration by broadcasting a message to the planet. It was mostly propaganda to bolster the courage of the people of Henderton. It promised reinforcements would be arriving soon, and while Alaric sincerely doubted that, he couldn't discount it completely. The Yedders warned that they could and would kill the invaders and as the Wolves pushed deeper into the warehouse district, Alaric could feel something in the air.

He smiled to himself as he waited in the cockpit of his *Mad Cat*. The Yedders had been very lucky so far, but they needed to continue being lucky. He only needed to get lucky once. Luck, he sincerely believed, favored the prepared. Alaric made his plan, briefed his people and set things in motion.

And if I succeed, I will have to thank Donovan.

Donovan's success had gotten Alaric thinking. He'd succeeded because he had remained consistent to his nature. Donovan was a planner. He analyzed data, he figured out how the other commander thought, and then he put his knowledge to use.

Alaric, from the very start, knew that an even more powerful tool was controlling the thoughts of the enemy. The efforts to unlock the tunnels were easily countered, which left the Yedders thinking the tunnels were secure. They dismissed them as being vulnerable. The tunnels were their domain.

On the surface, the Wolves had become predictable. They pounced, looted and razed. They were a pack of hyenas stripping carcasses, leaving nothing but rubble and a steel-girder skeleton behind. They always moved at the same pace along the same route. Chronometers could be set by their actions.

And attacks could be arranged.

The Yedders accepted the challenge at noon on the second day. A hideous storm broke over the big island, making the storm on that first night seem like a spring shower. The Wolves set out as usual from the spaceport, but wind, flooding and a lack of visibility slowed their progress. While the trek *to* the warehouse district would have been when Alaric chose to attack, the Yedders waited, realizing that heavily laden transports would make easier targets.

So they gathered in secret, making good use of the tunnels. Their 'Mechs mounted the elevators and rose into the hearts of warehouses where spies had confirmed a lack of Clan personnel. When the transports started forming up into a caravan, they prepared to strike.

And while they prepared, Alaric and his troops struck. The Clan leader targeted a warehouse two blocks away and hit his triggers. Red laser darts peppered the facade and blew through tall, narrow windows. The twin PPC lightning bolts struck the building, playing over the grounding lattice, but still melting ferrocrete.

Alaric keyed his radio. "Control, lock down the targets when you get a pause."

"As ordered, Star Colonel."

The *Mad Cat* sprinted across the dark, storm-lashed landscape. Alaric fought to stay upright as rubble shifted beneath the war machine's feet. Twisted steel girders flipped up into the air as easily as twigs dislodged by a toddler's jerky run. Though fighting the machine made the advance difficult, Alaric was thankful it also made him a difficult target. The one burst of laser darts from within his target missed well wide.

Because of the storm and terrain conditions, Alaric took a full minute to reach his target. He didn't bother to blast the huge scrolling door, he just plowed through it. The segmented steel curtain draped itself over his cockpit, then fell aside. He snapped his sensors over to vislight and was greeted by a large rectangular hole in the floor.

"Shut things down now, Control."

At his order, the Wolves' trap was sprung. Deep in the bowels of the building something rumbled. All of the emergency lighting in the place went dark. For a moment, until he switched to magres, Alaric could see nothing.

But he didn't need to see.

The Yedders had controlled the tunnels and moved with impunity. They thought themselves safe because there really was no practical way for the Wolves to locate them. The planet's fierce storms and the constant microtremors associated with volcanic activity rendered seismic monitors useless. The insurgents could move with impunity, and they knew it.

What they had ultimately neglected to address, however, was that the tunnels had a limited number of entrances, and the elevators required electricity to run. Until Alaric had given the order, the Clans had never cut power to the warehouse district. Even though every warehouse had its own backup generators, in most cases they were insufficient for powering the elevators. Alaric took no chances, and now had them destroyed.

He marched his *Mad Cat* forward and leaped down into the hole. He braced himself. Twenty meters down, impact with the ground jammed him into his command couch. He crouched his 'Mech, then backpedaled. Sweeping his crosshairs over the 'Mech outline in front of him, he hit his triggers.

Though he had shot hastily, the forestry 'Mech was bracketed by the tunnel through which it fled. It had started to make a right-hand turn, so the twin PPCs caught it in the left flank. Armor exploded on vaporous jets, scales whirling away to smash on tunnel walls. The rent armor gave him a tantalizing glimpse of the 'Mech's internal structure, some of which glowed.

More important that the obvious damage was the result of his assault. The pilot, caught in the midst of a high-speed turn, lost control of his 'Mech. The damaged industrial 'Mech slammed into the far wall, catching the corner of the intersection on its left shoulder. It spun around, smashing its back against the tunnel wall, then rebounded and dropped to its knees.

Alaric reversed his retreat and darted forward. He triggered his pulse lasers. A cloud of coherent light darts burned into the 'Mech's left shoulder just as the 'Mech pressed its arm to the floor in an attempt to rise. The lasers evaporated armor and ate into the arm's ferrotitanium bones. The shoulder separated and the 'Mech faltered again, this time falling on its left side, presenting its back to him.

So easy, too easy. His crosshairs settled on the 'Mech's glass canopy. Through the spiderwebbed glass he could see the pilot up and out of his command couch, pounding on the inside of the bubble. The canopy release had jammed, and the advancing *Mad Cat*'s footfalls shook the floor hard enough to knock the man down.

The gold dot confirming a target lock obscured the man's further struggles.

Alaric hit the triggers, and the PPC's backlight gave him a ghostly look at the tunnels. Stopping shy of the decapitated forestry 'Mech, he glanced at his secondary monitor, then cut left. An *Uller* had entered another factory just west of his and was chasing prey.

"Seven, what do you have?"

"Say . . . One . . ." The radio reply crackled with static that spiked with the *Uller* getting hit or lightning from above. The secondary monitor flickered and positions updated, but Seven no longer appeared where he had been.

Alaric hoped it was just interference, but if it wasn't—*what could they have that could take down an* Uller *so quickly?* Nothing in the data they'd sent for bargaining indicated anything more than medium-weight 'Mechs. The marine salvage 'Mechs had sported LRM launchers, but those would be singularly useless in the tunnels.

Whatever it is, I bet Donovan would have found it. Alaric snorted angrily, then turned left again, heading toward Seven's last-known position. *Whatever it is, I will find it, and then I will kill it.*

The outline of a 'Mech flashed across his scanners at the next intersection, but the computer had insufficient data to determine what it was. Alaric pressed on, twisted his *Mad Cat* to the right. He intended to keep moving at speed but have his weapons pods cover the corridor. If the Yedder hadn't cleared the passage, he'd get a clean shot at its back, open it up and kill it.

Alaric had only a second to react, though the moment seemed to unfold over the course of hours. The Yedder 'Mech had not fled, but had stopped and turned around. The pilot pressed the barrel-chested 'Mech hard against the corridor's right wall, making it a tough target to hit. Alaric's scanners caught enough of it at point-blank range that the identification of *Hunchback* instantly flashed on a tertiary monitor.

The thought *they have sent a museum piece against me?* flitted through his mind a heartbeat before the Yedder 'Mech opened up. Ancient it might have been; still the 'Mech sported a heavy autocannon in a boxy appendage on its right shoulder—hence its name. The cannon vomited fire and depleted uranium shells that blasted into the *Mad Cat*'s right hip.

Ferroceramic armor rained down in shards. The shells cratered the Clan 'Mech's hip and thigh, and struck with such violence that despite not fully penetrating the armor, they shifted the 'Mech's center of balance and knocked it off its course.

Alaric hit his triggers, but his momentum and the *Hunchback*'s position made it hard to keep the crosshairs on target. One of his PPCs and two of the pulse lasers missed, gouging scars through the tunnel's tiled walls. The other two caught the *Hunchback* in the right arm, stripping it of armor and starting the

'Mech's bones glowing, but did nothing to the laser mounted in the forearm.

Then the *Mad Cat* hit the tunnel's far wall. He caught the edge on his left hip and shoulder, which twisted him around. His cockpit crushed tiles as his 'Mech spun. He continued backward, crushing more tiles and aft armor against the opposite wall, then crashed his left weapons pod against the wall to keep himself upright.

Alaric pitched himself deeper into his command couch, then hunched forward against the restraining straps. The neurohelmet's feeds picked up brain waves and fed them to the computers governing the 'Mech's gyroscopes. For a half second they whirled out of sync, threatening to drop the 'Mech, but then they caught. More armor and tiles littered the tunnel floor as Alaric's left pod dragged along the wall, and he hugged it for support as he got the 'Mech's legs under it again.

And, in doing so, he saved his life.

The *Hunchback* pilot, having seen the *Mad Cat* careen out of control, stepped into the intersection to finish it off. The autocannon blazed. The line of slugs ripped a furrow down the corridor wall, filling the air with tile fragments. Some of the slugs hit the *Mad Cat*'s left arm, further tattering its armor, but doing no serious damage.

Unfortunately for the Yedder, to use the cannon on its right shoulder it had to step fully into the intersection. The twin PPCs spat and hit the 'Mech full in the left flank. Melted armor rained down, burning like hundreds of votive candles. The pulse lasers' angry red darts ripped up through the 'Mech's naked right arm. Myomer fibers snapped and the bones beneath melted away. The twisted remains of the arm dropped to the ground and the *Hunchback* drunkenly reeled away.

Then, from the other direction, the green beam of

a large laser stabbed through the 'Mech's left flank. The verdant beam melted the remaining structural members. The 'Mech's left arm dropped off and the unbalanced 'Mech spun to the ground, lying there with its back exposed.

Seven's *Uller* limped around the corner dragging its right leg. "Star Colonel, we have an emergency."

"And what could be more important than hunting down the militia in their warrens?"

"There are DropShips inbound. The commander has sent us data. She is coming to reinforce Yed Posterior."

Ah yes, they bargained saying they would use everything they could, including *reinforcements.* Alaric clenched his teeth. "How much?"

"Three battalions. Two are militia, one mercenary."

Fear flushed ice through Alaric's guts. No matter how poorly armed and led, three battalions would be able to drive him off the planet. *And, because I bargained as I did, I have no more reinforcements to call upon.*

"How long?"

"Three days." Seven hesitated for a moment, then added, "She said her name is Anastasia Kerensky and she is leading the Wolf Hunters."

Kerensky? Unbidden a shiver ran down Alaric's spine. The Kerensky bloodline was long and storied among the Wolves. If there were warrior gods and goddesses seeking to be born into flesh, they would have chosen Kerensky flesh for their avatars. *And now one comes hunting me. This truly is a Trial of Possession for my destiny.*

"It matters not who and what is coming, Seven." Alaric centered his crosshairs on the *Hunchback*'s cockpit. "We have a job to do. We need to finish the militia before she arrives. If we do that, she'll have a surprise awaiting her."

13

Verena smiled as Kennerly jumped back. Water still dripped from his face, and the towel he'd been using smeared a droplet of blood on his chin. He looked at her, then took another swipe with his towel, dragging it down over his throat.

"Don't you have better things to do than watch me shave?"

"Maybe I hoped you would slip with the razor."

Kennerly snorted once, then shook his head. "You're not serious. Without me, your life would lose all meaning."

Verena frowned. "Not this time, Kennerly. We are not turning a discussion into your psychoanalysis." *I have no need for your voice in my head anymore.*

"Then how may I be of service?"

"I have to know you are going to stick with the plan."

"Oh, I would never dream of doing anything else

but follow it, Captain." Kennerly hung the towel over his shoulder. "You're showing great confidence in me. Don't think I don't appreciate that. Lieutenant Carter, on the other hand, wonders what we have going on between us. She's not enjoying what she sees as a demotion, but she has other problems."

"No doubt you are helping her sort them out."

Kennerly looked back over his shoulder at the slender blond woman curled up against a cavern wall sleeping. "I could, but she's not nearly as much fun as you are. Her doubts are more raw. She watched Colonel Bradone die, and she feels guilty. It doesn't matter that sensor data from our 'Mechs make it clear he was dead before his chair ejected. You know her feelings are going to make her suicidal."

Verena nodded. "I would have her stand down but . . ."

"But her lance would revolt, and Animal company would follow." Kennerly smiled with his mouth but not his eyes. "You've put yourself in a precarious situation. There will be repercussions if you fail."

"I know."

In the aftermath of the action in which the colonel had died, the Badgers had regrouped and repaired their 'Mechs. They were operational save for the loss of the *Mercury* and Bradone's *Vindicator*. Major Peres' placing Verena in command had not been followed with any operational orders, and this created problems. Not only did the Animals want revenge, but the lack of orders suggested to everyone that Peres had no confidence in her.

This particularly vexed Verena for two reasons. First, it made her wonder what Peres saw that made him hesitate in giving her orders. Didn't he think she could lead? Had he disagreed with Colonel Bradone's hiring of her in the first place? Was he sending Abbie

Dannik down to replace her, and how soon would she arrive?

Those and a thousand other doubts assailed her, but she shunted them aside. Not only did she not have time for them, but she had Kennerly to keep track of them and a billion more. He constantly picked at her, which in one way was a good thing. It gave her impetus to deal with her other duties and do them well.

The second reason the lack of orders disturbed her was that she knew how the Clanners could be beaten. She'd seen it in the way the *Mad Cat* had crested that hill and continued to come on. The pilot had been happy to chase after a company of 'Mechs, even outdistancing other, faster 'Mechs under his command. While that showed courage, it also showed a complete lack of forethought, and she could exploit it.

She'd talked with survivors of the initial action and they confirmed her opinion. Bradone and the Animals had set up a classic ambush. They'd allowed the Clanners to move into position where the mercenaries could catch them in a cross fire. They'd been under orders to target the smallest of the Clan 'Mechs, hoping to take them out of the battle immediately, and they had killed one *Uller* in the initial exchange.

In keeping with ages-old doctrine, the remaining Clanners had driven hard at the ambushers. If they had gone to ground and looked for cover, it would have been bad, so they moved and attacked. They hit the Animals hard and Smythe's *Mercury* got blown to bits right away. The Animals withdrew in good order, exchanging fire and setting up the Clanners for the Demons' secondary ambush.

That ambush hadn't gone off as planned because the Clan pursuit had come on so fast. If the Animals had been farther into the basin, the Demons could have hammered the Clanners and the Animals would have had the option to form up and come back at them. That would have been Colonel Bradone's call, however, and in his absence, Verena had gone with the original plan.

Even if Kennerly hadn't made his snide suggestions, Verena would have chosen to act. She could read the political flows within the unit. Here she was, the most recent hire, the officer placed in charge of the least desirable unit. Colonel Bradone had died, and some people harbored a suspicion she'd let him die—simply to absolve an officer they'd loved of having done something stupid or having caught the bad side of luck. Unless she gave them a reason to think of her as a leader, they never would. The unit would fall apart and that meant the Clans would succeed in taking Baxter.

Even as she started to plan, old demons assailed her. She knew the grand strategy: Keep the Clans occupied, harry them, wait for reinforcements. Hit and run was the order of the day, but the patrols she'd sent out failed to elicit any interest from the Clans. The troops in South Allshot seemed content to pacify the city and prepare defenses against an assault.

We cannot bleed them if they will not come out and play.

Verena wrestled with the problem of getting the Clans to join battle. She recalled all manner of historical battles and tried to map them over the situation in South Allshot. The original plan for hitting Clan troops in the stretch of wasteland between the city and the spaceport went for naught because the Clan troops simply didn't head back to the spaceport.

Verena's eyes narrowed. "I know this plan will work."

"Would you fall prey to it, Captain?"

She blinked. "I am not the one we are attacking."

"But the answer is important." He arched an eyebrow. "Are you counting on the Clan leader being stupid?"

"No, I am counting on him being a Wolf."

"Ah, and what would that entail?"

"I do not think you would understand, Kennerly."

He opened his arms. "If you can't explain it to me, Captain, then perhaps you don't understand it well enough for your judgment to be trusted."

Verena raked fingers back through her short hair, relishing the scratching along her scalp. "To be Wolf is to be the consummate predator. Hunting, war, it is your element. It consumes you. It informs everything you do. You are not separate from it, it flows through you, and you react. You *act* and react in accord with it. It is intuitive, instinctual. Because of his training and culture, the Star colonel we are fighting against cannot possibly act any other way."

Kennerly canted his head. "But you were raised in the same culture, albeit the enclave form. Why can you think past it? Can you, or do you merely think you can? What's in your gut, Captain?"

She stared at the dark-haired man, hating him more than she ever would have thought possible. She wanted to say a thousand things, but the words couldn't escape the black hole growing in the pit of her stomach. What was in her gut? Nothing. Nothing but doubts. If she were truly worthy of being a Wolf, why would Anastasia have sent her away?

Verena shivered, and Kennerly laughed. The contempt in his voice shocked her. It also interrupted her thoughts and stopped her from spiraling down into doubt. What Anastasia thought really had no bearing on the current situation. She knew what had to be done, and how to beat the Clans. That was all that was important.

"Let me tell you this, Kennerly. In my gut I know he will fall for our trap."

"You don't *know* anything in your gut, Captain, you can only *feel* in your gut."

"Semantic games." She tapped a finger against her temple. "I *know* we will beat him. I feel it, too, else we would not be undertaking this operation."

"I hope you're correct, Captain." He snorted. "If not, the Demons will all die, and likely the Animals with us. Is it a risk we really have to take?"

"It is an opportunity we cannot pass up." She nodded toward where his *Clint* stood. "Mount up. It will be dark soon, and we have a ways to go before things heat up."

The *Union*-class DropShip looked beautiful, all lit up with ground lights. The ovoid craft sat on the ferrocrete landing pad at the Allshot spaceport all alone. Once the Clans had secured their landing zone and chased the Animals from South Allshot, elementals had moved in and taken control of the spaceport. The DropShip had transferred there, refueled and was ready to lift off at a moment's notice.

Though its primary purpose was to move 'Mechs and cargo from the ground to an orbiting JumpShip, the DropShip did serve a secondary purpose. In this case, it secured the spaceport. It bristled with weapons, and the chance of a raiding force managing to destroy it was very small.

And the odds of capturing it were even longer. DropShips *had* been captured in the past, but only under highly improbable circumstances, and certainly none Verena could duplicate on Baxter. Yet despite the impossibility of taking a DropShip, every warrior dreamed of being able to beat the odds. Taking a DropShip was a holy grail that haunted dreams, and the idea of losing one spawned nightmares.

Verena double-checked her secondary monitor. Her troops were all in position, just beyond the effective range of the DropShip's weaponry. The ship grossly outmassed her command, but the 'Mech force matched up well in terms of weaponry. Her 'Mechs actually outgunned the DropShip, but its thick armor more than evened those odds. It could kill some of her 'Mechs with a single shot, whereas the DropShip would take a lot of killing.

She keyed her tactical frequency. "Remember, grazing attacks. We keep moving, we soften it up. It is more important that you don't get hit than that you hit. Long range for the first pass. Then we tighten it up."

She raised her *Koshi*'s right arm, then brought it down. "Go!"

Verena smiled and kicked her 'Mech forward. The Badgers cut into range, moving across the spaceport's southeast quarter. Klaxons immediately sounded and lights blazed, but they only reached far enough into the darkness to illuminate her 'Mechs as fleeting shadows. Turrets on the DropShip swiveled and one PPC fired. The blue beam slashed a fiery path through the grass in front of her.

She swiveled her *Koshi*'s torso and triggered both her medium lasers. The red beams stabbed through the night. One scored armor below an LRM launch bay while the other missed wide. Heat flashed through her cockpit, but drained away almost immediately; then she shot again and burned more armor.

The other Animals had the same success, and in response the DropShip launched missile flights. The missiles exploded, lighting the night, chipping away at armor but failing to bring anything down. No pilot reported more than superficial damage, and they knew to pull out of the attack if they were in serious jeopardy.

At a point half a kilometer past where she'd begun her run, Verena turned her *Koshi* around and started back along the line of attack. She twisted her 'Mech's torso to the right and began another grazing run. More armor dripped from the DropShip and ground crews began clearing vehicles away from the area.

She smiled. The ship's captain had divined her strategy. By moving as they were, her troops could concentrate their fire on one portion of the ship's hull. To counter her efforts, all he had to do was bring the ship up and turn it. She would then have to batter fresh armor, or shift her attack to again hit the weakened side.

And if he puts his damaged side facing west, we will know . . .

It was always possible that the captain would simply launch the DropShip and pull out of the area, but she was fairly certain that would not happen. If he did that, the Badgers could take control of the spaceport. The Wolves would then have to take it back, and aside from being an embarrassment, it would also be costly.

Besides, the DropShip had lured the Badgers out of their hole, and Verena could imagine the Clan leader had intended it as bait all along. With its formidable weaponry, it could tie up the Badgers for a while, and would make one heck of an anvil.

A light blinked on her communications console. Verena switched over to that frequency. "Confirmation. Five 'Mechs leaving South Allshot, incoming your theater. ETA ten minutes. Confirm *Mad Cat, Vulture, Black Hawk* and two *Pumas*."

"I copy. Animal Lead out." Verena keyed a sequence that shot the scout's data reports to all the 'Mechs in her command, and then she switched over to the tactical frequency. "We have incoming. Stick with our plan. They are coming hot and heavy. No heroes, no one being stupid."

Verena started her third run, heading northeast again, and away from the 'Mechs coming in. The rest of her unit moved with her, like ducklings following their mother. No one betrayed any unease, despite the LRMs raining down in their midst.

Panic tried to take root in her guts, but she refused to let it. Doubts assailed her, and it was easy to imagine all the things that could go wrong with her plan. The Clan 'Mechs coming after them could kick out a lot of firepower, and if the Badgers got trapped between them and the DropShip, there wouldn't be enough left of them to hammer into an urn for their ashes.

At the far end of the run, Verena curled out to the east. The Badgers came with her and formed up in their lances. She led the medium lance, with the lights on each wing. Carter held the right, Pennington the left. Both wings drew back, leaving the center exposed, but still beyond the DropShip's range.

Then, to the southwest, the Wolves appeared. Lights flashed on, illuminating the 'Mechs. It was bravado to do that, but also psychological. While 'Mech scanners could present data over a variety of spectrums, just being able to see your enemy in his strength and glory could unhinge an enemy.

"Steady, people. Stick with the plan."

"Right, Captain. The plan." Pennington's voice wavered. "We pull back, they break off, right?"

"That is the plan."

"And if they don't follow it?"

Verena gripped her targeting joysticks. "Then we find out who the best warriors on this rock really are."

14

Alaric had relished the surprise in Anastasia Kerensky's voice. "That is correct, Colonel. I asked how many troops you were bringing in your Trial of Possession for Yed Posterior."

"My troops and I are coming in as part of the bargain for *your* Trial of Possession, Star Colonel."

"Then you are in error, Colonel Kerensky. I have *won* my trial. I possess the capital of Henderton, I have destroyed the militia."

"But the seat of government was transferred to Swofford on Graysea Island. The militia there is intact and you have landed no troops there."

"And they have abandoned any attempt to contest my possession of the world. I have been shipping material off it for days now." Alaric allowed himself a smile. "I will give you twelve hours to consider your bid, Colonel. Yed Posterior out."

He killed the radio and exhaled heavily. *At least I bought another twelve hours.*

He suffered under no illusions about how dire his situation was. The operation to clean out the tunnels had gone very well. Most all of the Yedder 'Mechs had been destroyed and the infantry had been scattered, rendering further resistance wholly ineffective. Even so, the fight had cost him a *Ryoken* and had inflicted heavy damage on two *Puma*s. They had been able to affect repairs on the *Puma*s and had combined the ruins of two marine salvage 'Mechs into one serviceable machine. That gave him two Stars of 'Mechs and a Star and a half of elementals with which to defend the world.

His decision to declare victory had been born of simple expedience. He did not know much about Anastasia Kerensky. She was a Kerensky. She had been raised among the Exiles. She would have Clan sensibilities and their sense of honor. By forcing her to declare a Trial of Possession, she would then have to figure out how much in the way of force she would bring. He expected she would leave the two militias out of it, which still meant he would be going up against the Wolf Hunters.

The data files she sent concerning her force yielded a lot of interesting information. Alaric wondered what hidden gems Donovan would have unearthed, but he did not dig very deep. The Wolf Hunters worked as a combined-arms battalion, with a company of medium and heavy 'Mechs, a mobile artillery company, and a fast-strike company of light 'Mechs and small troop carriers. The unit also boasted a company of infantry, but they had not been brought along for the fight on Yed Posterior.

That is an error she will regret.

It struck Alaric that the peculiarly sloppy wording

the indigs had used when bargaining with him had been a careful ploy. The plan for defending the worlds became clear. The garrison forces were to fight a rear-guard action that would deny the Clans the one thing they needed: speed. They were buying time to be reinforced and for other forces to flood the area to cut off the Wolves from Terra. As a plan it had merit and had proved enormously frustrating.

In part Alaric was pleased because it played into the misdirection part of his overall strategy. The more time it took for the Clans to advance, the more time others had to react. They would plan and move, tying up assets that would make the Wolves' lateral move into the Commonwealth much easier. In this way his strategy was working very well, almost too well.

The fact that he might not survive to see it come to fruition perturbed him. Alaric did not allow himself to think he would die. He considered it unlikely. *If I was going to die, the* Hunchback *would have killed me.* He didn't feel the specter of death dogging his footsteps.

Nor did he feel wholly confident for the future. Even if he *did* survive, the battle for Yed Posterior was a disaster and would set him back in any competition with Bjorn and Donovan. *And my mother will be furious as well.*

Despite his sense of doom, he organized his defenses for the planet. The Yedders had actually showed him how it could best be done. He'd prepare the tunnels, then force Anastasia to come down and find him. His elementals had rigged explosives, other tunnels had been blocked, so only he and his warriors possessed a working map of the maze. Once the enemy came down into the tunnels, their numbers would mean nothing and the close fighting would rip them to pieces.

The real question is whether we can inflict enough

damage to make Anastasia withdraw. Given her history he was inclined to bet against that possibility, but then, her Wolf Hunters were relatively new. While hardly made up of green troops, they'd not worked together that long, and the artillery company would be singularly useless in the tunnels.

Alaric juggled the numbers and began to see a glimmer of hope. *We might win, at that.*

He tried to maintain that positive view even after speaking to Anastasia again.

Her voice had an unpleasant edge. "I accept that you control the planet, Star Colonel. With what will you be defending?"

Alaric smiled. "With everything I have, and any reinforcements I can get."

"Glib, Star Colonel. You are defending with two 'Mech Stars and two Stars of elementals?"

"Approximately, yes."

"Splendid." She almost seemed to purr. "I am coming with three battalions, two militia and my Wolf Hunters."

"What?" Alaric shook his head. "You can't . . . you *cannot* do that. That is not honorable."

"Ah, clearly you have mistaken me for someone who cares about honor. You bid low because your courage, your honor and your ingenuity can win you a place in your Clan's breeding program." Her voice became cold. "I only care about being paid, and I get paid more when I win. We are incoming, four hours."

"I see, Colonel. Very well." Alaric forced calm into his voice. "I look forward to engaging you in combat."

"No, you do not, Star Colonel, not in the least. Kerensky out."

From deep in the tunnels, Alaric watched over links to the local holovision networks as the mercenaries came in. Kerensky had not been entirely without honor, as she sent one militia unit off to Swofford. The other militia unit and the Wolf Hunters landed in an *Overlord*-class DropShip and an *Intruder*-class DropShip. The *Intruder* brought the mobile artillery and other vehicles, while the 'Mechs marched in good order from the *Overlord*. They formed up at the spaceport's perimeter, looking down toward the seaside and the warehouse district that the Wolves had flattened.

Watching the 'Mechs exit the DropShips, Alaric was impressed with how quickly the Wolf Hunters moved. Picking out Anastasia had not been difficult. She drove a *Stormcrow*—a designation he found quite appropriate for Yed Posterior. She had it configured with four pulse lasers in the left arm, which would make it very effective in the tunnels.

What surprised him was her 'Mech having an LRM launcher in the right arm. The missiles would be useless in the tunnels. He looked again and saw her artillery company spreading out and taking up firing positions, as did the 'Mechs with LRMs. *What is she doing?*

Even when the DropShips lifted off into the storm it didn't occur to him what Anastasia had planned. In retrospect, given her contempt for Clan honor, it made perfect sense. In many ways he actually wished he'd hit on her strategy himself, because it would have made his fight in the tunnels that much easier.

The invaders launched salvoes of hundreds of LRMs from their 'Mechs, vehicles and DropShips. The missiles arced up, getting lost in the storm, and then came right back down, concentrating on the warehouses at quayside. Alaric felt the ground shake as the missiles rained over the warehouses, blasting them to bits, pulverizing the rubble, and gnawing into the earth itself.

The explosions destroyed buildings and ferrocrete slabs. They shattered the elevator plates and carved through foundations. They opened tunnel mouths with ease, leaving each one a smoking crater, open and inviting to assault.

And they crumbled the walls that kept the ocean at bay.

Alaric keyed his radio. "Everyone, get out of the east-west corridors. Move, now! Get out of the tunnels if you can."

Throughout the warehouse district the tunnels had been dug below sea level. Water burst through weakened walls as the ocean drained into Henderton's underworld. Solid columns of water gushed into the tunnels, tumbling debris like pebbles in a river. They overwhelmed the obstructions the Wolves had built.

Alaric escaped being swept along by the initial waves by ducking into a north-south passage. Water shot past heading west toward the spaceport, with eddies curling into his tunnel. A 'Mech—he thought it was the marine salvage 'Mech—somersaulted west. The water rose very quickly, and the tunnels soon would be completely submerged.

He had no fear of drowning. The cockpit was airtight and he could last a day, perhaps two, on the supplies built into the survival packet in his command couch. Underwater, however, his weapons would be useless and his speed cut down to almost nothing. And while he might be able to leave the tunnels through any number of exits, any within the warehouse district would be covered by an LRM barrage.

Just for a moment he contemplated blowing the charges that would get rid of his 'Mech's canopy. He would drown, but he saw it less as suicide than the equivalent of going down with the ship. *As the Spartans said, "With your shield or on it."*

He shook his head. Killing himself would have no

honor at all attached to it. *Dead is dead.* If he died now, he would just be another failed eugenics experiment—a match never to be tried again.

It is not in my blood to kill myself.

He did not have to wonder what his mother would do had she ended up in his situation. He already knew. She'd found herself trapped by her brother and did nothing but wait in disbelief until she was freed. She denied the reality of her situation, and if not for the kindness of Vlad Ward, she would have lingered in prison and would have long since died.

Instead he found himself wondering what Victor Davion would have done. Victor had not been trained in the ways of the Clans, but he had learned them. He had likewise learned the secrets of the Draconis Combine, and when Katrina had tricked him out of his realm, he learned all about her and won it back. That seemed to have been how he always operated— he endured defeat, studied challenges and learned, always learned how to get back on top.

But what do I learn from this?

Water swirled around the cockpit canopy as he thought for a moment. He realized that *what* was the wrong question to be asking. He needed to ask *from whom* he should be learning. Anastasia Kerensky had come up with a strategy that trapped him, multiple times. Her refusal to bid down her force had been what decided his fate. How she implemented it had merely been an exercise in practicality.

The need for honor was subordinated to the need for efficacy. It struck him that her comment about breeding programs hit at a core flaw in the Clan system. While it was true that a warrior who fought well but died would be allowed to breed, the fact that he didn't have to be alive to do so could cut out a desire to survive. The desire to survive, on the other hand, could be the key motivator that pushed someone to find new and better solutions to problems. It could even be argued that this was the major difference between warriors of the Inner Sphere and their Clan counterparts.

And warriors like Victor Davion *had* defeated the Clans.

But you knew this, instinctively, which is why you would not choose death before dishonor. He nodded slowly. "I guess I am like my father. While I live, I can learn. If I can learn, I can become better. I can defeat my enemies. I can attain my destiny."

I can become a god.

With this thought, he turned and stalked his *Mad Cat* through the watery tunnels, eventually emerging to surrender to a mercenary who had once been a Wolf.

And I will *learn.*

15

Though she had crafted the plan as perfectly as she could, commanding eleven 'Mechs to retreat from a mere handful of Clan 'Mechs left a sour taste in Verena's mouth. Her ranged raiding against the DropShip had been effective—far more so than she had allowed herself to imagine. They'd bled the DropShip, and now they would bleed the BattleMechs.

Still, she wanted more. She couldn't help it. Ever since she'd been dismissed from the Steel Wolves she'd been seeking an opportunity to prove herself. The successful completion of this operation would show what kind of a leader she was, and that was definitely a question she wanted answered.

It would not, however, prove what kind of *warrior* she was. Part of her needed that, badly. The fact that her *Koshi* was a third lighter than the smallest of the Clan 'Mechs was all the calculation she needed to convince her that heroics would be suicidal, and would be of no help to the mission at all.

"Fall back in order, Badgers. Concentrate on the *Puma*s."

Only her command lance fired in the first exchange. The four 'Mechs, a *Centurion*, two *Blackjack*s and her *Koshi* were the only 'Mechs in her force capable of firing effectively at range. Shooting a stationary DropShip was one thing, but hitting Clan 'Mechs coming fast was something else entirely. Her pilots chose their targets and the twin *Puma*s obliged by darting out in front of the rest of the Wolf Star.

The *Centurion* hit with his autocannon and an LRM salvo. He blasted armor from all over, including a fortuitous hit on the cockpit. One of the *Blackjack*s targeted the same *Puma*. The green beam of a large laser burned a black scar across the *Puma*'s torso, but failed to penetrate through to the 'Mech's heart.

Verena, backing her *Koshi* quickly, still tracked the other *Puma*. When the gold targeting dot pulsed at the heart of her crosshairs, she tightened up on her triggers and sent two ruby beams shooting out. One hit the 'Mech's cockpit, sending half-melted armor scales sliding from the squat 'Mech. The other one ripped up along the left arm, ablating over half the pristine armor.

The *Blackjack* followed up with a large laser. Green energy lanced into the left arm, melting the last of the armor and starting in on the ferrotitanium bones. The *Puma* retained use of the limb, but another shot would rip it clean away, and destroy the missile launcher built into it.

The *Puma*s fired back, launching four salvos of missiles. They rode fiery jets to scatter themselves over the mercenaries. The *Centurion* and one of the *Blackjack*s took the hits, shedding armor but suffering no serious damage.

In that first exchange the Clans had gotten the worst of it. *How fast will you do the math?* Her lance continued to pull back, and if the Clanners came on, they risked her other lances maneuvering around to flank them. While the 'Mechs were small, if they got in close they could pump a lot of energy into the Clanners.

Are you willing to risk it?

The Clan 'Mechs slowed.

Verena allowed her lance to pull back another fifty meters. "Wait for them. Wait to see what they are going to do."

"We can kill the *Puma*s right now, Captain."

"No, Carter, wait. Just wait."

The *Puma*s pulled back and positioned themselves in the middle of the Clan Star. The *Mad Cat* remained closest to the Badgers, while the *Vulture* and *Black Hawk* headed back west. They took up positions that let them cover the flanks; then the other three withdrew. The *Puma*s passed beyond the larger 'Mechs, took up covering positions, and the withdrawal continued.

Very good. Verena keyed her microphone. "We move forward now. Just as we planned. We shadow them but do not press them. Do not engage."

The Badgers moved in and the Clanners stopped. The Badgers stopped outside their effective range. The Clans withdrew again, and the Badgers advanced. The Clanners moved back in very good order. If either of the mercenaries' light lances attempted a flanking maneuver, the Clanners could hit them hard at range and close, five 'Mechs on four, which was a recipe for disaster.

The retreat almost became a game, and Verena half expected her enemy to radio her his compliments. They'd both succeeded. She'd inflicted damage to the DropShip and to some 'Mechs; he'd beaten back their attack. They would chase him to South Allshot and then retreat.

And he will begin planning how he will use his other Star to kill us later. She smiled. *He is already thinking about that.*

He didn't call. She resisted the urge to widebeam a message to him. She *was* curious, but if she initiated contact, he would see it as a sign of weakness. *He might take it as a prelude to surrender.*

Slowly and carefully the Clanners withdrew through the breaks and canyons of the badlands between South Allshot and the spaceport. The *Vulture* mounted one rise that gave it full command of the landscape, and a *Puma* raced past it. The *Black Hawk* squeezed through a tight pass, followed by the other *Puma.*

As the *Mad Cat* backed into the tight spot, Verena wondered if, just for a heartbeat, the Clan leader appreciated how perfect a spot that would be for an ambush. Perhaps he felt it as the hair rose tingling on the back of his neck. Maybe one of his pilots suggested it to him.

Because it really was.

She keyed her radio. "Now, Lieutenant Kennerly, if you please."

The Demons had maneuvered into position after the Clans had moved past. The missile carriers launched four full salvos of LRMs at the *Vulture* that had so commandingly skylined itself. Explosions rippled over the hilltop, and for a moment it appeared as if the Clanner had stationed himself on the cone of an active volcano. Searing light split the night. The top of the hill and the 'Mech that had been standing on it disappeared.

Beyond the pass the azure glow of PPCs flashed over dark stone. The trio of 'Mechs in Demon company targeted the first *Puma* to sneak through. Verena had no idea what damage they did to it, but the icon representing it on the tactical monitor went red. *If it is not dead now, it soon will be.*

Her own lance started forward, firing as they came. The *Centurion* missed with his cannon shot, but LRMs still scored armor on the left arm and leg of the *Mad Cat*. The *Blackjack* pilots did better, drilling green beams into the 'Mech's right flank, left arm and head. That last shot breached the cockpit canopy, but didn't seem to affect the pilot. Verena's shot raked armor from the 'Mech's middle and left weapons pod. The combined assault had all but stripped that limb of armor, but failed to damage the particle projection cannon mounted in it.

An azure glow started in both pods. The *Mad Cat*'s twin PPCs spat sizzling bolts of artificial lightning. In the flash of an eye they linked the Clan 'Mech with Verena's *Koshi*. The first beam hit the *Koshi*'s right arm and melted it clean off. Klaxons blared in the cockpit and the gyros screamed as they tried to keep the 'Mech upright.

Then the second beam took her 'Mech's left leg. Armor evaporated. Myomers flashed into greasy smoke and the metallic bones glowed white hot before flowing into nothingness.

Without the leg to support it, the *Koshi* crashed onto its left shoulder. Verena pitched hard against her restraining straps. The 'Mech balanced on its side for a second, then slowly flopped onto its back. She braced, but the impact still jolted her. Her head bashed into the back of her command couch and blood gushed from her nose.

The *Mad Cat* rose above her 'Mech like an animal claiming its kill. The weapons pods swung wide, spitting argent beams. Short-range missiles streaked from the 'Mech's right breast, and a trio of lasers shot a volley of ruby energy darts. The bright backlight of its hellish assault transformed it from a tattered war machine into a creature of nightmares. With its next step, it could crush the life out of her.

Or would have, save for the Badger counterattack. Laser light, coming in solid green and red beams as well as a scattering of scarlet darts, ate into the Clanner's 'Mech. Steaming armor streamed from its sides. Laser darts stippled it with burning wounds. Explosions rippled over it, shattering armor and blowing out the cockpit.

The Clan 'Mech towered over her, the cockpit smoking. It wavered for a moment, then sagged down on its haunches. The cylindrical torso pitched up and the 'Mech crashed back out of sight.

Verena lay there shivering, then hit the safety-belt buckle with the heel of her hand. The belts popped free. She shifted around to stand on the back of the couch. She pulled off her neurohelmet and wiped sweat from her forehead. She thought about getting the first aid kit from the command couch, but instead flipped the switch that unlocked the seals on her canopy.

Hydraulics hissed and cool air whistled in. It poured over her, starting another shiver. From outside a cacophony of explosions echoed through the canyons. Staccato bursts of light punctuated the noise and cast macabre 'Mech shadows against the walls.

She crawled out of her cockpit and stood on her 'Mech's shoulder. She couldn't see much beyond the *Mad Cat*'s carcass, but very quickly there wasn't anything to see or hear. Stars twinkled coldly in a dark sky. If it weren't for the fire guttering in the *Mad Cat*'s wasted cockpit, the stars and twin moons would have been all she could see.

Then, in the distance, a 'Mech came walking through the pass. Lights flicked on in the cockpit, but that was hardly necessary. She'd known from the first footfall who it would be. She sat and waited.

Kennerly brought his pristine *Clint* forward and stopped on the far side of the downed Clan 'Mech. The firelight slithered over his machine, transforming it into the avatar of some war god worshipped by primitive people. Verena felt very small and hugged her knees against her chest.

The external speakers on the *Clint* crackled. "We got them all. The plan worked."

"Losses?"

"Machines only. The *Mad Cat* killed a *Flea* and took an arm off Carter's *Hermes*. The others scored armor and Douglas lost myomers in a leg. The Demons are a hundred percent with three kills, including the *Vulture*."

"Anything we can salvage?"

"One *Puma*, the *Black Hawk* and this beast here, if we can find a new cockpit for it." Kennerly's voice suffered little from being squirted out through loud-speakers. "We have three pilot prisoners. Should we shoot them?"

Verena shook her head. "We will make them bondsmen."

"You'll have to handle that."

"That was my intention."

"There's one other thing, Captain."

She held her hands up. "No, Kennerly, there is not. You are looking at me here on top of a crippled 'Mech and you wonder if the pressure got to me. You wonder if I engaged the *Mad Cat* because I wanted to go out in a blaze of glory. Actually, you wonder nothing of the sort, but that is what you intend to ask me. You want me wondering if I tried to kill myself. It will not work."

"Captain . . ."

Verena shook her head adamantly. "No, because

the answer is *no*, most emphatically. I have nothing to prove. He came at me, he made a choice and I see where it got him. As an object lesson, that is a pretty good one, you know."

"Noted, Captain, but that was not the matter I needed to bring forward." A lighter note entered his voice. "It is good news."

Verena's eyes narrowed. *He'll make me pay for my protest.* "What is it, Kennerly?"

"The Skondia Rangers are inbound to reinforce us. Two days and they should be here. We've been or-- dered to sit tight and do nothing."

She snorted. "Did you mention to them that there is nothing left to do anything against?"

"Not going to take that DropShip, Captain?"

"What did you tell them, Kennerly?"

He laughed. "I told them to divert to Overton. I said we understood there were still some invaders there that might need dealing with. That suggestion was met with a fair amount of cheering."

Verena stood and glanced toward dawn, trying to spot the incoming DropShip. She saw nothing, so looked back over her shoulder at Kennerly's 'Mech. "Did you come to see if I had died?"

"I knew you hadn't died. You won't cheat me that way." His voice grew as cold as the night. "You've survived. You've guaranteed you'll be praised, elevated, given more responsibility. And the greater the height, the more spectacular the fall."

Verena hugged herself but could stop shivering.

$=$ **16** $=$

DropShip Jaeger, *Outbound*
Yed Posterior
Former Prefecture IX, Republic of the Sphere
16 January 3137

Anastasia Kerensky stood in the DropShip's security center with her arms folded over her chest. Ian Murchison had joined her, less because he wanted to see what was happening than to watch her reaction to it. *He already knows how I will react, he just refuses to believe it.*

Four different monitors were centered on the same image: a slender blond man in a stark holding cell. He'd been stripped of all clothing. The dark circles under his eyes gave him a haunted look. His hunched shoulders and the way his head jerked toward any sound reduced him to an animal.

A tired animal. A suspicious animal.

Ian shook his head. "Sleep deprivation, dehydration, starvation, the physical abuse. I fail to understand, and as a physician I most strongly protest this treatment."

She said nothing, but raised an eyebrow in his direction.

"Aside from the fact that we know torture never produces reliable information . . ."

"Do we actually *know* that, Ian?"

"Yes, and you know it. Most covert agents have a system of safeguards in place such that if they are out of contact with a handler, it is assumed they have been compromised and any ongoing operations are scrubbed. Anyone can hold out for a day, perhaps two, and that is all that is required to have their network account for their disappearance." Murchison shook his head. "He has held out for two days, but that is immaterial. He has nothing to give us. Moreover, that is something *else* you know, Colonel. If you actually thought he had useful information you would use psychoactive drugs on him, bust his mind open and sift the mush for useful tidbits."

She smiled at him. "Your conclusion, then, is that there is nothing to gain from this harsh treatment."

"Oh no, I will not fall into some trap—though the gambit was cunningly offered."

"Thank you."

"What is it you are trying to do?"

"Break him down."

"Why?"

Anastasia pointed at the screens. "That is Alaric Wolf. He was important enough to be brought to Terra during Victor Davion's funeral. He was given charge of the Yed Posterior invasion and proved rather resourceful in his opposition."

The doctor half smiled. "The declaration of victory was audacious, no doubt about it. But he also admitted defeat when you flooded the tunnels below the city. He surrendered, then ordered his elementals out of the caves in the volcano. He saved many lives on both sides."

"Very true." She nodded, then smiled as she watched him shift in his sleep on the cell floor. "You remember what his troops looked like. Haggard and beaten. *They* had been defeated."

"You suggest he had not been?"

"Not even close." Anastasia raised her chin. "He gave me his men. Their fate was in his hands, as was the fate of my people. For him it was no defeat because he had succeeded in at least some of what he came to Yed Posterior to do. He had looted the world, so his continued possession of it really was unnecessary."

She reached out and tapped the security technician on the shoulder. "How long has he been asleep?"

"Twenty minutes, Colonel."

"Good. Wake him up. Cold water. Then have him interrogated."

"Which program of questions?"

"The Victor Davion set. Make it about Strana Mechty."

"Confirmed." The tech made the call to the interrogators.

The hatch to the detention cell burst inward. Alaric sat up sluggishly, then flew back against the wall as a high-powered water jet caught him square in the chest. At first he fought against it; holding his arms up, but the interrogator shifted it to his belly. Alaric folded around it; then a blast to his knees dropped him. The water shoved him into a corner where he curled into a fetal ball.

He lay that way as water drained out the center of the floor. His body shook, but if it was from sobbing or shivering against the cold, Anastasia could not tell.

Nor did she really care.

"How much of this do you think he can take, Doctor?"

"He is at his physical limits. I could examine him if you wish."

Anastasia shook her head. "You will get your chance soon, but only after he is broken. He is a warrior, but the Clans treat their warriors very specially. He came to me expecting to be made a bondsman. That would have showed that I valued him."

"He would be useful to have as one of our own."

"Not yet, Ian. Possibly never." She nodded at the screen as two burly men dragged him from the cell. "He is a Wolf, an alpha even. But we already have an alpha. He is also flawed. He believes himself to be invincible. If you believe that, if you refuse to believe in the very real possibility that you could be defeated, you never plan sufficiently to preclude that scenario."

"And you intend to teach him this folly, which will make him better and even more deadly?"

"Exactly."

"And then what will you do with him?"

She smiled. "I will give him back to the Wolves."

Ian stared at her. "Why would you do that? They are quite deadly enough."

"But it ensures that he will rise among them, come to lead them. I want that." Anastasia Kerensky nodded solemnly. "Here he will learn to defeat all his enemies. All of them save one. Me. He will be ignorant of that fact, but I will know it. Consider it insurance for our future."

Alaric tumbled into his cell and didn't even make an attempt to control his fall. He landed hard and skidded, burning flesh on his flank and thigh. He could feel pain, but it remained distant. He reached for it, clung to it, for as uncomfortable as it was, it was the only thing that seemed real in his world.

Nothing made sense. When he surrendered he had

expected better treatment. He worked with Kerensky's subordinates to bring his people in and to save lives. He knew the mercenaries would appreciate that. Not only did it prevent people from dying, but it saved on equipment and ammunition loads. If Anastasia Kerensky was going to cite economics as justification for a lack of honor, he could play that game.

So he had. He expected, in exchange, to be treated as befit his rank—which was the equal of hers—but her opinion differed. Once his troops had surrendered, elementals had dragged him away without a word. Alaric was taken to the *Overlord*-class DropShip, stripped, holographed, weighed, measured, had samples taken, and then had been tossed naked into a bare metal cell.

The lights never went out in his cell, and the four dark dots in the corner hid cameras. That much Alaric was sure of. He'd heard the cameras whir. He was sure of that, too. *I am sure, I am.* He'd been given no food, and the only water had come in what he had sucked up when his keepers hosed him down. He wasn't even given toilet facilities; his waste washed down the same drain.

So many things he wasn't sure of. He had no idea how long he had been a prisoner, though his beard had not grown out much, nor were his fingernails any longer. But he could not discount that he'd been shaved when unconscious, and had his nails trimmed.

You have had no sleep. That was another thing he was certain about. His limbs felt crafted of lead and his eyes itched as if his sockets had been stuffed with nettles. He'd gotten tired of fighting yawns and had no idea if he covered his mouth when he lost that fight. He wanted to. He tried to. He had no desire to lose track of manners and the other things that made him human because he distinctly felt them slipping away.

Slipping away with my identity. That was the most

disconcerting part of what had been happening to him. His interrogators would blast him with water, then drag him from the cell to an interrogation room. They bound him to a chair. A strap went around his forehead so he'd keep his head up. They attached electrodes at the small of his back, one over each sciatic nerve. If he fell asleep . . .

He'd only done that once.

They would make holographic images hover in the air in front of him. They would tell him that he was watching himself, but he knew that wasn't true. One set was of a man named Jaime Wolf. Alaric watched footage of Wolf in combat, then Wolf at public gatherings, and then he would be asked about the military strength of the Draconis Combine and the death of his brother. He would be asked intricate questions dealing with the management of a mercenary unit, and when he refused to answer, they asked more questions, louder, building and building until he expected more shocks.

Then they would release him and toss him back into his cell. He would sleep a little, just long enough to dream about the material he'd been shown, and then the water would hit him again and he would be dragged back. The next time it would be Kai Allard-Liao fighting in some gladiatorial games or Hanse Davion getting married. *I was getting married to my grandmother.*

"No!" Alaric slapped his hand against the deck. "No, that was not me."

No, not me, because I am Victor Davion. The last set of holographs had been the worst. Images of Victor Davion had flashed past from when he was just a child to his time through the military. *I saw my body criss-crossed with scars. The sword scars. And then they wanted to know about Strana Mechty.*

The invasion of the Clan homeworld was something

Alaric knew well. All Clanners knew it for the tragedy it was. Tragedy and outrage. Victor had brought a fleet. *I told them, I told them everything so they could save us. But they did not believe me. They laughed at me.*

Alaric rolled onto his back and covered his face with his hands. *This cannot be happening to me. They dare not do this to me. They cannot do this to me. I am a god!*

He began to laugh and continued because he was too exhausted to stop. The only way he could stop was to start crying and he refused to do that. *Gods do not cry.* He fought to keep a hysterical note out of his laughter, but failed. He heard it, but chose to ignore it, because to acknowledge it would make him cry.

Gods do not cry, but I am not much of a god. As much as he wanted to find solace in memories of striding across a battlefield implacable and invincible, he could only see himself from the outside. He remained huddled and small, naked and cold. With a casual misstep a 'Mech would smear him along the ground and the pilot would never even notice.

I am the god of fools. Yet the moment that idea entered his mind, he knew he had arrogated too much divinity. *I am the god of nothing.*

He shook, less with dying laughter than a shiver. *Why are they doing this? What do they want? How can I please them? How can I make them stop?*

He rolled onto his side, slowly drew his legs up to his chest and hugged them tightly. He had tried to comply with what they wanted, but nothing made sense. Nothing was real. There was no right answer.

I have done everything. What do they want? Another shiver—his muscles rippled but didn't feel like part of him. Then he realized what he hadn't done yet.

I have not yet cried.

Hope burst in his chest. He flopped onto his back again and just let himself go. Strong sobs wracked him. Tears rolled from his eyes and his mouth opened, baring white teeth. He screamed in anguish, filling it with all his frustration and confusion.

Only distantly did he hear the clank of the hatch being opened. He wanted to smile, but his body would not obey his will. *Soon. You will stop soon. You have won. You have won.*

Then the cold water lifted him from the floor and smashed him against the back wall. As he huddled in the corner, water washed into his open mouth. He swallowed, tasting tears, bitter tears.

And knew there would be many more to swallow.

═══ 17 ═══

Overton, Baxter
Former Prefecture IX, Republic of the Sphere
18 January 3137

The weight pressed down on Verena's chest. She couldn't move and a warning buzzer pulsed through her head. She was facedown and could see nothing. *Blackness. The* Mad Cat *is going to stomp me.*

The buzzing grew more insistent. She clawed against the ground, and it came away in her hands. Her fingers tightened around a thin sheet of it. She ripped a hand free and pushed off, flopping over onto her back.

Cool air hit her, turning her sweat into an icy coat. Her eyes snapped open, and then she looked to the right. She slapped her datapad, killing the alarm she'd set. She pulled herself up in the bed and her head bumped off the headboard.

Good thing it is padded. She leaned back, then untangled the sheet from around her legs and drew it up to her neck. The nightmare had been horrible, but she wasn't completely certain she was awake yet. *This cannot be real.*

The Regal Crown Hotel was the best Overton had to offer. Within the Badgers it was the place most warriors said they'd go after winning a lottery. By the standards of other worlds it might not have been all that great, but there wasn't a resident on Baxter who would have refused to be *crowned* for a night.

On seeing the suite she'd been given, her first impression was *plush*. Velvet curtains hung everywhere and matched the thick, burgundy carpet. The overstuffed chairs and couch were more inviting than any billet she'd known as a MechWarrior. She could have fit her whole barracks room into the bathroom, and was fairly certain the bathtub was roomier than her 'Mech's cockpit.

She shook her head. She and the southern contingent had remained in the caves awaiting word on how the fight had gone up north. The night before she was brought to Overton they'd heard that the Skondia Rangers and the Beasts had crushed a Clan Star, completing the liberation of the planet. That resulted in a lot of celebrating in the caves, and that night she'd gone to sleep in a bedroll hoping the fire wouldn't go out before she woke up.

The next day a Rangers' helicopter arrived at her headquarters. Abbie Dannik took command of the Badgers, and Captain Verena and Lieutenant Kennerly were invited to return to Overton. Verena had gotten the distinct impression that she'd not be returning to the Badgers, though she couldn't immediately put a finger on why.

Kennerly had been most helpful in identifying the problem. "You have two things going against you. First, it takes no stretch of the imagination to blame you for Colonel Bradone's death. Major Peres inherits the unit based on the partnership deal when it was set up, but he has a problem. Because of your victory, you're more popular than he is. He really is nothing more than a logistics genius, so the warriors would be happy to follow you—save, of course, those who think you got Bradone killed."

He added that was pretty much everyone in the unit, which did nothing to mitigate her feeling of dread. He then pointed out that "while your plan here did kill off a Clan Star and inflict damage on a DropShip, it could easily be seen as exceeding your précis for harassment prior to the arrival of reinforcements. You would argue that since the Clans were not coming out of their stronghold, harassment was impossible, but you risked much. That you gained much will mean nothing because you could have lost big. Anvil forces are not supposed to take those risks."

She scrubbed her hands over her face. Kennerly had a point, but refusing to allow warriors to fight and take advantage of the enemies' weaknesses was to neuter them. She fully understood the risks of her operation, but she didn't see them as risks. She knew she would succeed, and she had.

The second she made that declaration to herself, she knew she was lying. She had not *known*. She had calculated and hoped. She had projected best-case scenarios and clung to them. While things had gone better than anyone realistically could have expected—and she could point to the reasons why—the fact remained that they very easily could have gone much worse.

The *Mad Cat* could have done much more damage to her troops than he had. After he downed her 'Mech he split his fire and took two other 'Mechs out of the fight. If he had not concentrated on her with his first shots, but split his fire then, he could have taken out a full lance. And had her lance not gotten lucky, he'd not have been put down for a much longer time.

We would all be dead, and he would be here in this bed.

Verena shook her head vehemently. "That is non-sense, and you know it." Her ambush had been classic. She had read the Clan leader perfectly. He got too focused on her and her troops to imagine she had set a trap. That left him vulnerable and she had exploited that vulnerability. He'd have done the same to her, and if she had fallen for it, her command would be dead.

"But they are not, and that is why I am here." She tossed back the thick comforter and padded across lush carpet to the bathroom. She shielded her eyes against the harsh light as she flicked the switch, then stepped into the glass-walled shower. She turned it on as hard and hot as she could stand. She allowed herself the luxury of a long soak, enjoying the water's sting and the way it made her pale flesh glow rosy.

Best of all, concentrating on the heat, breathing the steam and the lavender scent of the soap, she forgot earthly concerns for a little while. She sought that peace, both as an escape from battle and her dream, and as a respite from Kennerly's mind games.

Clean and relaxed, she emerged from the shower, dried herself on towels thicker than the barracks carpet, and dressed. She'd come north with nothing but the clothes on her back and had had no time to visit the Badgers' headquarters. The hotel's concierge had eyed her up and down and said he would take care of everything.

He'd been good to his word. While she'd slept, or while she showered, her closet and wardrobe had been filled with clothes of the appropriate size and even of a style she liked. She wasn't girly by any stretch of the imagination, but the concierge had avoided picking wholly mannish clothes. Conservative business suits of a dark color with blue blouses the color of her eyes formed the majority of her wardrobe. He'd even supplied lingerie that had more frills and lace than she would normally have chosen, but she actually liked how it looked and especially felt when she put it on.

She finished dressing by the time the second alarm went off. She killed it, scooped up the datapad and headed down to the hotel lobby. There the concierge stood beaming beside Kennerly. The man was obviously pleased at how she looked, and it took Kennerly a couple of seconds to recognize her.

Verena smiled and offered the concierge her hand. "You have exquisite taste. Thank you."

"Seeing you wear those clothes so well is my reward." He waved a hand toward the hotel's fine-dining restaurant, ignoring the fact that a sign nearby said it was closed. "The private room has been reserved for you, and your hosts are waiting. Please, follow me."

She walked with the concierge and Kennerly trailed a respectful couple of steps behind. Verena had been surprised at how Kennerly looked. She'd been used to seeing him with three-days' growth of beard, grease smears here and there, with dust caught deep in his crow's-feet—making him look far older than he was. The concierge had chosen well for him, too, supplying him with a light gray suit that he wore over a black mock-turtleneck sweater. Kennerly had helped by shaving his standard stubble down to a goatee. It sharpened his face and gave him a distinctly diabolical look, but that was in keeping with how she saw him anyway.

The concierge led them to an ornately carved and gilt door, which he opened after knocking once, quietly. The private dining room had been decorated with baroque furniture featuring a lot of scrollwork and gold leaf. The wallpaper had gold fleur-de-lis on an ivory background, and the carpet picked up the ivory hue. Silver dishes heaped with food had been placed on the sideboards, and four places had been set at the head of a long table.

General Artor Bingham stood as they entered. "Thank you, Philippe. If there is anything else, we will let you know."

"Very good, General."

He extended a hand to Verena. "I'm very pleased to meet the mastermind of the Allshot coup. I would have greeted you when you landed, but we were going over the post-battle assessment of the Overton action."

She met his firm handshake and pumped his arm. "Understandable, sir. This is Lieutenant Kennerly. He commanded the Demons, and they sprang the trap."

"Kennerly, good to meet you. You did good work."

"And you, sir. I just followed the Captain's plan, sir."

The general nodded and turned to the room's other occupant, a slender man with thin hair who clearly had never been in a 'Mech's cockpit. "I would like to present Baron Cutt Saville of La Blon. He is the chairman of the Global Information Network. He is also one of the leaders who have approved and, more importantly, bankrolled the defensive effort here in the Ninth."

Verena nodded to the Baron since the man made no move to offer her his hand. "Pleased, Baron."

"Not nearly as much as I am." He smiled broadly, but in a way that disturbed her. *Reminds me of Kennerly too much.*

General Bingham waved them toward the buffet. "Philippe was horrified when I suggested a buffet, but I told him that old warhorses would be uncomfortable having any other kind of mess."

"Very true, sir. After you."

"Baron."

They gathered up plates—in this case fine china

with a gold rim and a gold crown in the center—and filled them. The staff had laid out enough food to feed all the Badgers for a month, and actually have the Everett twins complaining of how full they felt. Verena just took a second to breathe in all the sweet and savory scents, then heaped her plate with ham steaks, cornbread with whipped honey butter and fruit—most of which she recognized.

They sat and the baron—who picked at eggs Benedict—launched into speech. "You will forgive me for conducting business while we eat, but there is a great deal I wish to cover, and frankly, I'm so enthused. First off, I hope you know that you and you, Lieutenant, are heroes throughout the Ninth. Your victory has electrified the citizenry. We lost Corridan Four, which was no *great* loss, of course, and managed to retake Yed Posterior, but that wasn't the sort of victory that makes for good news bytes. The sensor data the lieutenant here supplied us is already being shown on every world GIN is on, and it will soon spread further. You're already being compared to Victor Davion and his exploits in the first Clan war."

Verena covered her mouth with a napkin, hoping she hid her surprise.

The baron never noticed, never stopped. "You and your victory fit very well into the program we've been putting together in the Ninth. You, Captain Verena, will become Colonel Verena—the single name is a great touch, by the way, allows anyone to identify with you—of the Djinns. The Djinns will be the GIN militia, an elite cadre of MechWarriors I've assembled. I've already purchased a *Mad Cat* from the victors on Yed Posterior—I gave them the one you smashed up in partial trade. Major Peres was reluctant to do that, but we've offered a settlement, threatened a lawsuit, so he'll do nothing. I'm sure you can come up to speed in the larger 'Mech in plenty of time."

Verena blinked, setting her fork down. "Me, in a *Mad Cat*?"

"Of course. We can't have the savior of the Ninth piloting a light 'Mech. We've already spun your piloting a light 'Mech in a medium lance to great effect, but our polls show people want heroes in heavyweight 'Mechs. Worked for Victor and his father, it will work for you. I will also need details for the holobio we're shooting of you. It's already in production, stock shots for background, other footage. We found an actress who is your spitting image, so you won't be bothered."

General Bingham laid a hand on the baron's forearm. "Cutt, if you don't mind, let me explain something to Colonel Verena here."

"Oh yes, please. I have been going on, haven't I?"

The general addressed her in grandfatherly tones, patting her hand to reassure her. "I know this is coming at you very fast, but it is also very simple. We beat the Clans back on two worlds, but we have heard that they have already hit Izar, Ryde and Kimball Two. Those are worlds the Jade Falcons control, so their advance is not costing us personnel or equipment. But those victories do make it easier for them to strike into the Ninth. We're hoping the Falcons will grind the edge off their spear point but we cannot depend on it. Our strategy of hammer and anvil forces is working, so well that we need more hammers. The Djinns will be a hammer force, and quite welcome.

"More important than that, however, is that the people of the Ninth feel abandoned. Not only are the Clans coming through them, but we are moving units around. While my Rangers' victory here is being hailed on Skondia as wonderful, there are still voices there wondering why we are so far from home. They do not feel secure. They need heroes, and especially new heroes. Your rise, your success, will give them heart."

Verena nodded. "I can understand that, sir, but all of this strikes me as more entertainment than warfare. Am I wrong?"

"Only in that you see a separation of the two." Bingham pressed his hands together. "If people believe victory is possible, they will do everything they can to defeat the enemy. Once their will has been broken, it cannot be reestablished. Now, make no mistake about it, the Djinns, under your command, will be a vital part of our defense. You *will* be fighting a war. Your image, and news of how you do things, will be used to fight a larger war, a war against apathy and defeatism."

The baron smiled. "Haven't you always wanted to be a hero, Verena?"

"Yes, I guess so, I . . ." She frowned. She had always dreamed of being a warrior, of excelling at the art of warfare. She had always worked hard at it. It always seemed as if she were one step away from understanding, of turning the corner of seeing what an Anastasia Kerensky or a Victor Davion had seen and understood. She didn't feel she'd made that jump yet, but here wise men were offering her the rewards for having made it.

"You've realized your dream, Captain." Baron Saville smiled openly. "Today and tomorrow you will be free here in Overton. If you want for anything, please indulge yourself. I doubt you'll be charged for anything, but if someone is so crass as to want money from you, just charge it to your room here. That goes for both of you. GIN is footing your bill most willingly."

She nodded. "After that?"

Bingham answered, "Two days from now we head for La Blon and a summit meeting of mercenaries. There we will assess our strengths and weaknesses, then plan for our next level of defense. I understand you'll be reacquainted with a friend there. Lieutenant Kennerly indicated you'd be pleased."

"A friend?" She shot a hard glance at Kennerly, but he shrugged it off. "Who, sir?"

"The victor of Yed Posterior." Bingham smiled. "Anastasia Kerensky. I don't wonder if she will be regretting ever letting you get away."

18

Alaric was too grateful at having been given clothes to mind the fact that the stained jumpsuit had frayed cuffs and was sized for an elemental. He couldn't believe it when the door to his cell had opened up and the jumpsuit tossed to him. He caught it only because he'd had his hands up to ward off another blast of cold water.

He'd pulled it on and huddled in it when the lights went out for the first time in his captivity. He cowered there, shivering, waiting for the lights, waiting for the water. Soaked, the clothes would be leaden on him. Part of him was certain it was a trick, but mostly he was beyond caring.

Having been given clothes was a kindness and he clung to it.

In the dark he slept and fell into long, odd dreams. He saw himself as a titan walking across a landscape where 'Mechs warred with each other. Red and green beams linked targets and killers. Flights of missiles crisscrossed the battlefield. 'Mechs dissolved in sheets of flame, yet somehow more and more of them poured into the valley where he walked.

He strode among them, kicking out to topple some, stomping others into the ground. He was invincible, a god of war treating hundred-ton war machines like toys. They turned their weapons on him, but their assaults tickled. The futility of their opposition was clear to everyone, yet they kept coming.

Then the wave hit him. In a heartbeat the valley walls rose and curled over his head, with 'Mechs standing on the interior of the tube. No longer did they shoot hot light. Their weapons projected water jets and hit him from every direction. Water poured over him, shrinking him, melting him, until he bobbed in a river that sucked him circling down into a black hole from which there was no escape.

He woke shocked and sweating from that dream, then fell immediately back into it. He had no way to judge how long he slept each time, but he made it through at least ten dream cycles. He could have gone to sleep again, but the door opened and two elementals summoned him out of his cell.

They conducted him through the DropShip to showers. They tossed him in and threw a bar of soap and a brush after him. "Five minutes."

Alaric stripped out of the jumpsuit and quickly washed himself. He lathered up twice and would have gone for a third time, but he figured opportunity was running out. It wasn't that he was actually dirty; he just wanted to scrub off the flesh that had so often been sprayed. On some level he believed it had betrayed him, and he wanted it gone.

He dried himself with a towel clipped to the wall, then combed his hair with his fingers. He caught a glimpse of himself in the mirror, and the haunted face that looked back at him twisted his guts. Beard flecked his cheeks and dark circles helped sink his eyes deep in his head. He looked beaten, and as much as a part of him wanted to reject that idea, he couldn't deny it.

The elementals appeared and hauled him out of the locker room. Wordlessly they conducted him through the ship. He didn't recognize the path they were taking, and that heartened him. *Maybe I am not going to be interrogated again.* He dared not hope because that would be another trap. Still, his heart beat a little faster as they rose toward the bridge deck and traveled farther from his cell.

Finally they conducted him into a small conference room—one that would have served as the officers' mess during meal times. The table had been removed along with all but one chair. The elementals sat him in the chair and waited.

Footsteps approached, two pairs. The woman with whom he had negotiated for the fate of Yed Posterior came into view. The holographic communications devices had failed to display the aura of power she projected. Something in the way she moved, the way light glinted within her restless eyes—she was a *predator.* She always had been, and would be until she drew her last breath.

Alaric shivered. *I was once like that.*

Anastasia studied him with a hand on her chin. He might as well have been naked, for she saw past his clothes, and perhaps even past his flesh. He felt completely exposed.

Part of him wanted to slump out of the chair and onto his belly before her. He would have, too, had the elementals not stood there with their hands on his shoulders to restrain him.

"You present a problem for me, Alaric." Though her voice made the concern sound grave, her expression did not match it. "Are you worth more to me dead or alive?"

Alaric said nothing.

"Yed Posterior wants you back. They want to try you for war crimes. All the destruction, the murder of people. They want their pound of flesh and the blood with it, too. They are not pleased I have taken you from them."

She shrugged. "That is less my concern than what I will do with you if I keep you. I have many options, but I find few of them palatable. Some of my people suggest you might be useful and perhaps should be made a bondsman. I disagree."

Alaric shook his head.

"You have an opinion in this matter, Alaric?"

"No."

"That surprises me. You are supposed to be a good MechWarrior. So what am I to do with you?" Anastasia frowned. "Set you to training our new recruits? You would do poorly at that. You do not know why you are a good warrior; you just are. One cannot communicate that to others."

She studied Alaric again and his guts knotted. "Is there any other use for you, Alaric?"

"I was trained as a warrior."

Anastasia arched an eyebrow. " 'Trained as'? Do you not see yourself as a warrior anymore?"

"You do not, which is all that matters."

Anastasia reached out and caught him by the chin. "Never venture to tell me what is in my mind. You presume too much, and you presume incorrectly. You thought you knew my mind on Yed Posterior, and where did it get you? You surrendered your forces without firing a shot. You believed I would not do things you had not done, and yet from our bargaining you knew I did not think as you did."

Alaric nodded.

She released his chin, and his head slumped forward. "You might yet be a warrior. I have sold your 'Mech, by the way."

He heard her words and they sank in slowly. He waited because he knew there should be a reaction. Panic, perhaps, outrage. He really felt neither. While he had trained to be a warrior, he could separate himself from a 'Mech. He had no favorite, he didn't take to naming them as some did. To him they were a tool through which he could manifest his skill at arms, not part of him.

Anastasia watched him, then smiled. "And I sent your people home."

His head came up. "You sent them back?"

"I bargained with them for their freedom. I demanded they give me their parole not to fight again in this campaign. They gave it."

Alaric shook his head. "They never would do that."

"But they did, because you ordered them to do it."

He shook hard enough that the elementals had to hold him in the chair. His hands slipped from his lap and dangled at his sides. "I would never."

"You did. I can show you the holo of it."

"No." Alaric stared at his knees, at a hole, a tiny one, in his coveralls. His men would do as he ordered them to do. He did not question that. And, he supposed, under duress, in the frame of mind his lack of sleep had left him in, he would have made a holo of that order just to get them to stop torturing him. His men would have thought he was weak or afraid, and the khan . . . *He would think I am worthless and broken.*

"Are you certain you have no desire to see the holo?" She folded her arms over her chest. "We have it from several angles, as they waited to hear you, all lined up, pretty as you please."

"No." He looked up again. "You have ruined me with them."

"Hardly. I merely completed the process you had begun. You were sloppy when you bargained. That first act doomed your invasion. At least you survived your folly."

"Another invasion leader died?"

"Baxter."

Bjorn. Alaric nodded. "It is not too great a surprise."

"Why is that?"

"Because . . ." The Clansman hesitated. "No. This could be a trick."

Anastasia laughed. "Very good. Perhaps there is some warrior left in you after all. You need not be so cautious, however. We have had out of you whatever we wanted. You know that."

He searched his memory for anything he had said, especially anything about their ultimate goal, but he got nothing. *They never asked after our goal because they believe what they were told. They still think we are headed for Terra.* "Bjorn attacked Baxter. He was not a planner."

"Apparently not."

"How did he die?"

"In combat, in a trap. He fought well, but all the ninth prefecture is alive with how the Wolves were crushed on Baxter. They've crowned new heroes. Your 'Mech goes to one of them, in fact."

Alaric just shook his head.

"Do you really think you might be useful as a warrior? I suppose I could toss you in a lance and find out."

"No." Alaric half closed his eyes. "I will not fight for you."

Anastasia started to pace around him, vanishing on

the right, slowly appearing past the elemental on the left. Her footfalls, crisp and regular, rang on the deck. Twelve steps was all it took for her to complete her circuit, not hurried, not slow, not heavy, just firm and even.

Finally she stopped before him again. "You realize that makes you less than useful to me."

"You would not make me a warrior unless you first made me a bondsman." He lifted his right hand. "You have not done that. You have no intention of doing that."

"Why do you think that is?"

"You are a mercenary. You have no desire to compel people to work with you." Alaric ventured a weak smile. "And you would not trust me to fight for you."

"You are right on the second count, but not the first." Anastasia smiled. "If I could trust you, I would use you. A bondsman is someone I would not have to pay. As for the trust issue, I can foresee you deciding you know a better way to do just about anything, which means you would overrule me, and that would be wrong."

He almost protested, but she would see through it. He might have misread her, but she had him pegged correctly. Believing he knew the right way had gotten him trapped and landed him in his current predicament. He had always known, in the abstract, that he could be wrong, but even when he had made mistakes, the consequences never amounted to much. Even in losing his command to her, his people had not been killed.

"What will you do with me?"

"There are many choices. The Yedders want you, of course, but are not prepared to offer nearly what you are worth. I suspect some council or court will form itself up in the prefecture to steal their thunder and try you for crimes against humanity. They will not want to pay for you at all, but the case could be good publicity for our unit. I could even sell you to a circus and have you exhibited all over the Inner Sphere as the Wolf who thought he was a sewer rat. Countless media outlets would pay serious money to interview you."

"These are all things you will not do."

"Why do you say that?"

"Because you have not yet done any of them." Alaric's eyes tightened, less out of defiance than fear. "And none of them would have required you to do to me what you have done."

"An interesting insight."

"Why did you do what you did?"

She glanced at her chronometer. "Twenty minutes. My doctor predicted a half hour before you got to that question."

Alaric snorted listlessly.

Anastasia watched him for a moment, then nodded. "I shall answer your question. I saw what you had done on Yed Posterior. Your use of power, your planning, all made the best of a bad situation. You anticipated your enemies and were successful against them. Most importantly, however, you recognized that actual control of the planet was less important than control of its resources. No matter how well men study war, too many of them worry about the faces on currency. The possession of a world does not matter provided you have the resources you need to continue to wage war. Seen in the proper context, no world is worth anything."

Alaric involuntarily shook his head. "Except Terra."

"Even Terra is worthless." She spread her arms. "It may have been the cradle of mankind, but we have found bigger, richer worlds. We have tamed better worlds. We are now born under hundreds of suns and can live our whole lives quite happily without ever seeing Terra or touching anything that has ever been in the same solar system as Terra. You see it as a talisman—if you take Terra, somehow you will control mankind.

"That is an illusion. You can only control mankind if you have the resources to control mankind."

"Or," Alaric offered, "if control of Terra makes others cede control to you."

Anastasia nodded slowly. "If the Clans would unite under you, you would have *some* of mankind, but far from the whole of it. Devlin Stone came as close as anyone ever will to uniting mankind, and look at his dream now. Shattered."

"Why did you do what you did to me?"

"Because the thing that made you weak was your belief in yourself. Self-confidence is good, save when it blinds you to your own weakness. You know you are smart, but you are stupid to think no one might be smarter, and even more stupid to forget someone might be luckier."

"Luck favors the prepared."

"And the stupid or blind are seldom prepared."

Alaric nodded. *She has seen through to my heart and my soul.* "What will you do with me?"

She smiled, and he did sense uncharacteristic kindness there. "I think I shall take you as an apprentice. I will teach you. I will ask your opinions. I will use your mind as I will, and you will benefit. If you cheat me, betray me, withhold anything from me, I will have you sent off. There are no second chances."

"Do I give you my parole?"

"No. Under no circumstances would I ever want you to vow that you will not fight against me." Her eyes narrowed. "In fact, I am counting on your wanting to face me in combat one day and to kill me."

"Why would you count on that?"

"Because, Alaric, it means that while you are in my service," Anastasia Kerensky said, "you will make certain no one else kills me. A finer guarantee of your fidelity I cannot imagine."

19

DropShip Baron's Pride, *Incoming La Blon*
Former Prefecture IX, Republic of the Sphere
5 February 3137

Even if Verena had been warned, she doubted she
could have covered her surprise.

For the last two, nearly three weeks, her life had
been completely insane. General Bingham had been
treating her as a respected colleague—not quite an
equal, but with sufficient deference that she very much
felt she was an imposter. The baron had his aides
doing all they could for her. She conducted interviews
for immediate distribution, was recorded answering
preset questions from dozens of local newspeople. In
addition, she made a generic set of answers to the
same questions, so yet other newscasters could cut
themselves in and make it look as if they had shared
a direct link with her.

That was quite enough to turn her head, and then
she had Kennerly crawling inside it to twist everything
even further. He had taken to whispering, "All glory
is fleeting," whenever she began to believe her own

press. Then their journey came to an end, and the JumpShip arrived in the La Blon system.

Though Kennerly remained as annoying as ever, without him she doubted she would have survived the building of her legend. So many people who knew her only through the news reports approached her with glowing faces and shining eyes, seeing in her something she certainly did not feel. When they praised her for bravely facing down a *Mad Cat* in her little *Koshi*, and she countered that it was foolishness for her to have done so, they praised her for being modest. The early comparisons to Victor Davion had become speculation that she was the new Morgan Hasek-Davion or even Devlin Stone.

While she knew this was all nonsense, it was seductive. That was the problem with hero worship. Those who praised her did it so sincerely that it was easy to believe what they said was true. But sincerity does not equal truth; and if she forgot it, if she began to believe about her what they said, it would destroy her.

She didn't need Kennerly to remind her "Pride goeth before a fall," or that hubris is a sin the price for which is complete destruction. She recalled from somewhere the saying "Those whom the gods would destroy, first they make proud," and she repeated it to herself with even more regularity than Kennerly managed. She applied the brakes to her ego as much as she could, which took her from the elation of praise to the depression of self-doubt in a heartbeat—all of which was exhausting.

In her discussions with General Bingham she really did try to do her best. She was not without insight, since she had been raised among the Exile Wolves. She had made a particular study of warfare down through the ages, and was very good at recalling odd situations and tactics that might well be adapted to modern battle. Tactics that had won the day four and five thousand years ago and had proved to be sound military doctrine could succeed using modern capabilities.

No matter how hard she worked, however, there never was an *aha* moment. She never offered something so brilliant that the general or his aides decided she had unlocked the mystery that would end the Clan threat forever. On one level, she knew there was no single key to the Clans—*there wasn't even a single lock.* That fact notwithstanding, she had hoped to make a greater contribution to the solution.

Then they started the run in from La Blon, and the baron's people began to prep her. La Blon was a world largely covered by water. The few landmasses had pristine tropical forests that the early explorers had declared off-limits to development—beyond a spaceport or two. Using the technology of the day, the people colonizing La Blon created floating farms and raised algae, which they manufactured into all manner of foods. They used aquaculture to farm fish, and much of La Blon's native florae and faunae took well to domestication.

As the years passed, they encased their floating cities in domes and lowered them to the seabed. The farms still floated, and beneath them vast metropolises spread out and prospered. Light industry explored and conquered everything from recovering gold from seawater to manufacturing items under high pressure. La Blon also had a thriving tourist economy, with people traveling vast distances to spend a month or more exploring on land and below the waves.

Their arrival at a dry spaceport would be holovised worldwide. Representatives from La Blon and an adoring public would greet the heroes of the war against the Clans; then Verena and the others would travel to a resort for strategic talks. La Blon was proud to be hosting the event, and industries competed to sponsor various aspects of it.

When the aide ran down the agenda with Verena, she assumed that the "heroes of the war" referred to Kennerly and herself. Because of that assumption, she was taken completely off guard when two men with holocams entered the lounge where she waited with Kennerly, followed closely by Anastasia Kerensky. One cameraman concentrated on her, while the other focused on Verena.

Verena shot to her feet and saluted.

Anastasia smiled and waved off the salute. "You need not salute, Colonel. We need no formalities between us, you and I." The red-haired woman smiled and Verena caught perhaps a hint of pleasure in it. "You have done well since I last saw you."

Since you sent me away as unworthy. Verena's cheeks burned. "Yes, Colonel, I have achieved some good results. My second, Lieutenant Kennerly."

"Pleased, Lieutenant. I have reviewed the footage of the battle on Baxter. You deployed the Demons well."

Kennerly nodded. "I merely followed the captain's plan."

Anastasia's eyes glittered coldly. "It is well you give her credit, but there were tactical considerations that doubtless required adjustments. You made good choices."

"Thank you, Colonel."

One of the cameramen held up a hand. "Okay, now we need the two of you shaking hands or hugging or something. You know, make the home folks feel good that you two are such good friends."

Verena offered her hand and Anastasia took it, then drew her into a hug. They held each other tightly, tried a few backslaps and awkward chuckles, then broke the embrace. Verena tried to read Anastasia's face, but it was an emotionless mask.

"Was that good enough, gentlemen, or would you like another take?"

"It's fine, Colonel Kerensky. We'll let you talk. If we need more, we'll be back."

Kennerly nodded. "I'll head out with them."

Anastasia smiled. "No need on my account."

Verena nodded. "You can stay." She regretted the words the moment she uttered them, but the die had been cast.

Kennerly retreated to a corner of the room and sat where Verena would have to crank her head around to see him. *Prick.*

Anastasia selected a seat on the other side of the lounge. "I would have warned you that we were coming in a shuttle from the *Jaeger*, but Baron Saville's people wanted to see the surprise on your face as you were reunited with your former commanding officer."

Verena glanced at the closed hatch. "I am sure they got a reaction."

"It was not devoid of happiness, Verena. Were you happy to see me?"

"Of course. Why would I not be?"

Anastasia chuckled lightly. "I could think of dozens of reasons. You have to have wondered why I sent you away. I have no idea what answers you have come up with, but once you had them, you must have wondered how I would treat you when we met again."

Verena shook her head. "No to both questions."

"You have not wondered?"

"I have, but I have come up with no answers." She frowned, annoyed at Anastasia's tone and attitude. "As for my treatment at your hands, I had not thought on it at all."

"Very good." Anastasia gave her a little nod of the

head. "And in that, perhaps you have an answer to the first question."

Before Verena could ask for clarification, warning klaxons sounded in the ship. In response, all three of them settled back in their seats and fastened the restraining belts. Reentry and the trip to the surface of La Blon would take twenty minutes and was predicted to be bumpy.

Anastasia glanced at Kennerly. "How are you enjoying your time in the limelight, Lieutenant?"

"I very much enjoy spending someone else's money." His eyes sharpened. "And you, Colonel, must be enjoying your notoriety after having fallen so ignominiously from the heights of commanding the Steel Wolves."

Anastasia hesitated for a moment and Verena rejoiced, even though she knew she would pay for Kennerly's attack. "Indeed, Lieutenant, I take great pleasure in my success. If one continues doing the same thing over and over again, one becomes stagnant. I like new challenges and take great satisfaction in succeeding where others so often fail."

A solid bump and then the beginning of a spin killed the conversation. Verena was happy to let it die, and she thought Anastasia was as well. The Wolf Hunter colonel did not appear to be enjoying the turbulence. Sweat trickled down her temples and though Anastasia wiped it away as if it were nothing, it was the first time Verena had ever seen the woman the least bit discomfited.

She is remembering that combat drop, the one that almost killed her. Verena felt a wave of sympathy wash through her for Anastasia, but a voice inside— sounding remarkably like Kennerly—mocked her for such concern. *This is the woman who cast you out, drove you from your people, forced you to assume responsibilities you have no means of handling.*

Verena shook her head. *Does not matter. She is human, just like the rest of us.* Verena produced a handkerchief from her pocket and silently offered it to Anastasia.

Anastasia looked at it for a moment, then accepted it with a nod.

The ride smoothed out; then the roar of the ship's engines as the retrothrusters were engaged drowned out any chance of conversation. Verena just closed her eyes and let the engines' thunder ripple through her. For a moment she imagined herself as a creature of living fire. That was who everyone else believed her to be, after all, an elemental creature who could smite BattleMechs and defend their homes. This was the only way she would ever feel exactly like that.

Then the ship touched down. The engines went silent.

Verena was left empty.

Anastasia unfastened her belt with a click. "I will have the handkerchief laundered and returned to you, Verena."

"No, Colonel, no need." Verena looked up at the woman as she unfastened her own harness. "I may have wondered about the answers to your questions, even feared those answers, but I never thought you hated me."

"Good. It was never about feelings, Verena." Anastasia shook her head. "It was just what had to be done."

Verena considered that for a moment, then nodded. It didn't satisfy her, but she could understand it. Moreover, she understood that on at least one level, there would never be an explanation that would satisfy her.

Wordlessly, she stood. Arm in arm with her former commander, she exited the *Baron's Pride* and stepped into an ocean's worth of planetary adoration.

20

Storm Island Spaceport, La Blon
Former Prefecture IX, Republic of the Sphere
5 February 3137

Despite having been dressed in Clan Wolf leathers with a mantle of wolf fur, Alaric felt like anything but a warrior. He held his wrists crossed before him as if they were bound. He followed Dr. Murchison from the *Baron's Pride* and did not look up as the crowd cheered. *This must be how barbarian captives felt on parade in Rome.*

Crowds surrounded the hastily constructed platform that had been wheeled in on gantries to the DropShip's side. There probably were no more than two thousand well-wishers, but their enthusiasm made up for their lack. Swelling their numbers were holo-cam operators intent on capturing every second of the ship's arrival. Baron Cutt Saville stood at a podium, announcing each person who disembarked, and the crowd cheered on cue.

The spectacle disgusted Alaric, but also frightened him. The Clans were not passionless, but they put things in perspective. When they celebrated victory it was to praise the skill of warriors, not voice relief that they were somehow safer or more free because of the outcome of a battle. Because of this difference he scorned these people as hapless sheep bleating joyously, but he also recognized that this sort of enthusiasm was the emotion that turned ordinary people into partisans. He'd faced partisans on Yed Posterior, and while they had not been terribly efficient, a sniper's bullet or a well-placed explosive device still was deadly.

Saville turned from the podium and pointed a hand at Alaric. "And here, my friends, is your enemy at bay. This was the commander of the Clan forces on Yed Posterior. Unlike his counterpart on Baxter, he avoided death, but could not escape our justice."

The crowd roared appropriately and some people shouted epithets. He glanced at one man who screamed the loudest. Slender to the point of making Saville look morbidly obese, the young man had a scraggly beard and pumped his fist in the air with a complete lack of coordination. *We would have let him die after birth. He is too weak to survive, to be useful.*

And yet, his hatred was infectious. Those around him picked his chant of "Die, Wolf, die!" and the baron let it sweep through the crowd. The sound pulsed up, battering Alaric, giving him pause. The Wolves might well be superior to all other humans, but greater numbers of inferiors could drag them down and ruin them. This realization surprised him.

He lifted his chin and affected not to hear them.

Saville raised his hand. "And now, the people you have waited for. The Belligerent Belles who sent the Wolves packing. Colonel Anastasia Kerensky of the Wolf Hunters and Colonel Verena of your very own La Blon Djinns."

The multitude exploded in an orgy of emotion. They leaped up and down. Some unfurled flags, and others held up signs. They screamed for women who, a month ago, they'd not have known or cared about had they seen them on the streets wearing signs proclaiming their identities.

Anastasia and Verena emerged together, their arms linked. Then they raised both hands and waved furiously. That just heightened the frenzy. One woman fainted. Men and women screamed that they loved them. Parents held children aloft so they could see, and flowers in bunches arced in at the platform.

All of this registered on Alaric, but only distantly, for as Anastasia stepped to the fore, he got his first glimpse of Verena. La Blon's gentle sunlight made her face glow and her blue eyes shared the cerulean hue of the planet's oceans. Though her face was fuller than Anastasia's—*or my mother's*—it made her no less beautiful. In fact, coupled with the well-concealed surprise and the hint of a rosy blush, it gave her a soft innocence that caught Alaric completely off guard.

He looked away quickly, not certain why, but he couldn't risk that she would see him staring at her. Something about her, though, drew his eye back. As she stepped forward, looking very smart in a black uniform trimmed with blue and gold, he admired the strong fluidity of her gait. She calmly clasped Anastasia's hand and raised it, sparking another cheer.

Baron Saville invited her to speak, but she shook her head to decline. The crowd roared, insisting. Anastasia patted her on the back, almost seeming to shove her forward, and Alaric recognized that move. *She wishes to see how Verena will handle this situation. It is a test. Anastasia tests everyone constantly.*

Verena took her place at the podium and the crowd grew quiet. "Citizens of La Blon, thank you for this welcome. I have been told of your courage and generosity and spirit, and here it is. Thank you. It is an honor to serve you."

She glanced back, waiting to see if Anastasia or Saville would rescue her, but neither moved. A resigned smile flashed on her face; then she turned back to the crowd. "I have no prepared remarks. The reason for this is simple—words count for little in war. I am not an orator, but a warrior. *Your* warrior. The Djinns and I will serve you, serve to keep you free and safe, whether here or elsewhere. This battle with the Wolves is one that rages throughout the Ninth, but working together we have stopped them, and will *continue* to stop them. Thank you again for this welcome. I shall not forget it or the wonderful people for whom we fight."

She bowed and backed away from the podium. Saville allowed the people to cheer again before stepping forward to fill the vacuum. He announced that the defenders of the Ninth would be meeting on La Blon to plot out strategy, and that La Blon's role in the defense of the Ninth would never be forgotten.

The cheering and applause continued as GIN security personnel cleared a path along a red carpet at the base of the platform. Led by the baron, the guests descended to the ground and walked toward an odd-looking conveyance. Members of the public reached out on all sides, fingertips clawing to touch the visitors.

Adoring expressions melted into hatred as he passed, but not universally, and Alaric wondered at those who did not loathe him. *Are they the most sane because they refuse to hate, or so far beyond rational they do not realize they should hate me?*

After a short walk they mounted the steps and entered the cabin of the cylindrical vehicle that would convey them to the city of Fathnine. The plush appointments rivaled those of the baron's DropShip, but were limited to the thickly padded seats and some expertly carved cabinets. The top half of the cylinder consisted of clear ferroglass, allowing an unobstructed view of their surroundings when everyone was seated.

The baron waved them all to seats, then sat and buckled himself in. A pilot slipped into the cockpit at one end; a similar cockpit existed at the other end as well. The vehicle started forward and Alaric realized that the multiwheeled bed on which it moved was separate from the cylinder itself.

Saville smiled. "This is called a Cylcar. I think you'll find the journey most interesting."

The vehicle moved into a station and pulled parallel to a track fitted with a chain down the middle. A crane reached down, plucked the cylinder from the wheeled vehicle and deposited it on the tracks. A moment later the cylinder jolted as the chain caught; then it started forward toward a dark tube. Once the cylinder was entirely within the tube and had been plunged into darkness, the interior of the cylinder pressurized.

A second later it lunged forward. It emerged from the darkness in a clear tube, then plunged into the ocean and rapidly descended. Their ears popped and people gasped or laughed.

Alaric stared, mouth agape, as the water shifted and darkened. The sun sent shafts stabbing down into it, and silhouetted schools of fish cut through. The tube snaked along the continental shelf, weaving its way through coral reefs and forests of kelp. As they passed through, lights came on outside to splash color into the deep.

"It is breathtaking."

Verena was sitting next to Alaric and had spoken. "I have seen nothing like it before."

The two of them fell silent, and he was happy for it because his heart started pounding in a way he'd never experienced before. There was something about

Verena—he felt close to her, a sort of kinship. While he found her physically attractive, it was this more ephemeral link that made him want her. And yet, he could not identify the feeling, or understand its strength.

The Cylcar sped on, then turned and the tube descended off the shelf and down a steep drop. Alaric looked up through the ceiling and shook his head in disbelief. In the distance a network of glowing tubes and clustered domes glittering with lights covered the ocean floor. He'd seen similar sights on many worlds when flying into a city at night, but for so much to exist beneath the sea—it was difficult to grasp. And despite the speed at which they traveled, the domes were not growing larger very quickly. They were still a long way off, which meant the cities were positively huge.

Baron Saville unfastened his safety belt and dropped to one knee in front of a cabinet. "We're still an hour out of Fathnine. May I offer any of you a drink? It's our native brandy, made from sea grapes. I assure you it's most delicious."

General Bingham accepted and everyone followed suit, save for Alaric and Verena's aide, a dark little man to whom Alaric took an instant dislike. They glared at each other for a moment, and then Saville moved between them. They broke off their stares, neither being able to claim victory, but each continuing to glance sidelong at the other.

The general swirled the light brown liquor in a bulbous glass, then offered a toast. "To the success of our conference and the war against the Wolves."

They all raised their glasses and drank, and then Verena glanced at him and lowered her eyes. "Nothing personal was meant by that."

"I took no offense." He looked at her openly, then

nodded. "You defeated Bjorn on Baxter. Were you the one who killed him?"

Verena shook her head and stared down into her glass. "He almost killed me."

"The little man did not kill him."

"Kennerly, no. His lance killed others. My lance killed Bjorn. I did not know that was his name until now." She sipped again, let the brandy linger on her tongue, then swallowed. "We ambushed him."

Alaric caught a note of uncertainty or regret in her voice, but could not decide which it was. "You would have had to."

Verena's head came up. "What do you mean?"

"Bjorn was not an original thinker. A great fighter, perhaps, but not much of a tactician. He thought in one dimension, perhaps two. I do not believe he even recognized other dimensions."

She shook her head. "I am not certain I follow what you mean by dimensions."

Alaric nodded. "There are physical dimensions that resolve themselves into aspects of range, how much strength can be deployed at a particular range, and how terrain affects attack and defense. Time is also a dimension. Morale, unit training and the status of equipment and supplies are more dimensions. There are almost too many to name, but you understand the concept."

"Yes."

"Bjorn had a grasp on the physical dimensions, but failed to reconsider things as they changed over time. Had he marched across a beach at low tide, he would be surprised when high tide blocked his path. Perhaps he was not that simple, but . . ."

"I see." She frowned. "Is courage a dimension? Because that is one he saw."

"Almost too well." Alaric smiled slightly. "It was

for him the overarching dimension. Soldiers with a strong heart could overcome any obstacle because, in his mind, obstacles were merely manifestations of fear. Hostile terrain is a matter of fear. Not enough missiles, you fear you will run out. So it goes."

"You get into an ambush, you attack and make them fear you."

"Precisely." The Wolf watched her face. "How often did you see him do that?"

"Just once. He pursued our commanding officer and killed him, and would have kept coming, but his Star was in jeopardy." She smiled weakly. "It occurred to me that his behavior was similar to a story about Genghis Khan. He had one warrior who was valiant, could ride hundreds of miles without rest, never complained about the cold or hunger. The khan's men wanted to make this man a general, but the khan refused. He said that this man would expect of his subordinates what he did himself, and no other man could live up to that."

"That describes Bjorn accurately."

"Then how was it that your khan let him lead an invasion?"

"For that, I have no answer." Alaric shrugged. "How did you set your ambush?"

"I do not believe, Colonel, you wish to answer that question." Anastasia leaned forward in her seat. "Your answer might contain operational details our friend could find useful."

Only the sloshing of her brandy betrayed Verena's surprise.

General Bingham nodded. "Quite right, Colonel, though I fear the baron has made certain that everyone in the Ninth knows how we have beaten the Wolves down to the tiniest detail."

Saville laughed and hoisted his glass. "I have, and have done well with it. I had my brokers buy stock in

Karnak Food Distributors, maker of the rations Verena reported eating the night before the battle. They've had to put on a third shift in their factories to handle the demand for their products. We've cut a licensing deal here to manufacture and relabel a few items to give the citizens what they want. War may indeed be hell, but it can also be hellaciously profitable."

Everyone laughed politely, and then Anastasia leaned forward again. "Alaric, we sold your 'Mech to the baron here."

"I am well aware it is gone."

The Wolf Hunter's eyes narrowed. "Colonel Verena will be piloting it as commanding officer of the Djinns."

Alaric wasn't certain what reaction Anastasia hoped to provoke, so he gave her none. He just looked at her openly as if asking for further enlightenment. She remained silent.

"I am sorry it is your 'Mech."

Alaric shook his head. "It was never mine. It belonged to my Clan, and now it is the spoils of war. You are welcome to it, *entitled* to it." He flicked a finger against her glass and it rang with a crystal chime. "I hope it will serve you better than it did me—though truth be told, I failed it."

Verena looked in his eyes, but could not read his emotions. Then she drank, draining her glass, and extended it to the baron for more.

21

Fathnine, La Blon
Former Prefecture IX, Republic of the Sphere
5 February 3137

Though it was hardly palatial, the home given over to Verena for her stay on La Blon was the most beautiful place she had ever lived. The architecture seemed to flow up out of the seabed, and mimicked the columns of coral that could be seen outside the dome that formed the estate's rear boundary. Native stone and marine motifs decorated the building, with white wainscoting and vaulted blue ceilings. Murals of seascapes decorated the walls, all of which flowed like stones long since softened by the caresses of countless waves. Giant shells formed basins for sinks and tubs, and lights were hidden in pearlescent globes.

She walked into the central grotto, marveling at how a small fountain at its heart reflected dancing lights onto the walls. Toward the back an iron staircase spiraled up to the tower rooms. The furnishings, while not quite as elegant as those in the Royal Crown, fit the home perfectly. Pillows dominated, inviting visitors to rearrange things to make themselves feel the most at ease.

She turned as Kennerly followed her into the room. "Have you ever seen anything so beautiful?"

The man hesitated and his mask slipped. "I don't believe I have. There is serenity here."

"Yes, serenity, exactly." She sat on a low couch and leaned back into a mountain of pillows. "If I ever get a vacation, I am coming back here."

Kennerly's face closed again. "Have you forgotten that you live here now? You're a big hero. You could probably have this place for the asking."

Verena laughed, refusing to let him spoil her mood. The brandy warmed her belly and she felt very good. "I will bear that in mind."

Kennerly laughed, too, but it carried no joy or warmth. "Please tell me you are not taking to heart all that was said?"

"The baron? Hardly." She sat forward. "He was telling the people what they wanted to hear. He has no clue about the reality of what happened on Baxter, and I do not believe he wants to know the truth. Why that look? What is it?"

"It's not him I was talking about. It was the *Wolf*." Kennerly managed to spit the word out as if it were as vile as *murderer* or *pedophile*. "He filled your head with pretty imaginings, didn't he?"

Verena stared at him. "No. We talked about the Wolf we killed on Baxter. We talked about warfare."

"And you found it all enlightening."

She frowned, but bit back her initial response. "His perspective on war was enlightening. He talked about the dimensions to warfare, beyond considerations of terrain. He talked about all the variables and how Bjorn had a hard time dealing with them all. That is why we beat him. I see it now."

"'Dimensions of warfare?'" Kennerly shook his head sadly. "That brandy must have been very special."

"What do you mean?"

"There are no dimensions to warfare. People try to shade it, try to paint these stripes of gray in there, to try to make sense of it. And that's the problem—you can't make sense of war."

"What are you talking about?" Verena ticked off points on her fingers. "Sun-tzu's *Art of War* talks about all the different things you have to bear in mind. And Napoleon had his book of maxims. And Von Clauswitz and Musashi and Hasek and—"

"Forgive me, Colonel, but you can't possibly be that dense." Kennerly rubbed his temples. "Every work you cite was written by a victor to explain how he had won, or was written by a loser to show others how to avoid his fate. And what do they all have in common? They seek to apply rules to something that inherently defies them. Von Moltke is oft quoted as saying that no plan survives contact with the enemy. What does that mean? It means rules go right out the door when the fighting starts."

"Kennerly, you cannot deny that some rules are true. It is common wisdom that you want a three-to-one advantage over your enemy when attacking a fortified position."

"That is *wisdom*, but not a rule, not a law. The defenders are not going to count up how many attackers there are and suddenly decide to lay down their arms. If they are fighting for their lives, they will fight until they die."

"Which is why Sun-tzu says one should always leave an enemy an escape route."

"Which is patent nonsense as well. Wars are won by destroying the other person's ability to wage war. You destroy his factories, his soldiers, his transports, and his will to fight. That is the only way to win, and everything else is after-the-fact rationalization that only serves to delude the stupid."

The warm glow in her belly from the brandy had completely died. "What brought all this on, Lieutenant?"

"You, your conduct." He shook his head. "I watched your face as you spoke with the Wolf. You reacted with wonder at his words. You thought he had unlocked a grand mystery for you. Even tonight, you will be dreaming about past battles, slicing them into countless dimensions. You will quantify things that need not be quantified. You will make significant things that are insignificant."

Her stomach tightened. She'd already begun to think the way he was describing. The back of her mind had been running analyses, and little insights were popping into her brain like bubbles rising through champagne. "What concern is it of yours?"

"Good. You acknowledge I'm right. There might be hope for you." Kennerly's eyes glittered. "The concern is this. I've signed on to watch you, and I have been thinking you will fail, and fail spectacularly. You have that written all over you. But I had hopes, slender hopes, that you might actually grow into the job. When you spoke to the crowd, just for a moment there was something there. You touched on the key even though it seems clear now that you didn't realize it."

"What key?"

"No, no, no." Kennerly waggled a finger at her. "The key isn't something I can give you. If I did, you'd treat it the same way you're treating the Wolf's insights. You'd take it apart, twist it around, see if you could break it. You'd weigh it against the wisdom of all the warriors you've studied, and you would fail to see it is the one truth that unites them all. I thought you had it, but you missed it."

She stood and looked him square in the eye. "If

you believe I am so incompetent and so destined for failure, why are you here? Aren't you afraid you'll go down with me?"

He snorted. "I've placed myself where I am so I can insulate others when you implode. You see, you're so unsure of yourself you look for the rules to tell you that you're doing things correctly. You should want to be the one making the rules, not following them."

"But you just said that in warfare there are no rules."

"Pretty paradox, isn't it?" Kennerly threw her a salute. "Better you wrestle with it than the Wolf's ideas. Good night, Colonel. Sleep well."

She had not slept well at all. She found herself on a battlefield that was half melted, half blasted to bits, with broken BattleMechs everywhere and mechanical carrion birds ripping myomer muscles to shreds. Shell-shocked warriors wandered the battlefield, desperately studying datapads and choosing answers on an exam. When she looked at the screen she couldn't read a thing and yet she felt an urgent need to be selecting answers.

Up ahead a giant creature—humanoid with a wolf's head—strode the battlefield. He stopped each warrior and demanded to look at his datapad. He would snarl, toss it aside, then shoot them dead with a laser pistol. They all fell with a hole smoking in their skulls.

Closer and closer he came to her. She could smell the stink of death on him, the scent of roasted human flesh. She looked up at him. She looked into his face and into his eyes. She expected them to be Alaric's eyes, but they weren't.

They were Anastasia's eyes, cold and implacable.

She awoke with a start, gasping. Her bed was made from a giant oyster shell, with the lid as the headboard and the body containing a water-filled mattress. The bed shifted with her every motion, and a wave tossed her on her back. She rolled out of the bed and tried to stand, but fell back on the edge, barely catching herself. She sat and ground the heels of her hands into her eyes.

"Damn you, Kennerly."

The man had a talent for finding weakness and burrowing toward it like a parasite. He'd identified her weakness, and she knew he was right. She'd always been insecure. She always measured herself against the performance of others. She had always hit the marks set by others, but never exceeded them. She could hit a target but never pushed herself further. She never blasted past.

Why not?

The question echoed in her skull. The obvious answer seemed too easy because it completed the circle without offering a solution. Her insecurity prevented her from blasting past because she did not believe she could. It was one thing to follow a trail blazed by others, and quite another to strike out on her own.

This was why Alaric's insights were so seductive. They provided her a new perspective on battle. It became a new way to break things down and figure out how others had done them. By recombining those elements, she could do things no one else had. She could learn another warrior's weaknesses and exploit them. It didn't matter that Kennerly thought this was a dead end; it was a tool she could use to evaluate her performance.

And she had to perform. She levered herself up off the edge of the bed and stumbled into the shower. She turned the water on hot and let the whole room fill with steam. She laughed, once, when she considered that it represented the fog of war; then she turned the water down to a reasonable temperature and washed.

She dried herself off and dressed, then headed out to the nearby municipal office building they were using for their conference. The dome soared overhead, holding back hundreds of thousands of kiloliters of seawater. One crack and everything would fall apart.

When she arrived Verena was ushered up to a vast conference room with holoprojection equipment hanging images in midair and tables designated by small signs for each of the military units on-site. General Bingham was to preside, but he was not the highest ranking officer in attendance. At least four militia generals came in with five stars on their shoulders, and she was fairly certain that the first time she had seen one of them, the woman was only wearing four.

She walked to the Djinn's table and nodded to Kennerly. "Did you sleep well?"

"Very." He looked up from a datapad. "If these preliminary reports are accurate, this meeting will be fascinating."

Before she could ask him to elaborate, Anastasia arrived. Dr. Murchison came with her, and behind him marched Alaric. He wore a Wolf Hunter uniform, but with no rank badges. Heads turned as he entered and conversations died.

Colonel Hardin of the Alkalurops militia puffed up at the table next to the Hunters'. "Colonel Kerensky, is it wise to have one of the enemy present while we make our plans?"

"Colonel, if we are to be diligent in what we do, we would task subordinate officers to think as Opposition Force leaders. We would temper our assessment with these Opfor opinions, but you know as well as I do that many here would be tempted to dismiss them. They would say that our junior officers cannot possibly think like the enemy." She set her datapad on her table. "Alaric can and will render true Opfor opinions."

"I don't like it." Hardin tucked a riding crop beneath his arm and looked at General Bingham. "I protest, sir."

Bingham nodded. "I think you will find, Colonel Hardin, that this Wolf has no means for communicating with the enemy. Colonel Kerensky, do I have your word that Alaric will not present a security risk?"

Anastasia smiled. "A Wolf is always dangerous, General, but I think no one in this room has anything to fear from him."

"Very good. We should begin." General Bingham waved Anastasia forward. "Colonel Kerensky has offered to conduct the intelligence briefing so we can all come up to speed on the political situation."

Anastasia replaced him at the podium, then waited for him to reach the Rangers' table before she began. "Let us get right to it. The Wolves hit and took both inhabited worlds in the Kimball system, Two and Trey. These are very light industrial worlds that suffer a protein deficit. The system is a good staging area and since the Jade Falcons owned the worlds, the Wolves are expending energy on a fight that does not drain our forces."

She hit a button and a map of IX Prefecture flashed to life. Corridan IV had a gray cast to it, as did the Kimball system. Yed Posterior and Baxter were striped gray and red, and the rest of the free worlds showed up in red.

"You can all see that the Ninth Prefecture is a perfect channel leading to Terra. While the Wolves are waging Trials of Possession for the worlds, their conduct on Yed Posterior shows their real needs. The Clan leader there began harvesting resources even before he had control of the planet. Baxter could have fallen into the same pattern, but the leader there focused on gaining political control. While the Wolves only added one world to their holdings, in effect they got a significant portion of the output of two, which aids them in their drive on Terra."

Anastasia hit another button and the colors on the free worlds shifted. Three worlds, Unukalhai, Skondia and Nusakan, became bright green. Lyons, Atria and Ko, which were even closer to Terra, became green, but not as bright. The rest of the worlds remained red.

"Based on what happened at Yed Posterior, we can project a shift in Wolf tactics. The bright green worlds possess industry capable of turning out the sophisticated equipment required by a modern army on the move. They are primary targets. Lyons, Ko and Atria are very rich in foodstuffs, making them vital for the final push to Terra. These are the worlds we must defend. Everything else is unimportant."

Colonel Hardin stood abruptly. "I believe you are mistaken, Colonel Kerensky. Alkalurops produces a wealth of goods that are highly prized throughout the Inner Sphere."

Alaric, seated in the man's shadow, snorted. "The trifles your world produces are worthless. The only reason to attack Alkalurops is to kill trade in those shoddy goods."

Hardin turned and lashed Alaric across the face with his crop. "Silence, animal. You have no family, you have no honor, you are nothing but a machine." The crop flashed again, drawing another welt on Alaric's cheek. "A Wolf might be dangerous, but not a broken dog like you."

22

The second lash with the crop hurt less than the first, though it did tear the skin. Through the sting and the rising heat, Alaric felt blood welling to the surface. He found it curious that his only concern lay in the fact that the blood would run down his cheek and drip to his jacket, staining it.

Fury gathered in his chest, but he smothered it. He could see himself rising, batting aside a third blow, driving stiffened fingers into Hardin's throat. He'd fracture the hyoid bone, crush his windpipe and leave the man choking out his life right there. Most present would think him justified in doing that, and chances were that no word of what happened would leak out. Hardin would be a victim of a stroke or heart attack, and Alaric would be farmed out to some distant settlement, never again to fight or travel among the stars.

People—*civilized people*—had a way of handling

such things. If he had struck, they would have understood.

But he didn't. He didn't have to.

The crop rose a third time, but before it could fall again, Verena blocked it. Hardin looked at her, surprised—more at the fury on her face than at the fist that fast eclipsed Hardin's view of anything else. The punch caught him square on the nose with a sharp pop. Blood gushed and the man fell back. He landed on the edge of his table, upsetting it, and abruptly went to the floor as datapads dashed themselves to pieces around him.

Verena shook out her right hand once, then looked at the men and women surrounding her. "If we let pride and petty jealousies blind us to what we need to do, we do *not* deserve saving. We are fighting for more than pride—at least, we should be. I am not proud of what I just witnessed. Are any of you?"

None of the militia from Alkalurops made a move, though Kennerly had slipped in behind them to discourage them from doing so. Two of his subordinates bent to help their leader, who clearly had no idea where he was, and led him from the room.

General Bingham rose slowly as the Alkalurops table was set upright. "This is a regrettable incident, but it should be a lesson to us all. Our success against the Wolves so far has come through cooperation. I believe Colonel Kerensky was going to make the point that just because some worlds were less desirable to the Wolves than others was no reason to leave them undefended. She simply wanted us to recognize that we must acknowledge this and adjust our plans accordingly."

He held up a hand. "And I do not say this because Skondia is listed as a desirable world. It will be defended appropriately, as will all other worlds. We fight for the Ninth, *not* for each individual world. I trust this is understood by everyone here."

He waited for the assembled soldiers to nod in agreement. "Very well. I suggest we adjourn for half an hour. Hopefully they can put Colonel Hardin back together in that time."

Verena dropped to a knee in front of Alaric and reached out tentatively. "There is blood. It is a nasty welt."

He sat up, pulling back from her hand. He dug in his pocket for a handkerchief and pressed it to the wound. "Thank you for your intervention."

"Only a coward would strike a man who is . . . seated among enemies."

Anastasia walked over. "Hardin surrendered to fear. This is as close as he has ever been to a Clansman. He comes from a world that produces cheap toys and cheaper food, so I did not expect much from him."

She reached out and took Alaric's chin in her hand. She turned his face, then grunted. "Ian, please take Alaric and get him cleaned up."

"I will have it repaired quickly enough."

Alaric looked up. "You have decided you will not need me after all?"

"I have decided you made a point about the Wolf perspective on the invasion. We will not need you for what follows—I merely invoke your name and they will believe whatever I tell them."

The Wolf nodded, then stood. "Thank you again, Colonel Verena. Perhaps someday I will be able to repay your kindness."

Ian Murchison led Alaric back to his rooms, applied salve to the wound, then sealed it with a plasticine spray that tightened Alaric's flesh and immobilized his cheek. The doctor recommended rest, but the look in his eyes told Alaric that he knew it was a futile order. Ian packed up and returned to the meetings, leaving Alaric alone.

That suited him. While he realized that not having struck back was the right thing for him to have done, it disturbed him that he didn't attack Hardin. Four weeks earlier he would have, without thinking. Hardin certainly would not have hit him a second time—and might not even have managed the first strike.

I have changed. Had he been a bondsman, he would not have struck back, because he could not do so without permission. Anastasia Kerensky had declined to make him a bondsman, saying she was uncertain if the effort would be worth it: *Was I trying to show her she made a mistake?*

That was probably part of the answer, but he knew there was something more. He seemed to have undergone a fundamental shift, one that disconnected him from the need to strike. He was detached. Even the way he'd thought about the pain showed a distance from the act of being struck.

That was not the way of the Clans. The Clans fought to prove they were superior. Superiority guaranteed the immortality of your DNA. While he was not the product of the Clan breeding process, he could argue that the Davion bloodline long had been tested, and had proven superior on numerous counts. Victor Davion had beaten the Clans, and if that did not indicate superiority, what would?

That was it. *I am superior.* Superior certainly to the likes of Colonel Hardin and any of the other militiamen who thought of service as parades and medals. He was fairly certain Hardin had never drawn more blood in battle than he had from Alaric's cheek.

General Bingham? He felt superior to him, but allowed that did not mean he could not be surprised by him. Bingham did have experience and seemed gifted in melding units together. That alone was a skill few mastered.

His mind flitted to Donovan. Donovan had won on Corridan IV, and doubtless took one of the two worlds in the Kimball system. He had probably even learned from Alaric's experience, and had his looters figured into his logistical calculations. *He probably calls them* resource recovery units *or something equally absurd.* Still, Donovan lacked boldness and vision, which meant that while he could calculate a workable solution to any problem, he consistently failed to define the problem in large enough terms. He hobbled himself and therefore denied himself greatness.

His mind shifted to Verena. He thought himself superior to her, but somehow still on a par with her. He did not know her well enough to know her weaknesses, but he knew they were there. Even so, she was willing to act quickly, and if that ability were coupled with analysis, she could succeed where Bjorn had failed, which could make her a very deadly foe.

Anastasia.

Just thinking about her as an enemy sent a trickle of fear through him as cold as the jets of water her men had used to blast him. Testing, she was always testing him and everyone else. Hardin had failed his test. More would. Anastasia liked it that way, because it kept everyone off balance and gave her an edge.

Of course it does. By being the one doing all the testing, it naturally made her seem superior. If she tested and attacked, others had to defend. Defense is by its very nature an act of subordination, for your will works only in reaction to someone else's will. You dance to their tune and, in doing so, are more likely to stumble and fall.

That insight into Anastasia, though valuable, did not let him escape her shadow. She *had* been able to see right through him. His treatment at her hands had broken him down; for that he must thank her. If she had not done to him what she did, he would have struck back at Hardin. He would never have understood what was required to be superior, or that he *was* superior.

But will I ever be superior to her? He laughed at himself. That was a question that could only be answered in combat and yet, the only time he should logically fight her would be when he already knew the answer. He knew that time would come, and he spent the rest of the day pondering the many scenarios in which it might take place.

Early in the evening Alaric answered the door, smiled and invited Verena in. "I am afraid Colonel Kerensky has not returned from the conference."

She returned his smile. "I know. She is having dinner with Baron Saville and General Bingham. It is something of a celebration, though the official banquet will not be until tomorrow night. Planning went very well, and has concluded very much along the agenda that Colonel Kerensky devised."

"I am sure the colonel is pleased."

"She is." Verena's blue eyes narrowed. "I came to see how you are. How does your face feel?"

"Mild discomfort. The doctor says there will be no scarring." He smiled with half his face. "It is a good thing. My mother would be horrified."

Verena cocked her head. "Your mother? I cannot imagine you were freebirth. Sorry, I did not mean to offend."

"No offense taken." Alaric waved her to a couch, then joined her, moving a pillow to form a breastwork between them. "When I tell her what happened, she will be pleased with your intervention. And, yes, I have met my mother. It is a complicated story and quite tedious."

She shook her head, her gold hair barely brushing her shoulders. "I wanted to tell you that I admired how you sat there and took those blows."

"Ha! There is not a warrior there who saw me as anything but a coward."

"Not true. Not me." She glanced down, picking at the threaded fringe on a pillow. "There is an ancient Chinese legend about a military genius named Zhuge Liang. It is called 'The Empty City.' Do you know it?"

Alaric shook his head.

"I will not bore you with all the details, but Zhuge is put in defense of a city and is facing a huge army. He has all four gates thrown open, has the few soldiers in his command hide, and sits on the wall above one of the gates, dressed in casual robes. He plays a lute as if he is without a care in the world. And his enemy, who knows his reputation for being a military strategist, rides up to the city. He looks at the open gates, he looks at Zhuge, and rides away. He knows it must be a trap. Zhuge defeated him without a fight, just as you defeated Hardin without a fight. It is the greatest of warriors who do that."

She blushed. "I am sorry. I do not know why I blurted that out."

Alaric reached up and slipped his fingers into her hair. "I do." He drew her to him and kissed her softly.

She pulled back, breathless, licking her lips. "Why?"

"Because we are very much alike. We are both captives. We are both in thrall to Anastasia, and that fact unites us. It binds us in a way no others are bound."

He kissed her again, then pulled her across the pillow. Lips crushed against lips, breath came heavy and hot. She caressed his cheek, then jerked her hand away, but he drew it back. He let her explore the wound with her fingertips, and then she kissed it, softly, gently, and cast away the pillow separating their bodies.

They wanted each other and needed each other. They understood each other in ways no one else could. Clothing was discarded and flesh ground against supple flesh. Mouths explored, fingers caressed, breath caught until released in sighs, moans and whispers. Sometimes they used words, other times just sounds or touches, their bodies moving together, soon slicked with sweat.

Minutes passed as hours, each detail etched in his memory. How she felt, what she sounded like, her scent. Little smiles and the glint of her eye, the way a stray lock clung to a sweaty cheek, or the way she blew another lock out of her eyes. Her kisses, the scrape of her teeth, the raking of fingernails over his flesh and the softness of her skin beneath his caress.

They enjoyed one another for hours with the desperation of people engaging in the forbidden, and the urgency of those who know such an act of sharing and unity would not come again. It had the wonder of novelty and the sadness of finality. Even as Alaric embraced it, he could feel it slipping away. He hugged her closer, feeling her trace patterns in the blond hair on his chest.

She kissed his left nipple, then laid her head on his breast. "I can hear your heart."

He kissed the top of her head. "Hardin would not think I have one."

She rolled onto his chest and looked into his face. "I know I will probably never see you again. From here we will be split up. Anastasia has assigned the Djinns to—"

Alaric pressed a finger to her lips. "Say nothing."

She nodded. "Operational security, you are right."

He laughed. "No. I know Anastasia. I know where she will send you."

"But she will never have her Wolf Hunters and my Djinns fight on the same world. After tomorrow, I will never see you again."

"Nothing is impossible." He caressed her cheek. "We have a bond. We are united. Nothing will sunder that."

"I know, but we will never again be as we are— vulnerable, wounded, salving each other's hurts."

He thought for a moment, then nodded. "But if we are never again vulnerable or wounded, would that be so bad?"

Verena shook her head and smiled. "Not at all." She kissed him. "Again, just once more. More memories for those alone moments."

He nodded.

23

DropShip Jaeger, *Unukalhai*
Former Prefecture IX, Republic of the Sphere
20 February 3137

Alaric relished the look of surprise on the face of Donovan's hologram when Anastasia introduced him as her aide. The hologram glanced down at Alaric's wrists, but he'd clasped his hands behind his back to deny Donovan a simple way to understand what had happened. He smiled easily as the hologram's eyes came back up.

"It is good to see you looking well, Alaric."

"And you, Donovan. You have conquered two worlds."

"Three, actually." Donovan glanced at Anastasia in the middle of the holotank. "We crushed the last of the resistance here at midnight, planetary standard time. The civilian government—after some changes—has conceded control to us, and we have, in turn, appointed them the interim government pending the arrival of our garrison authorities."

Anastasia nodded as the tableau shifted around her

to a representation of the local solar system. Two more Clan DropShips were speeding in toward Unukalhai and would arrive a day before the *Jaeger* and its companion. "I assumed as much when I saw your ships heading in. So, this will be a Trial of Possession, *quiaff*?"

"Aff. I will be defending with five Stars. Three are BattleMech Stars, one heavy, two medium. A Star of combat support vehicles and one of elementals completes my deployment."

Alaric frowned. That was a considerable force. While Unukalhai was valuable for its industrial output, it really wasn't worth contesting so strongly—especially in light of the fact that the Wolves would be abandoning it when they moved laterally into the Lyran Commonwealth. If Donovan had a strategy, Alaric was not seeing it.

Anastasia nodded solemnly. "You present me with a problem, Star Colonel."

"That was my intention, Colonel Kerensky."

She rubbed a hand over her throat. "I have two 'Mech companies with me, only one heavy, the rest medium and light. I have four companies of armor and artillery, two of infantry, but one of those is militia."

Donovan smiled. "I hesitate to further complicate your life, Colonel, but the Kalhai militia has retained its arms and is planning to defend the world against invasion. We have told them to stand down, and I expect that order to be obeyed, or there will be consequences. Still, you could find this an inconvenience."

"I appreciate your warning us, Star Colonel."

Donovan smiled openly. "Shall I consider your force inventory to be your bid?"

"I will need some time to refine my bid, if you do not mind. An hour or so?"

"Very good." Donovan hesitated, then held up a hand. "Colonel, I will withdraw a medium 'Mech Star from my force in return for a concession on your part."

She shook her head. "My forces are limited, Star Colonel."

"This will not limit them further, I assure you." Donovan glanced at Alaric. "If I defeat you, I take possession of Alaric."

Alaric's guts turned inside out. *No, you cannot!*

Anastasia smiled. "I will take your offer into consideration. An hour, Star Colonel. Kerensky out."

The holotank went dark, then the room's lights came up. Anastasia looked at Alaric. "It would seem you have a friend."

"You cannot be considering his offer."

"If he wishes to surrender a Star of 'Mechs in the hopes of getting his paws on you, who am I to tell him he is insane?" She clapped her hands once, then looked over at her subordinate, Captain Liam Horet, as he strode across the room. "What have you learned about the situation on the ground?"

The big man shrugged his shoulders. "Less than I would have liked, Colonel. The local government was an uneasy coalition between conservative and hyper-reactionary forces, the latter having gained more support as fear over the world's future spread. When the Wolves arrived, two sets of negotiations took place. The duly elected prime minister bargained for the defense of the planet. The reactionaries, known as the Forever Party, staged a mutiny within the planetary defense forces. The prime minister resigned, his hard-line rival was appointed in his place, and after a fight to wipe out the last loyalists, the Wolves were declared victors."

Anastasia frowned. "The FP is claiming they limited the damage the Clans inflicted and promising to keep everyone safe as long as no one challenges the Wolves?"

Liam nodded. "That is exactly what seems to be

going on. We have no direct confirmation of that since the FP's supporters took control of the planetary media—including the GIN outlets. Baron Saville will not be pleased."

Anastasia snorted. "I am certain he will spin it all into good news."

"He will have his work cut out for him. The media outlets are all broadcasting civil defense messages urging calm and support of the Wolves, who will keep them safe from marauding mercenaries and foreigners. It does not help that we have the militia from Atria with us. In the last prefecture soccer championships they beat the Kalhai United team four to zero to win the Nine Cup. The Kalhai still take that loss very personally."

Anastasia closed her eyes. "People see sport as a surrogate for war and take it far too seriously. Hatred should be reserved for things that truly matter."

Captain Horet opened his hands. "You have no argument from me, Colonel, but that is the political environment we will be dropping into. As for the force matchups, we would stand roughly even now in a straight fight. His eliminating a 'Mech Star would give us a slight edge. With terrain working for us we can hurt him, drive him off."

"I concur." Anastasia opened her eyes again and glanced at Alaric. "Your assessment of Donovan?"

"He fights by the numbers. He is willing to risk all because the government is behind him. I would assume he has locals loading the ships."

Liam nodded. "Looking at a listing of the corporations whose output he will be taking and comparing it to a list of the conservatives who are now out of power, you can see that they are the ones suffering big losses."

She smiled briefly. "So you are suggesting that if Donovan is able to loot the world, then he will see nothing here to defend? We inflict a lot of damage and he will weigh the benefit against the cost and pull out?"

"It is a no-risk decision for him. He will have gotten everything he came for and be freed to prepare the next strike." Alaric pointed to where the hologram had stood. "Every planet he takes increases his fame. He could easily be elected saKhan of the Wolves and stand one step away from ultimate power when we take Terra."

Anastasia slowly nodded. "Well, it is in our contract to defend Unukalhai or retake it, if possible. It seems the only tool we have on our side is time—time to plan our assault, and time to let Donovan succeed to the point where opposing us costs more than he wants to pay. Liam, have the task force slow their burn for the planet. Instead of arriving in two days, let us make it three, three and a half—whatever puts us at our appointed landfall at midnight local time. We can let the civilians all be tucked away in their beds. If we are fortunate, we find a place that is very cold, to further discourage adventurism on their part."

"What about me, Colonel?" Alaric watched her face carefully. "Will you leverage me against a Star of 'Mechs?"

"Afraid I will lose, Alaric?" Anastasia laughed. "Or are you offended that you are only worth a *medium* Star?"

"On his best day, Donovan could not beat you."

"Ah, but it is on his best day that I wish to defeat him." She half smiled. "If he wishes to be foolishly generous, who am I to refuse his generosity?"

She reached out and patted his cheek. "Fear not, Alaric, I know what I am doing. I know how this all plays out. Arrogance makes for a fall, and your Donovan is arrogance personified."

*   *   *

After careful study of the world and analysis of the pirate broadcasts the government could not squelch, the Wolf Hunters chose to land high on the northern continent. It was a relatively barren and frozen area that had the added benefit of being part of the former prime minister's home district. A low mountain range dating from the planet's last glacial period separated the district from the capital and provided the Wolves an excellent line of defense. The Hunters had a limited number of routes in toward their target, but with more mobile forces, they had the opportunity to range south through a river valley and flank the Wolf position.

Alaric stood alone in the *Jaeger*'s holotank. Above him in a narrow band ran images from the various available holo sources. If he reached up and drew one down it would form a window, and if he pushed it back, it would take over the larger holographic display. The image it replaced would pop out into a window, or if he pushed two images back at the same time, they would split the image area.

He pulled down the sensor feed from Anastasia's 'Mech, a *Stormcrow*, but did not push it into the background. He did touch a small icon on the bottom of the window, giving him access to radio chatter. Opposite it, on the other side of the satellite-based composite tactical map, he pulled down the feed from the leader of the Hunters' armor task force. They were ranging far to the south, making for a bridge over the river that would then get them into the Wolves' rear area.

The armor thrust was a viable but limited threat. It would force Donovan to detach a Star of 'Mechs to seal off the mercenaries' flanking maneuver. That would weaken his middle, but as Anastasia drove at him, the Wolves could withdraw in good order to the capital and depart without serious loss of life and very little damage.

The difficulty with the tactical composite was the paucity of data from the Wolf position. While Donovan had had to hurry to move forces into the mountains, they had gotten there in sufficient time to cool down. Infrared data from satellite passes revealed nothing about their location, and the mountains had plenty of places to hide them. This included natural formations as well as some defenses that had been created and then abandoned during the drive to form the Republic of the Sphere.

Anastasia's main force placed its 'Mech companies in the middle of the formation, with the heavies on the left. The infantry took up the leftmost flank, with one company of armor on the right. The two artillery companies hung back to provide cover. The Hunters' own armor was hooking around, but moving through terrain that hid them from direct observation by the Wolves.

Captain Horet's assessment of the matchup had basically been correct. The invaders had an edge, but fighting in the mountains would blunt it quickly. Everything would come down to maneuvering, and the mountains would make that rather tight. The successful end run by the armor would shift the advantage considerably.

The main force advanced across pristine snowfields that were dotted with swaths of forest. Unless Donovan was a complete moron, he had spotters deployed in the woods to track Anastasia's advance. Had Alaric been fighting her, he would have used vibrabombs and other devices to inflict damage as she came in. There was no sense in letting her advance unmolested.

Only honor.

He shook his head. Once upon a time, the concept of honor held almost mythical weight for him; a worthy ideal for which to die. He supposed that his thinking on that matter had been shifting for some time, but the short period he had spent with Anastasia had sped the process. Honor might have been a concept that some people refused to face life without, but he had come to see it as an excuse that retrospectively ennobled stupidity on the part of dead warriors.

Of course, things were not always clear-cut. He recalled the story Verena had told him of Zhuge Liang. Was deceiving his foe honorable? Very few societies saw deception as honorable, but many would also describe Zhuge as being clever, and that seemed to make it acceptable. Clever or deceptive really were beside the point. The action was actually both, but more importantly, it was *effective*. Not only had Zhuge won that battle without fighting, but chances were that anyone else he faced who had heard of the story—from his enemy's point of view or the full story—proved very reluctant to fight him.

For someone like Verena, this meant the greatest warrior was one who never had to fight. In that assessment, however, she missed the point. It was not that Zhuge didn't have to fight, it was that he won the battle before it began. He beat his enemy in his mind, and that was a defeat from which his foe could never recover.

Alaric glanced over at the sensor view from the armored column. Major Perkins had shifted over to magres, so the bridge over the Soluval River lit up brightly. Alaric reached out to tap into his radio output, then recalled they were traveling under radio silence until they crossed the river, and then they were to be as noisy as possible to get Donovan to react.

Suddenly, light flashed on the bridge. A second light and a third. It took Alaric a moment to realize these were explosions. The bridge sagged in the middle, and then the center of it fell clean away. It broke through the ice coating the river.

He hit the armor radio icon.

". . . I repeat, the bridge is gone, Colonel. Next bridge is three hours away, and you have to know they will have it covered, too."

Anastasia's voice tightened. "Acknowledge, Perk. Thank you." She fell silent for a moment, then switched frequencies. The holotank's computer took a couple of seconds to catch up with the switch. ". . . is Colonel Kerensky for Star Colonel Donovan."

Donovan's voice, as relayed through Anastasia's communications link, sounded distant. "Yes, Colonel Kerensky."

"I congratulate you on anticipating us, Star Colonel. Blowing the bridge at Darien has robbed me of all tactical advantage." Anastasia managed a chuckle. "Doing it when we were just in sight of it shows élan of which I did not think you capable."

"I am not certain what you mean, Colonel." Donovan's voice came slowly and he sounded confused. "I have no troops operating near Darien."

"Then, apparently, it was my bad luck that the bridge spontaneously exploded and collapsed. Such are the fortunes of war. I had counted on flanking you to gain a tactical advantage that would let me drive you from the mountains. With that gone . . ."

Alaric's stomach sank in on itself. *No, this is not happening.*

"What are you saying, Colonel?"

"I am saying you have won, Star Colonel Donovan. You have successfully defended your holding of Unukalhai. I beg of you the indulgence of allowing my people to withdraw. Once we have recovered our troops, I will conclude our bargain." Her voice hardened only slightly. "You have won Alaric's freedom and I shall deliver him to you myself."

24

Though her accommodations on Nusakan were meager compared to the opulence of her lodgings on La Blon, Verena felt far more at ease in the small house she'd been given. Not much had been done in the way of decoration, but the refrigerator had been stocked with the food and beer she'd showed a preference for over the last month. In addition to that, various Nusakan industries had sent her gift baskets of products to welcome her, meeting most of her material needs on the domestic side of things.

Baron Saville had provided for her needs on the military side, too. The Djinns had preceded her to Nusakan. The unit was a reinforced, combined-arms battalion, fashioned very much along the lines of the Wolf Hunters. She had three lances of 'Mechs, one each heavy, medium and light, though her new 'Mech fell into the assault class. The pilots were all veterans, and while they all should have known better than to believe the hype, the fact that they'd seen both her and Kennerly on the holovid seemed to make them a bit more respectful.

Kennerly, who had been promoted to captain, led the medium lance. Officers she didn't know commanded the companies of infantry, armor and artillery and, at least at first blush, had a strong working relationship with their troops. Things seemed to be functioning very well when she arrived, and despite the fact that she had never commanded a battalion before nor worked for GIN as most of them had, they accepted her easily.

She'd commented on this to Kennerly, and he just laughed. "They got told that once you arrived on station, they'd be getting combat pay. Saville knows how to buy loyalty."

Verena put that comment into proper perspective and hadn't let it get under her skin. The soldiers in her command would have been stupid to accept her just for a little more money. They had confidence in her—for whatever reason—and she was going to maintain that. It fit perfectly into the dimension of morale, and she wanted that one as high as possible before the Wolves landed on Nusakan.

That meant her own morale needed to be high, and it was. Alaric had hit upon something that she had missed: She had been acting like a captive to Anastasia. She had continuously been measuring herself against Anastasia and wondering why the woman found her lacking. The answer had been obvious: because she was *not* Anastasia. By comparison with her, especially in her own mind, no one would measure up. It was no fault of Verena's that she had been judged harshly—she had neither the tools nor desire to be Anastasia.

Kennerly had changed, too, just a bit, and had become less annoying—at least until he learned of her liaison with Alaric. Prior to that he had complimented her on how quickly she had decked Hardin. He'd even alluded to the fact that she had once again almost gotten the key. She'd hoped he would drop a hint to allow her to figure out what he was getting at, but he didn't.

Then he learned she had slept with Alaric.

His reaction had surprised her. He had just looked at her and nodded. "Took longer than I thought."

That had not been what she expected. Cutting remarks, contempt, or anger, any of those would have been appropriate. She even could have understood the exact opposite, a sudden softening of his attitude and his admitting that he loved her but had treated her badly because he didn't know how to express his feelings. But indifference, his expecting her to have slept with Alaric, that made no sense.

After that, he was back to his old self, picking at her—never blatantly enough to bust him on insubordination, but enough to scrape her nerves raw. She could have ordered him to stop, and he would have, but she dreaded the new outlets he would have found for his ambitions.

More importantly, she had come to value his digging at her. He'd said that he was there to insulate the others from her and her collapse. He was her early warning system. He could see things about her that she could not see herself, and that made him valuable.

Despite all this, Kennerly did not figure prominently in her thoughts because she hit the ground running on Nusakan. She diligently applied herself to learning everything she could about the world. She began to mentally organize the planet and its defense into the dimensions Alaric had revealed to her. She studied terrain, especially near targets of high value, rated it and planned defenses. She looked at ways to deny the Wolves the items they would be coming for, and initiated programs of dispersing the most valuable elements. She also worked on establishing improved sensor networks and increased maintenance schedules for the unit's equipment. She wanted everything in top form when the time came to use it.

Alaric came to her thoughts in the times when she felt the most alone—usually late at night when she was working by herself, poring over data and trying to let her mind absorb it all. She would turn the datapad off, douse the lights and crawl into her bed, which was infuriatingly—and yet refreshingly—cold.

She would close her eyes and feel his touch again, his warm breath, his weight upon her. She found the memories stimulating—physically, certainly, but also mentally and emotionally. It was the emotional stimulation that she most craved. Her position required her to hold herself back and avoid familiarity—Kennerly, if he could be called one, was her closest friend. While he knew her very well, she drew little comfort from his company, and saw very little of that regardless.

Alaric had needed her as much as she had needed him, and being needed meant a great deal. Having that need communicated with a simple human touch had import she could not describe. It was as if lines of a program were suddenly inserted and compiled, making her feel complete and alive and aware on levels that had not existed for her before.

He had not been her first lover, but she could not say she had ever truly been in love. She didn't even think she could say that now because she did not yet love Alaric. She could have grown to love him—at least there was a chance of it—but that did not matter. For the space of a night, the two of them had completed each other. They had validated each other on the most basic human level. One could strip away rank and nationality, skills as a warrior and in command, just break them down to the most fundamental demands on a human, and that was where they saw value in each other. It seemed too simple to reduce it to just boy-girl, tab A into slot B, but it was the very simplicity of that connection that confirmed they were human and they were alive.

Kennerly had ridiculed Alaric's idea of dimensions of warfare, but Verena could see them in human relations as well. There were many dimensions of humanity that remained closed to her because of her situation. With Alaric she had explored some of them, drawn satisfaction from them, and even begun to understand the lives of those she would be protecting because of them.

She found solace in the memory of that night. Verena had little doubt that her prediction that they would never see each other again would come true. Yes, it was entirely possible that the Wolf Hunters and the Djinns would be tossed together once more, so the opportunity to see him would present itself. That said, she could not imagine a reunion with Alaric, and that inability seemed to close off that future.

Ultimately, Verena just didn't *feel* it.

She had never before put much stock in intuition. Her life and approach to living really did not allow for intuition and hunches to function. She relied on accumulated wisdom, tempered with contemporary variables. She truly did follow a trail blazed by others and felt safe there.

Kennerly's scourging her with that point still rankled, but she saw no way out of the path she'd started down. Moreover, she had no desire to stray. He might be right, that she would only reach waypoints that others had marked, but straying from that path would lead to a grave.

Or will it lead to greatness? In a heartbeat she realized that all trails blazed by others had, at one point or another, just veered off into what was the unknown. Sun-tzu, Napoleon, Aleksandr Kerensky and Victor Davion all had to depart from the paths others had blazed. They shifted direction because others might anticipate their path and prepare a defense.

It was just like the evolution of chess. One strategy begat another. An attack resulted in the creation of a defense. The employment of that defense spawned another attack, which created its own response. And so it went, with the strong strategies surviving, and the weak responses resulting in losses.

And if I were to mount a weak response, people would die. There would be no resetting the board. No starting over.

Just as that realization made her feel proud, another thought, delivered in Kennerly's voice, undercut it completely. *But life is not chess. There is no set of rules that cannot be broken. There is no board, no ranks or rows or squares. You do not want to abide by the rules, you want to make the rules.*

Verena shivered. To make the rules she would have to travel outside the rules. She would have to go places she had never been before. She would have to look at the battlefield and the world and everything in a new way, a way without guidelines, without dimensions.

She hugged her knees to her chest and huddled under a thick blanket. Her reality began to fragment. All the things she was certain she knew, all the sharp edges and crisp details, began to soften and fly apart. Colors ran, then swirled and splashed through each other, making new colors. Everything became energy flowing in vast rivers. To move against it was to be consumed. To float above it was to be carried along.

But to dive in, to grab hold and warp it to what you desired and needed, that was something else entirely. That was to possess limitless power. The flick of a finger could start a current that would crest and wipe away an army. A flutter kick could sweep up worlds, a shout could be heard throughout the Inner Sphere. She could be invincible and immortal, feared and unchallenged. She could become as powerful as Devlin Stone and even surpass him.

Is this what they all saw? Was the key to war, to life—the key that Kennerly held just out of her reach—was it just to dare to be the motivator instead of the moved? Was it enough to be the one who made the rules instead of the one who followed them? Could one truly master reality and shape it as she desired? Is that what Sun-tzu and Genghis Khan and Zhuge Liang and Victor Davion did?

It seemed for a moment—one fleeting moment— that this must have been precisely what they did. They found themselves beset by problems and they reached outside reality to change things. What were problems suddenly had solutions. Traps could no longer close, or they were no longer caught in the jaws. It would take colossal effort, of that she had no doubt, but that had to be what they had done.

Confronted with the impossible, they just changed things around so the impossible became possible.

Part of her refused to believe this because she knew, she had known all her life, that reality just cannot be changed that way. It isn't fluid. It doesn't slosh around and take a new shape when transferred from one vessel to another. It is not clay that can be shifted and altered. It is more rigid and immutable.

But who was to say that belief was true? Was it possible that before Galileo charted the orbit of the planets and discovered that Terra was *not* the center of the universe that it, in fact, had been? Could Terra once have been flat, then become a ball as people began to believe it was? Could generals destroy great hosts with a handful of soldiers just by convincing the combatants that they would win?

No, not destroy, but defeat, *yes.* Had Zhuge Liang shifted reality? He clearly had for his enemy. Sima Yi had an army of more than a hundred thousand men and came to an open city. He saw Zhuge's utter lack of concern and lack of fear, and knew that no man could be so confident and unafraid in the face of such a host unless he was confident of winning. By dint of his demeanor Zhuge Liang had changed Sima Yi's perception of the world—*of reality*—and that led him to retreat.

Verena sensed the truth in what she was thinking, but the most important element eluded her. *How do I do it? How do I grab hold of reality and change it?* She wondered if there was a mechanism, a key that would unlock the means to do that. *Is Kennerly's key* the *key?*

She did not know. Contemplating the whole puzzle, she fell into sleep and into terrifying dreams. Upon waking she remembered little of them, save the image of a shining key eluding her grasp.

She looked at her hand and clenched it into a fist. An empty fist.

Then she shook her head and resumed her planning.

25

Alaric forced himself to hold his head up high as he entered the Civic Auditorium in Anapar. His guts twisted and he easily could see himself sagging and collapsing like the bridge at Darien. He refused to succumb, however, because he chose to give neither Anastasia nor Donovan more pleasure than they were already taking from the situation.

The auditorium lights had been kept low as the mercenaries paraded down the center aisle. Spotlights illuminated the waiting Wolves on the stage. Alaric actually thought the staging was a bit elaborate, and couldn't imagine how Donovan could justify it on a cost-analysis basis. *Then again, were I in his position . . .*

Donovan stood center stage, unrecognizable in a black wolf's-head mask worked with gold. The rest of his uniform consisted of black Clan leathers, with a short cape of wolf's fur over his shoulders. He wore a dagger in his right boot, and the spotlight cast his shadow huge against the backdrop. It dwarfed the Trinary of elementals arrayed in their battle armor at the back of the stage.

When Anastasia, Ian and Alaric were still ten meters from the steps, Donovan raised a hand. "Trothkin near and far, seen and unseen, living and dead, rejoice. The Wolf has recovered one of its own."

"Seyla." Anastasia and Ian uttered the word proudly, but Alaric whispered it reluctantly. It tasted bitter in his mouth. His throat threatened to close around it.

Donovan continued. "I am the Oathmaster. All will be bound by this Conclave until they are dust and memories, and beyond that time until the end of all that is."

Again, "Seyla" echoed through the darkened hall. Though the word scourged Alaric, it also thrilled him. The Right of Return was part and parcel of Clan tradition, though rarely used. When their captors considered warriors too great to be made bondsmen, this ceremony was used to return them to their Clan. It was the ultimate sign of respect between Clans, and honored even among the most bitter enemies.

His ransom mocked that honor. The Exiles were hardly proper Wolves. *Anastasia should have made me a bondsman.* In that instant he recognized how much it annoyed him to have been seen as unworthy for inclusion in her mercenary group. Even though he understood that it would have been utterly inappropriate for her to make him a bondsman, and while he had no desire to be in thrall to mercenaries, he hated to be excluded.

He stared straight ahead, wishing his gaze could bore holes through Anastasia's skull. He could not understand her at all. She captured him, tortured him, decided to keep him and teach him, then quickly handed him back to the Wolves. It all made no sense—other than perhaps by assuming she was insane.

But he knew she was not insane, not by a long shot. She clearly had an agenda. Even though Ian Murchison, an apparent confidant, never commented on her actions and decisions, Alaric had read confusion on his face more than once. This made Anastasia very dangerous, because knowledge—wisdom—combined with unpredictability meant no one could take anything for granted with her.

Donovan lifted his head like a wolf scenting prey. "Let Alaric Wolf come forward to rejoin his pack."

Anastasia stepped aside, then smiled. "You will be missed, Alaric."

He blinked. "You cannot be serious."

"I am, indeed." She canted her head toward the stage. "I look forward to our next meeting."

"I am certain you do." Alaric forced himself to smile to conceal his confusion. "You have been an able teacher."

He faced forward and marched to the steps. As he mounted them, Donovan stepped to one side and three of the elementals came forward. Two of them grabbed the shoulders of the Wolf Hunter's jacket and ripped it from him. Next they tore off his tunic, then his trousers. They allowed him to unlace his boots and kick them off, and then he stood, naked, with his back to Anastasia and the doctor.

The third elemental handed him a long gray cloak with a mantle of wolf fur. Alaric pulled it on and fastened it at his throat with a silver wolf's-head clasp. He accepted a wolf mask, which he settled over his features. Once it was in place, hiding his humanity, he slowly turned and faced his former captors.

Donovan's voice boomed. "Behold, Alaric the Wolf, reunited with his trothkin. As dark as were the lamentations while he was apart from us, so shall the rejoicing be bright. All are to abide by the rede given here. Thus shall it stand until we all shall fall."

"Seyla."

Alaric echoed, "Seyla," with the others.

Hiding behind the mask lessened his embarrassment, but could not eliminate it. Anastasia stood there before him, half hidden in shadows, gently illuminated by the backlight from the stage. He thought how easy it would be to imagine her an illusion and his time apart from the Clans a very short and horrible nightmare.

But it had been real, very real. Now the welts on his face had healed, leaving no mark of his captivity on his body. And if he did not concentrate to remember everything that had happened, he could let it slip away as an unpleasantness that was beneath him.

That is exactly what his mother would have done. Alaric could understand the allure of her coping mechanism, for concentrating on the disappointments and frustrations of life could embitter and cripple you. Too many people found themselves trapped in cycles that spiraled down, sapping them of options and energy until their frustration consumed them.

His mother avoided that trap by putting annoyances behind her in one way or another. Granted, there were times when she did this through the suitable application of power. If half the stories from the Inner Sphere were true, she'd had enemies eliminated with little remorse. Alaric did not know if it was true that she'd had her own mother killed, but the truth of that rumor was really not important. He knew she was capable of having done it.

Victor, on the other hand, dealt with problems in an entirely different way. He faced up to them. He learned to deal with them. He never ran away from them. Victor had his supporters and detractors—both camps having become far more polarized since his death—but on that one point they agreed. Victor spent his whole life learning and, along the way, became wise enough to achieve many of his goals and help lead the Inner Sphere to an unprecedented period of peace.

As the mercenaries turned to leave, and the lights in the auditorium went down, Alaric followed the elementals from the hall. They would take him to a ground vehicle that would carry him to Donovan's DropShip and out of the system. It would be a long trip, and at the end of it, Alaric would have to face Khan Seth Ward.

He squeezed into the vehicle between two elementals and was pleased that neither they nor Donovan wanted to speak to him. He had a decision to make. If he decided to deal with Anastasia the way his mother handled things, he'd be forced to kill Donovan and anyone else who had been a party to his disgrace. That would include Anastasia, Ian and the rest of the Wolf Hunters. Verena would be tossed into the mix as well.

If he adopted the Victor Davion method, he would need to analyze what Anastasia had done and locate her weakness. She had to have one—no one was invincible. In fact, the loss on Unukalhai showed one glaring one. She had plotted a tactically brilliant maneuver and risked much on it. Had her armor been detected early and had Donovan moved hard to counter it, he could have destroyed it. He claimed to have had no troops working in the Darien area, and the Kalhai government repeated that claim, but rumors had run rampant regarding a local militia having blown the bridge to keep back the Clans.

Once that had been accomplished, she stopped her advance and conceded defeat. She clearly did not like being outthought, and when she perceived that to be the case, she hesitated. This meant that if one could outthink her not once, but twice, her hesitation at the first instance would allow a second surprise to completely devastate her.

For a heartbeat or three Alaric believed he'd unlocked the mystery to Anastasia Kerensky. When next they met, he'd be able to craft an assault that would rip her Wolf Hunters apart. She'd be *his* captive and he would repay her kindnesses to him with interest.

She would not be pleased.

His mind began to spin fantasies of revenge, but then he stumbled. His conclusion was based on a series of assumptions that were built on nothing more than rumors. He recalled very clearly the surprise in Donovan's voice when he'd claimed he had no troops operating near Darien. *If that is true, and if his allies were not there either . . .*

Alaric's mouth went dry and he felt even smaller. *Anastasia blew the bridge herself!* Even though it seemed to make no sense, he knew it to be true. She had set the battle, set Donovan up to show how he had been outplayed, then let him get away. *But why?*

His head swam as he imagined wheels within wheels, and games being played on levels of which he was barely cognizant. She avoided a fight that was too close to call, and that would have inflicted severe casualties on both sides. At the very least, a victory would have rendered her Wolf Hunters inoperable for months, perhaps even a year. Moreover, the planet's government had become hostile to her effort, and being in charge of a damaged unit in a hostile environment was something no leader wished to face.

Her withdrawal also would encourage Donovan and the other Wolves to underestimate her. That would be to her advantage. Donovan, by following Alaric's example, had turned the battle for the planet into a

Trial for Possession. This allowed him to regroup his forces and gave Donovan an advantage.

And he still will try to use it against her. It was cost effective, after all. It all began to unravel for him. Donovan would repeat that tactic, and look for a way to set up a battle that mirrored the one she had backed away from. He would choose a battlefield that he thought gave him an advantage. *And she already knows where that will be and how to defeat him.*

He shivered. Anastasia lost deliberately, knowing he would be returned to the Wolves. He didn't understand that, though he did acknowledge that he had hardly been of much use to her. In fact, after the La Blon conference, where she had used him to validate her plans and embarrass any opposition, he'd been useless. Giving him up cost her nothing.

But what did she gain from it? He exhaled slowly, the noise filling his mask. She was handing the Wolves an able commander, one who had spent time with her. *I think I know her. It is easy for me to assume I do.* He already had begun to make assumptions. He had begun to assume that when outthought she hesitated, and operating on that assumption would be deadly. Moreover, she did not have to know Alaric well to defeat him, she just had to know how he perceived her, and his perception of her had been something she had controlled since the moment they met.

His brain felt like it was going to explode. He slipped his wrist from beneath his cloak and examined it. He was certain the elementals thought he was looking for a bond cord, but he was checking for traces of the marionette strings. Anastasia had played him expertly, and doubtless was playing everyone else equally well. He assumed that she even knew of his liaison with Verena. *I wonder if she set that up.*

He shook his head. He didn't even know if this

analysis of Anastasia was right, or if it was merely a layer she'd presented to him to make him think he knew her. She would easily read from his strategy which of her layers he was treating as true, and she had him.

It occurred to him that perhaps neither his mother's nor Victor's method of dealing with problems was entirely applicable. *I need a synthesis.* He resolved to do as much analysis as possible, but also to deal with his enemies as analysis revealed their weaknesses. Anastasia would take a lot of time and serious analysis. Donovan and others, not nearly as much.

And, if I do this correctly, I might even have one problem eliminate another. With that thought he smiled and nodded, and waited for the long journey home to end.

26

DropShip Jaeger, *Outbound, Unukalhai*
Former Prefecture IX, Republic of the Sphere
25 February 3137

Anastasia looked up from her berth as Ian filled the hatch. "You are still uneasy about my having given Alaric back to the Wolves, *quiaff*, Doctor?"

The man nodded. "He is a very dangerous enemy. In fact, I would almost rather have you as my enemy than him."

This brought Anastasia upright and teased a smile onto her face. "You give him a great deal of credit."

"Perhaps you give him too little."

"That is possible." She cocked her head. "I had planned to keep him a little longer, but the opportunity to surrender him to his rival was too good to pass up. Alaric will be anxious to get back into the fight, so he will push Donovan hard."

Ian shook his head. "You say that as if you'll benefit from it. You might not face Donovan again."

"Oh, but I will."

"How do you figure that?" Ian's brows furrowed.

"Alaric is smart enough to figure out that you blew the bridge at Darien. He will know, therefore, that you deliberately surrendered him to his rival. You gave him over for humiliation. As proud as you are, he is more so. He will want revenge."

"True, but on whom? On me for losing? On Donovan for making me the offer? On all the Clans for a system that guaranteed he would be humiliated?"

"With Alaric, all three would be targets."

"Exactly."

Ian shook his head. "I don't understand, then. I grant that he is shrewd, and any target he wants to destroy is in for serious trouble, but the khan won't even let him enter the bidding process if Alaric seems out of control. The khan might hold him back simply because he has been in your camp and could have been deceived by any number of things. Would you let him fight if you were in the khan's position?"

"No, but the khan will let him fight." Her eyes sparkled. "And Alaric will not be coming to Skondia. He will attack elsewhere."

"How can you be so sure? He is not that predictable."

"True, but Donovan is." Anastasia rose from her berth and stretched. "Of the worlds in Prefecture Nine, there are only two targets of high enough value that they will be defended by strong units—the sort of units that can build a reputation. Those worlds are Skondia and Nusakan. Along with the Nusakan Rangers, we will be defending Skondia. Donovan will see the world as valuable enough to be worth attacking, and he has the added benefit of facing units that have defeated the Clans before. In our case, he's fought us once and won, but is not certain *how* he won. He will choose Skondia."

"But what if Alaric tells him how he won here?"

"It does not matter. Donovan may assume that

Alaric is angry and being petty, attempting to steal the glory of his victory. If he does that, he refuses to believe we let him win, or he assumes that I was so afraid of him that I made no serious effort to defeat him. He knows I was trying to outflank him, so he will be wary of that sort of attack in the future. Alternately, he can believe Alaric and take everything he has to say into account. He will be wary of feints and deceptions."

"And if Alaric says nothing?"

"Then Donovan still has to wrestle with his lack of knowledge of how he won. It is an unknown that can never be known. Donovan is a numbers person. It will drive him insane. If he has too few numbers he frets. If he has too much in the way of numbers, he will go insane." Anastasia shrugged. "Either way we have him."

Ian looked at her expressionlessly. "You say this as if it's all a game of chess."

"And you react as if it's not." She pointed toward the deck and the planet they were racing away from. "My contract required me to land troops and fight a battle with the Clans. I got a bonus for entering Anapar. Upon my departure, the administration of the planet was turned over to local civil authority. Granted, none of this occurred exactly as my employers anticipated or specified, but I accomplished what I needed to accomplish."

"All this implies that you could have defeated Donovan on Unukalhai."

"I could have, but at a horrible cost. The advantage is always to the defender. Always has been, always will be. Defense is always easier than offense. I did not have the position or a sufficient superiority of firepower to defeat Donovan without laying waste to my whole unit. Moreover, Unukalhai is not an important battlefield. Defeating him there would have meant little. Defeating him on Skondia, on the other hand, will be big news. Not only will we have the advantage of defending on Skondia, but our victory there will cement our reputation within the Inner Sphere. This positions us to be able to do many useful things."

His eyes sharpened. "There are whole realms of things in play here that I know nothing about."

Anastasia smiled. "I am the leader of a mercenary unit looking to build my reputation so I can build my fortune."

"I don't buy that, Colonel."

"I wouldn't look for more than there is, Ian. It will drive you insane, just as it will Donovan."

"Sometimes I think you live to drive us all insane." He smiled. "And letting Alaric go was a step in that direction for him?"

She shook her head. "Not to drive him insane, but to unsettle him. Alaric is confident—egotistical, even, but not with all the negative connotations that usually implies. He thinks quickly and well, but extrapolates too far forward. He looks beyond, so he trips over those things that are right in front of him. My trading him for Donovan withdrawing a Star, and then allowing him to be sent away, will have confused him. He will want to exact revenge, but because he doesn't know why I did what I did, he is going to hesitate in coming after me. I put that at a ninety-five percent probability. If he does choose to come to Skondia, he will be completely out of control and ineffective."

"So he will go to Nusakan."

"Most likely."

"And that is why you had Verena stationed there?" Ian crossed his arms over his chest. "You know they had a liaison on La Blon."

"Hardly a surprise. They are young and were united in their hatred for a common enemy. Me."

"You say that as if you are proud."

Anastasia thought for a moment. "Maybe I am. When I sent her away it was because she limited herself. I have watched her, and will watch her more, especially against Alaric. Nusakan will be an interesting test for the both of them. Will any lingering personal feelings affect how they fight? In Verena's case, the answer is yes. It might even get her killed."

He shook his head again. "I can't understand why you have it in for her. She's not bad as a warrior. In fact, she's done well since she left us."

"There is no denying that, Ian." Anastasia tapped her breastbone. "The problem with Verena is that she does not embrace war here, in the heart. She is all in the head."

"She was in her heart when she decked Hardin."

"Very true. She showed passion then, and that was good. The problem is that passion scares her. It represents the risk of being out of control and being wrong. She controls for failure, so she throttles any chance at success. If she could get past that, she has a chance at greatness."

"Do you think she can?"

"I don't know. She may have merit yet. And future use." Anastasia shrugged. "If Alaric does not kill her."

Ian raised an eyebrow. "You think of him as far colder than I. Do you mean he will actually kill her, or just that she will die fighting against him?"

"He will kill her."

"I cannot say I see it."

Anastasia chuckled. "It is because you still have the spark of romance in your heart, Doctor. You cling to the idea that MechWarriors are heirs to the grand chivalric traditions that harken back almost two millennia. Gallantry is a wonderful idea, an ideal to be strived for, but we have seen enough war to know that it is anything but gallant.

"I will tell you what most likely will happen at Nusakan. Verena will find herself outmaneuvered by Alaric. He can read her. He will know what she is going to do before she does. She will feel compelled to attack in an effort to save what is left of her command. Perhaps she will even bargain with him for a winner-take-all confrontation. He will accept and kill her remorselessly."

"She has no chance against him?"

Anastasia thought for a moment. "Perhaps one, a slender one. To avail herself of it, however, she would have to operate so far outside her comfort zone that she would really not be herself. In that case she might win."

He nodded. "I think I shall hope for that outcome."

"If it happens, I will have to reconsider her position." Anastasia smiled. "She will prove very useful— more so than I would have imagined."

"You are again talking about realms I do not see."

She slapped him on the shoulder. "Do not trouble yourself, Ian. Come, the only realm we need worry ourselves with is Skondia. We will meet Donovan there. We already have defeated him. We just need to pick out the battlefield where we will destroy him, and guarantee the future of the Wolf Hunters."

DropShip Thylacine, *Outbound, Unukalhai*
Former Prefecture IX, Republic of the Sphere
27 February 3137

Alaric bowed his head in an attempt to hide the blush crawling up his face. He'd known this moment would come. Khan Seth Ward had been too busy to meet with him but now, as Donovan was preparing to bid against other Star colonels for the privilege of attacking further into Prefecture IX, the khan could no longer avoid his company. Alaric had no doubt the khan found it as distasteful as he did, but likewise found it necessary.

As the slender man walked into the waiting area overlooking the holotank where the bidding would take place, a profound wave of shame ignited Alaric's cheeks. In the days since being accepted back among the Wolves, Alaric had tried to come to grips with all that had happened to him. The Right of Return had seldom been invoked, and no one seemed to know how to behave toward him. The default treatment was to ignore him as much as possible, speak little to him directly or not at all, and generally act as if they wished he were dead.

The khan stopped as the door slid shut behind him, then smiled ever so slightly. The smile reminded Alaric of those Anastasia would wear, and he didn't like it. Something was going on, and he was fairly certain that his life would be more miserable for it.

"It is good to see you again, Alaric."

"And you, my Khan." Alaric tried not to make anything of the fact that the khan had not used a rank when addressing him, but fear fluttered in his stomach.

"Please forgive my inability to meet with you prior to this. I have had much to attend to." The khan's smile broadened. "I want you to know that your mother was informed of your loss, and she flatly refused to believe you were dead. She said she would have known."

He produced a small disk from a pocket in his fatigues. "She recorded a message for you. You may listen to it now, if you wish."

Alaric shook his head. "Later, sir, thank you."

Seth Ward approached and leaned heavily on the railing of the gallery overlooking the holotank. "Donovan will be bidding to continue the invasion. The next wave will find very rich worlds. Any Star colonel who successfully participates in this wave will reap great glory. He will certainly earn consideration for a Bloodname, and doubtless be fodder for the breeding program. That *is* what we fight for, is it not? Immortality among the Clans?"

"Yes, sir, it is."

The khan turned to face him. "You are a problem, you know."

"Sir?"

"I have spent much time researching the Right of Return. It has never been used much among the

Clans—certainly not since we began the invasion of the Inner Sphere. In the past, it was used almost exclusively to invite back a venerable warrior so he could return to his Clan and live out his days in honor. You are, as nearly as I can discern, the youngest warrior recovered in this manner, and one of the few who was not even Bloodnamed."

"I see, sir."

"I doubt you do." The khan clasped his hands behind his back. "You have been returned to the Wolves, but all previous status is gone. You have no rank. You have no standing. If we had time, you could test out and resume your rank. It would appear you have to remain in the rear as this final assault goes forward."

Alaric stared down at the deck and tried to remain still. A tremor shook him. The flutter in his stomach became a quake. He had not imagined that all he had worked for had been lost.

He looked up quickly. "Sir, would this not be a waste of all I have learned during my captivity?"

"Fear not on that count. I am certain our leaders will gladly listen to you in planning their assaults. Would things be better if you were available to them on an operational or tactical level? Certainly. You have leadership skills, but your position has been compromised. Fear not, however, for there will be much war in the future in which you will be able to participate."

Alaric shook his head to banish the wave of dizziness cresting over him. "Is this final, my Khan? Is there nothing that can be done?"

"Nothing you would agree to."

Alaric's eyes narrowed. "What would it require, sir?"

The khan tapped on the viewport to the holotank. Donovan looked up, then nodded when the khan signaled for him to join them. "You have one chance, Alaric, only one. How much does your future mean to you?"

The door hissed open and Donovan entered. He saluted the khan, then nodded to Alaric. "As you requested, my khan, I have researched the Right of Return in all its parameters and traditions. There was one peculiar case that is applicable here. An officer had been returned and was needed at a critical juncture to command a task force. He was allowed to assume command and acquitted himself well."

Alaric forced the fear from his voice. "How was it done?"

Donovan produced a white cord from his pocket. "The pilot willingly became a bondsman. His captor bargained with him for his release and the Clan khan accepted the forthcoming battle as a proxy for rank testing."

"I would be *your* bondsman?"

Donovan nodded solemnly. "I take no delight in this, Alaric, and would not propose it save it will enable me to accomplish what I want to do."

Alaric looked at Seth Ward. "You would accept any battle I am in as a proxy for my testing?"

"I would."

"And, Star Colonel, what is the bargain you will offer me for my freedom?"

"You serve as my subordinate and win the battle I set you to. Win and you will be free."

Alaric closed his eyes. His heart pounded swiftly, as if trying to burst through his chest. He forced himself to breathe evenly. He sought to slow his heart and calm his thoughts. A decision was required of him and though he knew what he wanted to say, he knew that haste would be his undoing.

If he did not accept the bargain, he would not even be allowed in a war zone until after he tested out again. Given their planned move, he had no idea how long that might take. Until then he would remain in this state of limbo, and he would have to watch Donovan being lionized for his successes. *And everyone would forget it was my plan that allowed him to succeed.*

If, on the other hand, he accepted the challenge, he would be a bondsman, his rank conditional. If he failed, he would have to earn his way back into the Clan, and then test out and again rise to the position where he could command. While others had done it before, it was not an easy road. Though Alaric knew he could make it—*would* make it—millions of things could go wrong and hamper him.

I could be killed in combat, or I could die from others endlessly singing Donovan's praise.

He knew he would accept the bargain, but it was not cold calculation that cemented his decision. It was a random thought, one linked to others he'd not entertained recently, that won him over. In folklore and legend, there were gods who reduced themselves to mortality. They faced death and rose again, wiser and stronger. Odin was but one example. *How appropriate to sink to the depths and rise again. It befits the legend.*

He opened his eyes and extended his wrist. "I will be your bondsman."

Donovan advanced and looped the cord twice around Alaric's wrist, then knotted it off. "You will possess the rank of Star captain for our purposes. You will accompany me into the holotank and will say nothing until I give you leave to do so. Is that understood?"

"Yes, sir." The words tasted like dust in his mouth, but he uttered them without a trace of disgust."

The khan looked at Donovan. "You are ready, then?"

"Aff."

The khan led them from the room and down a ladder to the deck below. They entered the holodeck where two other Star colonels waited. Hestia was a MechWarrior who wore her long black hair in a queue. Edward was the smallest of all of them, yet not of the diminutive stature marking Clan aerojocks. His blond hair made Alaric think of pictures he'd seen of Victor Davion, but Edward's dark eyes boasted only bovine intelligence, not the predatory gleam visible in all images of his father. Alaric dismissed Edward from consideration because he would end up with the scraps of the bidding between the other two.

Seth Ward punched a button on his datapad, and the holotank sprang to life. Three worlds hovered in the center: Skondia, Nusakan and Alkalurops. "This wave of assaults concerns these three worlds. You have all participated in operations up to this point, but only Star Colonel Donovan has participated in *every* wave. Because of his success, he will bid first and you will bid against him."

Donovan cast a glance behind him at Alaric, then clasped his hands at the small of his back. "I will take Skondia *and* Nusakan with Alpha Galaxy."

Alaric covered his own surprise, but neither Hestia nor Edward could manage theirs. They stood there agog. They had clearly done their calculations based on what they would need to take each world, but had never considered so grand a grab. *And that is why Donovan needed me. I get one of the worlds, and he gets the glory of both being taken.*

It *was* a brilliant bit of strategy. Donovan escalated the challenge to his rivals and caught them unprepared. They probably had no subordinates they could trust with a whole planetary assault. If they bid a Galaxy against Donovan, then the bidding would tighten as parts of it were cast away. Donovan had done the calculations and they had not. He could bid successfully and they could not. They were undone before they stepped into the holotank.

The khan waved a hand toward the female Star colonel.

Hestia closed her mouth and nodded. "I bid the Seventh Battle Cluster to take Alkalurops."

Edward swallowed hard, then ran a hand over his forehead. "I bid the Third Battle Cluster less the fighter Binary."

Donovan nodded and Alaric smiled. He'd won this round, but Alaric knew what would be coming next. Donovan would force him to bargain for the world he wanted, and the troops he would use. Donovan would force him to bid low, and Donovan would choose whether or not he would be allowed to bring in reinforcements. Donovan had him effectively hobbled.

The other two Star colonels continued to bid down, with Hestia winning. She retained a Trinary of elementals, a Command Star of 'Mechs and one other Trinary of 'Mechs. That was easily enough force to take Alkalurops, though Alaric said nothing. The only way it would not work was if Anastasia was there, and he knew she would not be.

Hestia and Edward departed, the latter clearly shaken. The khan smiled. "Very well bid, Star Colonel. You have a Galaxy to accomplish the conquest of two worlds. Do you feel it will be enough?"

"More than enough, sir." Donovan turned and looked at Alaric. "Star Captain, we need to decide which world you will take. Nusakan or Skondia."

Alaric bowed his head. "That, sir, would be your prerogative. I *am* your servant."

Donovan frowned. "I will give you the Fourth Wolf Guards and the 279th Battle Cluster. Which of the worlds would you take?"

"You are most generous, Star Colonel." Alaric lifted his chin. "I would take Skondia. Anastasia Kerensky and her Wolf Hunters will be there. They are lying in wait for you."

"Of course. They want revenge."

Alaric shook his head. "Not revenge. They wish to spring the trap you stepped into on Unukalhai."

"What trap?"

"Anastasia let you win. She blew up the bridge at Darien and credited you with forethought. You now underestimate her. You will deploy against her and attack her weakness, which will be no weakness at all. She will defeat you."

Donovan shook his head. "That is not possible."

"The trap, or your defeat?" Alaric smiled. "Both are true, one past, one future. On the other hand, if I am sent against her, it will not be what she expects. I will have the advantage and be able to exploit it. But if you insist on Skondia, then just give me the 278th Battle Cluster. It is all I will need on Nusakan. You will need the Guards on Skondia."

Donovan glanced at his datapad and punched a few keys. "She only has a mixed arms battalion. The Skondia Rangers and their militia each have barely a Trinary of 'Mechs. I will not need three Clusters to take the world."

Alaric frowned. "Is it that you are bidding two Clusters to take Skondia?"

"I could take it with just one."

"But that is not a bid I would hold you to." Alaric spread his hands. "Mine is to do your bidding. How would you have it? Shall I win Skondia for you, or will you prove the mercenary a fool for thinking she trapped you?"

"You will have the 279th and the Guards." Donovan's eyes narrowed. "You best take Nusakan quickly. If you fail and they capture you again, there will be no return."

"I understand, sir. Thank you." Alaric bowed his head, hiding his smile. *I do not think, Donovan, I shall be the one who has to worry about returning.*

28

DropShip Thylacine, *Inbound, Nusakan*
Former Prefecture IX, Republic of the Sphere
10 March 3137

The 279th Battle Cluster had been a bit uneasy when they learned that Alaric—a disgraced bondsman—would be placed in command, but then word leaked out about how he had specifically chosen them. While he did have the Fourth Wolf Guards in reserve, he'd not released their DropShips to head in toward Nusakan. This meant if his troops got into trouble, it would take at least five days for reinforcements to arrive. This vote of confidence—along with a basic realization of how much trouble they would be in if they needed to summon reinforcements—spiked morale.

Strapped into the cockpit of a new *Mad Cat*, Alaric reviewed the data about Nusakan. Cold and dry, the planet had vast ice caps north and south and tundra that dominated all but a few zones. One of those was around the equator, where year-round the temperature remained pleasantly cool. Elsewhere, tectonic activity created a volcanic zone where geothermal power stations were able to render the tundra habitable. These zones held the concentration of electronics manufacturing facilities, while the equator was home to agri- and aquaculture industries.

The northern continent boasted two manufacturing zones and the southern three, but those were older and sorely in need of upgrades. They produced mostly consumer electronics that might be wildly popular in the Inner Sphere, but were of little use to the Clans. The northern zones were clearly the most valuable, and the ones the planet's soldiers would have to defend.

On his way in, and even through the initial orbits around the planet, Alaric had refused to acknowledge any calls from the defenders. He sent them scrambled messages to make it appear as if there was some sort of equipment failure, while pulling in all signals intelligence he could get from the world. The local news reports and unguarded civilian communications gave him a good picture of the situation on the ground.

Three military units were operational on Nusakan. The Stormhammers, who still went by that name despite having been folded into the Lyran Commonwealth Armed Forces, had been there the longest and had a deservedly fierce reputation. Though Jasek Kelswa-Steiner no longer commanded them, Colonel Carl Tucker was reported to be a shrewd officer. They certainly knew the planet the best, were well suited to fighting in the cold, spare landscape; and were looking for payback against the Clans since abandoning Skye to the Jade Falcons. That they had not taken the opportunity to attack Skye while the Wolves were ripping down through Prefecture IX indicated a lack of deep thought to Alaric, though he did not make this a critical element in his assessment of that unit.

Colton's Screaming Demons, a mercenary group formed and led by Aynn Colton, was as long on self-promotion as it was short on actual combat experience. Colton, a tall blonde with a sharp tongue and no sense of restraint, boasted mightily about what her troops would do to the invaders. She spent a great deal of time posturing and inviting local media to watch her troops in action. Alaric and other analysts in the 279th broke down all the holovid they could get and determined the Demons were screaming because their 'Mechs were poorly maintained, undersupplied and led by a cadre of officers who made rank by sucking up to Colton.

The La Blon Djinns also had been featured in media coverage, but Verena had remained low-key. The news commentators had played it positively, noting that she was "no-nonsense" and "all business." This legitimized the Djinns being placed in overall command of the world's defense. The Stormhammers' leader took his demotion rather well, and the media enjoyed contrasting Colton and Verena as "fire and ice."

Alaric had no intention of letting Verena know he was leading the attack on Nusakan. He knew that would be a complicating factor for her. Even though the physical act of love and the usual attendant emotions had been severed rather sharply in the Clan culture, a certain amount of bleed-over did occur. Verena had effectively been isolated before they had come together and Alaric suspected that Kennerly would have become even more hostile to her when he learned of their liaison. Discovering that he was attacking the world she was defending would trigger feelings of betrayal for her, and would erode her concentration.

Both of these things he could use.

It had not been his intention to use their connection against her, even though he had known where she would be and that he would be opposing her. He would not, however, refrain from using any tool at his disposal for an advantage. Just as he knew he could upset her, he knew he could likewise discomfit Aynn Colton. A quick glance at her biography and listening to a few interviews pointed out her glaring weaknesses that, oddly enough, were not that different from those Verena possessed.

Fatal flaws. He shook his head, then punched up a communications link. "This is Star Captain Alaric of the 279th Battle Cluster. I am seeking Colonel Aynn Colton." He hit several buttons on his console, freezing out all other attempts to reach him, and let her face fill his secondary monitor.

"This is Colton, Star *Captain.* To what do I owe this pleasure?"

"It is my understanding that you are defending the Makonato district. With what will you defend?"

The blonde's face slackened. "Are you saying you want a Trial of Possession for this *district?*"

"Did I not make that clear? Yes, Colonel."

"But aren't you supposed to fight to possess the entire planet?"

"I fight to possess what I need, and you are defending what I want." Alaric smiled easily. "With what will you defend?"

"The Demons will defend the whole district. You'll not take a step in here without our opposition! We will fight you on the beaches. We will fight you—"

"I am sure, Colonel, you will fight us everywhere. You might want to curtail your rhetoric, however."

"What? How dare you?"

"I do not mean to be rude, Colonel, but I thought you might go on for a bit." He glanced at the chronometer on his holographic display. "And as we will be landing in twenty-seven minutes, I thought you might want to prepare."

*   *   *

Even before the *Thylacine* landed, Alaric launched a single Star of aerospace fighters. They flew cover as the DropShip came down. The pilots met no opposition in the air and reported back on the advancing Demons. They gave him excellent data, including infrared scans that showed the mercenaries heating up their 'Mechs just by the haste of their approach.

Colton brought her entire battalion save the armor company, which remained behind to secure her base. She had forty BattleMechs in all: a company of heavy, medium and light 'Mechs, along with a command lance consisting of heavy and medium 'Mechs. The light company ranged out to the north, advancing on the far side of the river that, though covered with ice, had to be forded or crossed on a bridge. The heavies traveled on the southern riverbank, and the mediums covered their southern flank. The medium company had staggered its lances along a line running northwest to southeast, presumably to discourage Alaric from trying to flank her formation. The command lance came behind the line, near the juncture of the heavy and medium companies to strengthen that weak point.

Alaric keyed his link to the aerospace fighters. "Star Captain Hollis, you are clear to run the north side of the river."

"As ordered, Star Captain."

He punched another button, and an auxiliary monitor filled with the image from Hollis' targeting scanners. Because of the dim light and snow of the battlefield, the pilot switched over to infrared. The light 'Mechs came along the northern bank in three ranks—presumably one per lance. They had actually arranged themselves nicely to provide fire support, yet had not jammed up so closely that they would hamper each other when they needed to maneuver.

They were not, however, well positioned when it came to defending themselves for a strafing run. Hollis brought his *Visigoth* up and around, with his wingman off to the left. He set up on the river, drifted to port just a hair, then tightened down on his trigger and made his run.

Green laser bolts slashed down, illuminating the snow and lighting up a humanoid *Spider* in the first lance. The lasers burned through armor on the 'Mech's torso and arms, wreathing it with greasy smoke. A secondary explosion blew structural parts out the right side of its chest. The lasers further melted both arms. The 'Mech staggered drunkenly, then reeled left and fell, crashing through the river's ice.

Hollis' wingman cut a swath through the light 'Mechs; then came the next two pilots. They staggered their runs, both to escape the missiles and lasers coming from the heavy 'Mechs in the center, and to pick out fresh targets. Three more pairs of fighters made runs, killing half the light 'Mechs outright and crippling the rest. As nearly as Alaric could make out, only one was still operational—something called a *Falcon*—but its armor was in tatters and the pilot was withdrawing quickly.

"Well done, Star Captain Hollis. You may stand down."

"We could maintain combat aero patrol."

"Head back to the ship, rearm. If we have intervention from the north, you will be free to launch along with Beta Star."

"Understood. Hollis out."

Alaric flipped over to the Demons' communications channel. "I agree with your bargain, Colonel. You retire your light 'Mechs and I will retire my fighters."

"You bastard!" All he could see of Colton's face was her blue eyes flashing from within her neurohelmet. "I will kill you for that."

Alaric wished she could see his smile. "Has it occurred to you, Colonel, that my unit now consists of fifty-five 'Mechs, which are pristine, are possessed of superior Clan technology, and effectively outnumber you three to one? You are in the open and your unit likely will not survive another two hours."

Her eyes widened. "What is your point?"

"I will offer you another bargain. It will save two of your companies."

Wariness wove through her reply. "How?"

"Your command lance will fight against me alone. If I win, I take possession of this district and your surviving 'Mechs may travel north to join the Djinns or Stormhammers. If I lose, you retain control of the district. I will declare it neutral."

"What if you die in the fight?"

"The bargain will be supported by my subordinates."

Her eyes narrowed again. "How do I know you won't cheat?"

The same way I know you will. "It is not in my nature to cheat, Colonel. This is the bargain. You have a minute to decide."

"I'll do it." She laughed huskily. "Worst bargain you've ever made, Clanner."

No one in the 279th Battle Cluster questioned what he was doing because he was just making formal what would have happened in a melee battle. To validate his skills as a MechWarrior, he would have faced a test in which three 'Mechs would have attacked him in sequence. Killing one or two would be enough to get him into a combat unit. Three would put him in a command position. *Four and I can rightfully reclaim my rank.*

He stalked his *Mad Cat* forward and suffered under no illusions about the difficulty of the task ahead. Colton's command lance consisted of a *Blackjack*, a *Dervish*, her *Axman* and a *Caesar*. The *Blackjack* and

Caesar were best equipped to hurt him the most at range. He had no idea how good Colton and her pilots were, but the holo he'd seen of them had not impressed him overmuch. Still, to assume they were bad would put him in great danger, so he accepted they might be as good as he was. Then he set about planning his strategy.

The Demons came on in a box formation, with the *Blackjack* and *Caesar* hanging back and the other two operating within their fire arcs. The *Dervish* and *Axman* both had jump jets, which would allow them to soar beyond his position. He'd find himself trapped in the middle of their killing box, and that was not a place he wanted to be.

He waited as they advanced and slid his crosshairs over the *Blackjack*'s outline. Numbers scrolled down his holographic display as the stocky 'Mech moved toward him. Finally the golden dot in the center of the crosshairs blinked to life, and Alaric triggered his weapons.

Two particle projection cannons spat azure beams at the small 'Mech, while a trio of pulse lasers unleashed a storm of angry red energy darts. Two of the lasers missed, but the other boiled away the armor on the 'Mech's left flank. One of the PPCs likewise missed, carving a black furrow through the snow. Its companion hit, however, and slashed up the *Blackjack*'s left leg. Armor sloughed off like dead flesh; then the blue beam stabbed into the hip joint and took the leg clean off. Even as the *Blackjack* fired back ineffectively, it tottered and slammed to the ground.

The *Dervish* launched two flights of long-range missiles, but they scattered harmlessly all around the *Mad Cat*. Colton managed to hit Alaric's 'Mech with a large pulse laser, scouring armor from his right flank, and the *Caesar* used a medium pulse laser to evaporate armor on his 'Mech's right arm. All their other shots missed, and he put it down to their shock at his having downed the *Blackjack*.

Alaric kicked his 'Mech up to speed and cut north toward the river. This put the *Caesar* farthest from him and put him closest to Colton herself. Silver fire blossomed beneath her 'Mech's flat feet. Her 'Mech rose on the jump jets and flew southwest, initiating a flanking maneuver. The other two 'Mechs continued on to the west, now forming a triangle with Colton's 'Mech as the southern point.

Having his 'Mech in full lope made him harder to hit but also made targeting more difficult for him. He took a deep breath, forcing himself to be calm, then swung his targeting reticule over the *Caesar*'s hulking form. He held it on target as his 'Mech rose and fell with its birdlike gait. Once the targeting dot pulsed gold, he fired.

Blue PPC beams sizzled from each of the *Mad Cat*'s weapons pods. One ablated all the armor from the *Caesar*'s left flank while the other caressed the left leg, vaporizing two-thirds of the armor protecting it. Only one of the pulse lasers delivered its scarlet energy bolts on target, but did so devastatingly. They lanced through the armor over the 'Mech's heart. The thermal image of the 'Mech went white, indicating damage to the engine shielding. Moreover, the *Caesar* shook, suggesting damage to the gyros.

In that instance it really didn't matter, however, because the pilot shot back. A PPC beam liquefied armor on the *Mad Cat*'s right side. It ran down over the leg in a steaming flood that melted snow. Then the gauss rifle in the *Caesar*'s right side flashed. A silver ball arced out and slammed hard into the Clan 'Mech. It shivered armor from the 'Mech's right arm, but failed to fully penetrate it.

Alaric jammed himself back against the command couch and leaned left, countering the impact. *Can't allow my 'Mech to go down.* He fought against gravity and by sheer willpower kept the *Mad Cat* from stumbling.

Now for the big kill.

He slowed his 'Mech, then turned straight west before picking speed up again. Colton's jump had taken her outside her weapons' effective range, and the *Dervish* fired, but again scattered missiles and missed cleanly with the lasers. The *Dervish*'s pilot worried Alaric least of all, and he fully expected Colton to leap closer and bring her 'Mech's hatchet to bear. It was a purely foolish tactic, but she'd so often bragged of killing Clanners that way, Alaric imagined she'd begun to believe her own rhetoric.

The *Caesar* blasted away at the *Mad Cat*. The gauss rifle ball missed and skipped over the river's ice. The PPC beam hit Alaric's 'Mech square over the heart, dissolving armor but doing no other damage. Both pulse lasers laced red energy needles into the *Mad Cat*. One set stripped the last armor from the right arm, while the other nibbled at the armor on the left.

Without thought Alaric covered the *Caesar* with his targeting crosshairs, then tightened up on the triggers. Both blue PPC beams plunged straight into the mercenary 'Mech's chest, stripping the last of the armor from over its heart. Something exploded within the hellish lightning storm and the big 'Mech wavered. It staggered, then slowly toppled on its back. Seconds later the faceplate exploded and the pilot rose on a jet of flame, escaping the dead 'Mech.

The *Dervish* pilot got his nerves partially under control and actually hit the *Mad Cat* with one barrage of missiles. He stripped the last of the armor from the 'Mech's right flank and chipped away at armor on the left arm, but otherwise did no damage. Colton, coming in at Alaric's back, sprayed green laser darts over his 'Mech's left side, evaporating all the armor and burrowing into the torso. She did no further damage, but warning klaxons blared in the cockpit.

"You're mine." Her voice burst over the radio, filling the airwaves with arrogant triumph.

As you wish.

Alaric curled his 'Mech back around and drove toward the *Axman*. He brought his weapons to bear and triggered everything. *If this doesn't work, she'll pounce and use that hatchet.*

One PPC beam missed wide, but the other scourged all but the last bit of armor from the arm with the hatchet. Had any of the pulse lasers hit that limb, it would have come off. Instead of compounding the damage done by the particle beam, the trio of pulse lasers poured energy into the armor on the *Axman*'s left arm and flank and the center of the chest. The third weapon found a flaw and punched through, damaging the heavy autocannon nestled in the 'Mech's torso, but not before Colton fired back.

The autocannon's stream of slugs buzzed into the armor on the *Mad Cat*'s left flank. Had he still had the 'Mech's back to Colton, that shot would have ripped his 'Mech in half. As it was, with him facing her, the shot only stripped away armor. With its last shell the weapon failed, locking up skyward with black smoke pouring from the muzzle. Colton's other shots missed wildly, but her 'Mech's right arm came back, prepared to use the hatchet.

The *Dervish* again hit with missiles, this time shattering more armor on the *Mad Cat*'s back. Alaric held on tight, compensating for the weight shifts as the 'Mech shed armor. Trapped as he was between two 'Mechs, with armor stripped from several locations, he should have felt fear, but something else slipped into its place. It struck him that they could never defeat him because they were mortals, and unworthy.

And I am a god.

Time slowed. Alaric kicked the *Mad Cat* into reverse, driving back toward the *Dervish*. He swept his crosshairs over the *Axman* and kept them on target with an ease he had not yet known. The target lock indicator pulsed slowly, and he hit his triggers. Heat spiked through his cockpit, but every weapon hammered the mercenary's 'Mech.

One PPC and two of the pulse lasers savaged armor on the 'Mech torso and left leg, but it was the other two weapons that did the most damage. The PPC's azure caress stripped the last of the armor from the 'Mech's left arm, then gnawed away at actuators and the ferrotitanium bones. The pulse laser sent crimson bolts ripping through artificial muscle and devoured the last of the internal structures, amputating the arm easily. What was left of the tattered limb bounced on the tundra, raising steam in its wake.

Whether surprised by his retreat beyond her hatchet's range or shocked by the loss of her 'Mech's heaviest weapon, Colton fired back utterly ineffectively. The lasers scattered red and green darts all around, stippling the tundra with little puddles of water. The *Dervish* brought missiles to bear, scoring armor on the *Mad Cat*'s right leg and left rear flank. A laser beam stabbed into the 'Mech's left arm, but failed to breach the armor.

Alaric glanced at an auxiliary monitor. The armor on his right flank was gone, and severely damaged on the left flank. Likewise the right arm was naked and yet the 'Mech's firepower remained undiminished. *I must finish this now.*

Alaric pivoted the 'Mech on its left foot, driving south on a course perpendicular from the direction his enemies were traveling. He flicked his thumbs down along the joysticks, splitting his crosshairs in two. He covered the *Dervish* with one, and Colton's battered 'Mech with the other. Two dots burned to life and he gently stroked his triggers.

The PPCs spat man-made lightning that hissed through the air and struck the *Axman* in the chest. The beams cored through the armor on the left flank and center of the chest, then ate into the internal support structures. Half-melted bits of metal bounced from within the cavity and the thermal outline broadened. Alaric could see clean through to the back of Colton's 'Mech. The mercenary's war machine staggered and began to fall backward.

The pulse lasers tracked the *Dervish* even as the silvery fire of jump jets blossomed at its feet and back. One slagged armor over the 'Mech's pristine chest, while the other two stripped most of the armor from the *Dervish*'s left leg. The loss of so much armor shifted the 'Mech's center of balance. The 'Mech began to twist in the air. The machine's arms flailed as the pilot tried to correct his flight, but he failed horribly and the 'Mech landed hard on its left leg. The limb jammed up into the hip with a scream of metal, and then the jump jet exploded and the 'Mech crashed onto its right side.

Before her 'Mech went down, Colton did get off one shot. The medium laser played a red beam over the *Mad Cat*'s left flank. It melted the last of the armor there, leaving his 'Mech vulnerable. With one more exchange, she and her compatriot could do some serious damage. *But do they want to face the fury I will unleash on them?*

The *Dervish* pilot answered by ejecting from his 'Mech. For a heartbeat Alaric considered tracking the command couch as it leaped away and burning the man from the sky. His 'Mech could have regained its feet and continued fighting, had the pilot not punched out.

Cowardice should not be rewarded with life, but then, neither should stupidity.

He turned his attention to Colton's stricken *Axman* and covered it with both crosshairs.

"Would you care to capitulate now, Colonel Colton?" Alaric allowed a hint of contempt to slip provocatively into his voice. "I would allow you to get your 'Mech on its feet again."

On the auxiliary monitor he saw her eyes squeeze tight shut.

Are those tears?

"No, Star Captain, you win. Our bargain remains." She shook her head. "I almost had you."

"There is no *almost* in warfare, Colonel. There is only victory or its absence. You did not want to beat me, you wished to *humiliate* me. You failed. Take that as a lesson."

Her eyes opened and she stared hatred at him from the monitor. "What will you do with me? Make me a bondswoman?"

Alaric, unable to help himself, laughed aloud.

"How dare you laugh at me?"

"How dare you presume to be worthy of joining a Clan?" He reached over and slipped the bond cord from his own wrist. "I want nothing more to do with you, Colonel, so you are free to go with the rest of your people. Join the Djinns. You have left your pride and honor here. Come back and you will leave your blood."

29

Verena hugged the parka more tightly around herself, but did not pull up the fur-lined hood. The wind numbed her face and sank needles into her cheeks, but she pretended not to notice. She smiled carefully as she stepped from the hovercar, then shucked off a mitten and offered Alaric her hand. "Pleased to see you again, Star Colonel, is it now?"

Alaric shook her hand warmly, holding it for a second or two longer than necessary. "The pleasure is all mine. Yes, I am now a Star colonel. The khan accepted my destruction of four 'Mechs as a rank test."

So that was what happened! "Congratulations on your victory. You won your rank, and I won quite a prize. Twenty-eight 'Mechs is not something many would have given up easily."

Alaric shrugged. "It was greed on my part."

"Greed?"

"I wish to fight a pitched battle, as they were fought

in the days of the invasion, Clusters against regiments."

"I suppose that will depend on the nature of our negotiations."

"Indeed, it will. Please, come with me."

Verena fell into step with Alaric as the Wolf led the way into what had been the Demon's headquarters. His explanation of why he'd taken on Colton's command lance rang true for her, but had been completely at odds with the media speculation. Sensor data from the various 'Mechs present at the fight had been widely disseminated, and Aynn Colton herself had sold her version of the story for a significant amount of money.

According to her spin on it, she and her lancemates had not been defeated. They had, instead, engaged in a calculated charade to make the Clanners overconfident. Moreover, the Demons had provided valuable data concerning the strengths of the invaders, all of which would make repulsing them so much easier.

While her explanation clearly defied logic and belied the holovid evidence, it got wide play in the planetary media and on GIN. Verena understood her employer's using that version of events because it heightened the drama of the conflict and doubtlessly drew many viewers. While war has long been cast in terms of good versus evil, until the invention of mass media that distinction wasn't made in real time, and those spreading stories could lie without fear of contradiction. While every MechWarrior watching the battle—even in its most favorably edited version— knew Colton and her lancemates were thoroughly thrashed, the general public was jubilant at the spin that suggested the defeat was part of a larger plan for victory.

Kennerly had summed it up best. "What Colton's saying is the equivalent of a guy saying he let a dog maul him to tire the dog's jaws. It doesn't wash with anyone who's got enough neurons to form a synapse."

Alaric led her into the 'Mech bay and Kennerly trailed silently in their wake. Even though Verena knew Alaric's purpose in taking her through the hangar, she could not help but be impressed. They passed between ranks upon ranks of pristine Clan 'Mechs, standing tall and ready for combat. Alaric had brought the entire Cluster, so if she fielded every 'Mech she could scrounge on the planet, she'd outnumber him, but only barely match him in firepower.

And if I cannot bargain him out of using the aerospace fighters, the odds become even more heavily stacked against us.

At the 'Mech bay's heart stood Alaric's *Mad Cat.* It had been thoroughly savaged, but techs swarmed over it, layering on armor. They'd already finished the upper body, so some of them were busy painting it the same dark gray as the other 'Mechs, and one labored to paint his rank insignia on the right breast.

Verena smiled. "Is it not amazing that what will take them days to do can be undone in a heartbeat?"

"I should think, Colonel, that could be said of any human endeavor."

"Very good point." She glanced at him, studying his profile for a moment. Her stomach churned. She had been prepared to meet with the Alaric she had known on La Blon, but this man was different. Restoration to his Clan and rank were one aspect of it, but it was also more than that. It took her a moment to identify that element, but once she had it, it betrayed itself in everything he said, how he moved, his bearing.

He is no longer defeated.

That realization shook her for two reasons. Defeat had haunted him and made him vulnerable. The beating he'd taken had accentuated that; but it was the core vulnerability that had attracted her to him. There

was no denying he was handsome and could be charm-
ing, but the vulnerability allowed her to imagine it was
possible to connect with him.

The second reason drilled straight into her soul.
She, too, had been defeated and vulnerable. Her first
defeat had been at Anastasia's hands, when she was
dismissed from the Wolf Hunters. Her second defeat
had come on Baxter. She'd had her 'Mech shot out
from under her and could have been killed. That she
was praised for a great victory with which she felt
little personal connection just heightened the disso-
nance between the praises heaped upon her and how
she felt about herself.

Did Alaric sense that vulnerability in me? She knew
the answer even before she finished framing the sen-
tence. *And will he use it against me?*

That answer she knew without thinking.

As she accompanied him into the main building,
through a corridor lined with framed pictures of
Colton—presented as if she were some holovid star—
she wanted to feel resentment or shame at how Alaric
would use what they had shared, but she stopped. *I
would use it, if I could.* She could not because he no
longer felt vulnerable. To defeat him she would have
to make him vulnerable again.

That realization revolutionized her thinking. The
plans for bargaining that she had reviewed repeatedly
with Kennerly suddenly fell apart. Her plans had been
appropriate for the person Alaric expected to be dealing with; but that was a person he would defeat at the
bargaining table—much as he had done with Colton
on his way in.

Something in her shifted. She wasn't sure if Alaric
noticed, but Kennerly did. He coughed out a "Heh"
as she straightened her shoulders. *What is he thinking?*

Alaric paid Kennerly no mind and conducted them
into what had been Colton's office. He waved them

toward a conversation nook fitted with couches and a low table. "Please, make yourselves comfortable."

Kennerly shed his parka easily and tossed it on the couch. He looked around the room and smiled. "It's a couple pews shy of a shrine."

Alaric nodded slowly. "I think of Colonel Colton with the sour expression she wore when we pulled her from her 'Mech, not these pictures."

Verena removed her jacket and sat. "Should I thank you for sparing her life and sending her to me?"

"I doubt it. Place her in your front lines and I shall rid you of her."

"Not going to happen. She found a doctor to sign off on her being unfit for immediate duty due to stress."

Kennerly snorted. "She signed a big contract to offer commentary on the coming battle for Nusakan."

Alaric nodded and sat. "We should, perhaps, attend to that bit of business."

Verena rested her elbows on her knees. "We might not have to. You have your 'Mechs all lined up so beautifully in the hangar. The DropShip that brought us is loaded with forty tons of conventional explosives. I can have it crashed into the 'Mech bay inside of two minutes, and I am sure you can't shoot it down. That would end your threat to Nusakan."

Alaric and Kennerly both blinked at her.

The Wolf clasped his hands together. "You would not do that. You are a Wolf. You understand bargaining and honor."

"I also understand warfare and the reality of it, Star Colonel. Bargaining is all well and good, and we shall get down to that, but understand that my duty is to deny you access to the goods and services produced here. I will. And I do not appreciate the fact that in coming here you repeatedly ignored my attempts to speak with you. You chose deliberately to attack the south and Colonel Colton, not bargaining for a trial to possess the entire planet, just her district. I do not doubt you can find precedent for such a selective choice in the annals of the history we share, but we both know it was a deliberate strategy on your part to gain a foothold here—a foothold that I would have denied you."

Kennerly stared at her as if seeing her for the first time. He'd repeatedly urged her to say exactly those sorts of things to Alaric, and she had demurred. She wanted the negotiations to be dignified, but that would have been what he expected. Moreover, the remark about a DropShip making a suicide run to wipe out his entire command had shaken Alaric. He covered it well, but vulnerability had flashed through his eyes.

Alaric raised an eyebrow. "Very well, let us begin the bargaining. Am I attacking you, or are you fighting to regain this province?"

Verena shook her head. "You have to come north, and we both know it. You've cornered the market on the manufacturing of electronic toys. If you stay here, children on hundreds of worlds will weep at Christmas. What you want is what we have up north—the components that will allow your 'Mechs to continue fighting. So you will be fighting to take possession of the planet."

Alaric started to reply, but she held a hand up. "And you will take your aerospace fighters out of the mix immediately or I will have every warehouse and factory in the north destroyed, period. They are already wired and ready to go. You put anything in the air and you will lose everything but toys and processed algae food products."

The Wolf's blue eyes narrowed. "It would seem, Colonel, that command suits you. I shall assume that, unlike Zhuge Liang, you are not bluffing."

"Make any assumptions you like, Star Colonel."

Her counterpart nodded slowly. "Very well. I challenge you to a Trial of Possession for Nusakan. With what will you defend?"

"Everything I have. Three mixed battalions consisting of seventy-six BattleMechs plus assorted armor, artillery and infantry. I will not be activating the local militia, nor will I be arming partisans. I cannot be held responsible for what individual citizens choose to do on their own."

"I will treat such citizens as spies and have them shot immediately. Please get that message out."

Verena nodded. "I am in the process of doing that. It would help if you issued a statement that in the event of your victory, you will acknowledge the local government as the legitimate civil authority."

"Done. And, as you wish, aerospace fighters are withdrawn from the mix, assuming you will similarly retire any aerospace assets you possess."

"Done. What will you bring against me?"

"I will bring my entire Battle Cluster, though my third Trinary will remain here unless circumstance demands I bring them in."

Thirty-five 'Mechs against my seventy-six? Verena did quick calculations. Given that Colton's remaining Demons were unreliable, but that the Djinns and Stormhammers were crack troops, the odds still ran in Clan favor, but not overwhelmingly so.

"There are two strategic zones in the north. Will you fight for each one, or shall we choose a proxy battlefield, Star Colonel?"

"A proxy, I think." Alaric looked at her, then frowned. "I shall let you choose it and position your forces. Then you may communicate the location to me. I shall communicate in return a choice of landing zones and you may adjust accordingly. Shall we say a week?"

"A week." Verena smiled. "Once I have chosen the

location, I would be honored if you would be my guest to survey it. Four days from now?"

"My pleasure." Alaric offered her his hand. "Bargained well and done."

She met his grip firmly. "Bargained well and done. May the best commander win."

Alaric smiled. "I suspect, Colonel, *that* has already happened."

30

For Star Colonel Donovan, the conquest of Skondia was little more than a mathematics problem. The planet boasted temperate and heavily rugged areas that were the source of the trace metals for which it was prized. Toward the equator the rough landscape gentled into rain-forested areas of great beauty that provided a secondary industry of biopharmaceuticals and, combined with aquaculture, made the world self-sufficient in terms of food supply. In between the zones, in tectonically stable areas, light industrial districts had grown up. Metal from the smelters and mines in the mountains would move down for manufacture and subsequent export.

The mines and the factories were the prize, and he meant to have them. Though he was well aware that the entire campaign was a charade to cover the Wolf Clan's move into the Lyran Commonwealth, Alaric's looting of Yed Posterior had been taken as a brilliant tactic. The Clans were able to monitor Inner Sphere media traffic, and the debates centered on how this tactic was very much like those used by invading hordes in the past. Images of Mongols and Huns flashed into every home in the Inner Sphere, and reports of volunteers offering to help defend against rapine and pillage came from everywhere.

Donovan would not be outdone by Alaric. It had annoyed him that Alaric had been given equal status with him at the beginning of the operation. Alaric was too old, undertested, and so cocksure of himself that Donovan had known he was going to run into trouble. When it happened so early on, Donovan could hardly believe it.

Donovan admitted to himself that his offer to ransom Alaric was uncharacteristic—really, it was similar to something Alaric would have done were their positions reversed. Forcing him to become a bondsman was even more delicious. Donovan couldn't quantify the emotions he felt at humiliating Alaric, but they had been good, and even the news that Alaric had contrived a way to test out to the rank of Star colonel on Nusakan did not dampen Donovan's sense of victory.

Skondia was a problem to be solved, and he had hit upon the solution. He negotiated strongly with Anastasia Kerensky and brought the whole Thirteenth Wolf Guards Cluster and a Trinary from the 328th Assault Cluster as his reserve. While the Wolf Hunters did have Clan technology, the Skondia Rangers did not, so he could devote twenty 'Mechs to handle them, and bring twenty-five against the Wolf Hunters. The remaining fifteen he held in reserve and assumed he would use in the north fighting against Anastasia.

The crux of their negotiations centered on what would be defended. Both the mines and factories had to be covered, and as he expected, Anastasia chose to defend the mines. In fact, she brought her forces into the mountains in a formation reminiscent of how he had positioned his troops on Unukalhai. She'd done it to bait him—of this there was no doubt—and that left the Skondia Rangers covering the factory district down south near Askani.

The mountainous terrain would make for tough fighting, but the Thirteenth Wolf Guards were well suited to it and practiced at it. He intended to engage, pin the Wolf Hunters, then bring the 328th's Alpha Trinary up to crush a wing and punch through the line. Once he'd shattered the mercenary formation, he'd just hunt down the rest of her troops.

He reviewed his plans over and over again and still could see no flaw. He knew no plan survived contact with the enemy, but that was true for his opponent, too. Sitting there high in the cockpit of his *Daishi* as his troops began their ascent into the foothills, he sought to banish the last of his doubt about how things would go, but found that doubt quite tenacious.

It is all Alaric's fault. Alaric had poisoned his mind by suggesting that Anastasia had let Donovan win on Unukalhai. He said she'd blown the bridge herself, then declined battle. He said it was because she wanted to lure Donovan into thinking she was stupid or cowardly, and that he would pay for making such assumptions.

The problem for Donovan was that Anastasia's actions did not add up. She had deployed for battle. It would have been a fierce fight, but an even one—much like the fight would be in the heights above. Granted, he'd had the advantage initially, but her flanking movement would have hurt him. He did acknowledge that his positioning had been very weak in that regard, but he had a whole Trinary in reserve to protect his flanks.

A light burned on his communications console and he punched it. "Donovan here. Report."

"Carolyn, Task Force Askani reporting. We are three klicks out from the Rangers' base. We have contact to the southeast. They are waiting for us."

"Very good. Engage."

"As ordered, out."

Another light began to blink and he hit that. "Go ahead, Star Captain, report."

"Star Colonel, I have multiple contacts to the north of your position coming around the mountain." The elemental Star he'd deployed to monitor radio frequencies had found something. "Readings are incomplete, but would be consistent with a vehicular convoy."

Donovan smiled to himself. The mercenary had tried the same flanking maneuver a second time. "Very good, Star Captain. Shift over to Tactical three and let Star Captain Abigail know what you found. She will dispatch a 'Mech Star to head them off."

"As ordered."

Donovan nodded and threaded his way up an evening-shaded pass toward a large plateau. He followed a *Man-O'-War* and had a *Vulture* and a pair of *Ryoken*s coming in his wake. Five hundred meters to either side the other two Stars of Alpha Trinary converged on the same position, and to the south came the remaining two Stars of Bravo Trinary.

Carolyn from the Askani task force radioed in again. "False contact. We ran across the Rangers' live-fire training range. They had the sensors lit up. We banged some metal, then pulled back. We are converging on their base now. I have it in visual."

"Very good."

"This is odd." She hesitated. "Star Colonel, the base is open and lit. The gates are open and there are sentries posted there—infantry who are lounging in chairs. Here is the feed."

Donovan hit a couple of keys and directed the incoming videos to a secondary monitor. The bases' gates, which were tall and wide enough to handle four BattleMechs walking abreast, stood wide open. The gunnery turrets appeared unmanned. The two sentries, who appeared as glowing blobs on the infrared scan, didn't seem to have a care in the world.

"Star Captain, is one of those men playing a guitar?"

"It would appear so, sir."

Donovan shivered. "And you see no BattleMechs anywhere?"

"No, sir. The base is empty and the road into the factory and warehouse district appears open."

"Be very careful, Star Captain. They just want you to think it is open." Donovan thought. "That is an industrial area. It will have tunnels. You will have to clear and secure, block by block."

"It is a *big* area, sir. If I tie my people down like that . . ."

"Yes, yes, of course. And you can't bypass the base, as the Rangers may be hiding there. In fact, the live-fire range may have just been a screen for dug-in positions."

"What should I do, sir?"

"Secure your position. Have a Star cover the range, then begin a sweep of the base. Keep me informed."

"As ordered, sir."

Donovan's *Daishi* topped the rise and entered the western edge of the plateau. His other two Stars came up on the right and left, so the 'Mechs spread out in a line to cover each other and began their advance. A kilometer and a half farther forward, the plateau began to narrow into a valley that ran up to the next plateau, and that was where, he was fairly certain, he would find the Wolf Hunters. His Bravo Trinary's two Stars would reach the plateau by another route and their coordinated attack would destroy the mercenaries.

Star Captain Abigail reported in. "We have more contacts coming in south of your position. The Star I have to the north has not found anything, but is still searching."

"What is south?"

"'Mechs, six or eight."

"BattleMechs or the industrial conversions?"

"Contacts are intermittent so I do not know. Do I dispatch a Star?"

"Yes. Close, identify, engage."

"As ordered."

Donovan frowned, then keyed the radio to the elementals frequency. "Star Captain Lloyd, report contacts."

"Intermittent, sir. Harrison is fine-tuning the scanners. He says the signals are military, but not strong enough for military equipment."

And they should be running on radio silence anyway. "I need visual confirmation immediately. I want you out on a hunter/killer mission. Find the contacts, destroy them."

"Yes, sir, as ordered."

Off to the south, right where a *Ryoken* raised its left arm to acknowledge linking up with Alpha Star, something flashed. Staccato pulses of light repeated— five, ten, fifteen, twenty—and started up elsewhere from the hills rimming the plateau. *Missile carriers, dug in on the reverse slope, with spotters.*

Hundreds of missiles rained down, filling the evening sky with fiery arcs that ended in explosions. The *Ryoken* that had signaled the link-up danced in a bonfire as missile barrages converged on it. Though range and indirect fire made accuracy iffy, the law of averages dictated that the 'Mech would get hit. Missiles crushed armor, crumbling it into shards of ferroceramics that cascaded to the ground.

In an instant all of Donovan's calculations underwent revision. The sensor data from the north was a feint, likely with passenger vehicles and trucks broadcasting signals that mimicked those of military machinery. There was no flanking movement coming from the north. Likely the readings from the south were the same, or coming from industrial conversions. Anastasia had concentrated her troops here, and would continue to hit him harder and harder as the valley narrowed.

"Star Captain Abigail, bring your reserve in right now. We will need you."

"I still have not confirmed those contacts, sir."

"They are decoys."

Star Captain Anthony, with Bravo Trinary to the south, burst into the frequency. "I have contacts, Star Colonel. Multiple. BattleMechs, Inner Sphere design." Multiple explosions echoed over the frequency. "We are taking lots of fire, sir. It looks like the Skondia Rangers."

Skondia Rangers here? "Engage them. No, wait, can you retreat?"

"Negative. They have cut us off. We have to win through."

"Go, go, go." Donovan's mouth tasted bitter. "Star Captain Abigail, help Bravo Trinary. They're trapped."

"As ordered, sir."

And it was then, as Donovan reached out to switch to the Askani task force frequency, that he saw the devastated *Ryoken* waver and go down. A second later, lights flashed again and he found himself the victim of Anastasia Kerensky's plan.

And this time she does not plan to let me win.

*   *   *

Anastasia found Star Colonel Donovan on his knees a couple of meters in front of his *Daishi*. He had lost his neurohelmet. Blood from scratches on his arms and legs had dried and his hair hung limply save for where sweat pasted it to his forehead. His shoulders slumped and he toyed with a jagged bit of broken 'Mech armor.

Even after days of torture, Alaric never looked that defeated. She stopped in front of him and dismissed the two Wolf Hunter infantrymen who had been standing watch over him. "It would be a shame if you cut your wrists."

The man looked up at her, his eyes sunken into his skull. "This is not possible."

"You know that is not true, because your force is broken. Your task force in the south has already capitulated and withdrawn."

"But we agreed what sites you would defend."

Anastasia smiled. "And we did defend the south. We had people down there. They had sidearms."

"But . . ." His eyes narrowed, and then he looked down again, flinching from her gaze. "I did nothing wrong."

"Do you truly believe that?"

"Yes," he said, but refused to meet her stare.

"You know that is a lie, Donovan." She toed the armor fragment out of his hand. "You made a very significant military blunder. You divided your force in the face of a superior enemy. I had the Skondia Rangers positioned to roll up your flank and close in behind you. I used decoys, not to draw off your reserves, but to pin them. That holds true for the south as well. You planned carefully and based your calculations on the odds, and you kept them in your favor. I just found a way to shift them to mine again."

"What will you do with me?" He finally looked up again. "Ransom me to Alaric?"

"No, he would enjoy that far too much." Anastasia glanced up at the faraway star around which Nusakan orbited. "We do not know if he will win or not, but if he does, I will not turn you over to him."

"Will you make me a bondsman, then?"

She smiled, but shook her head. "I have no need of bondsmen."

"What, then?"

"I will offer you the same proposition I did Alaric. You will stay here, work with me, learn from me. And, when the time is right"—Anastasia gave him a conspiratorial nod—"I will unleash you against Alaric, and you will destroy him."

31

Mudana Refuge, Nusakan
Former Prefecture IX, Republic of the Sphere
19 March 3137

The site Verena had chosen looked no better to Alaric from the fastness of his *Mad Cat*'s cockpit than it had when he'd toured it via hovercraft. Though snow covered the landscape to a depth of two meters in places, it failed to soften any part of the terrain, and imparted no sense of innocence. The utter lack of trees was the primary defect, for it hinted at the complete corruption that lurked beneath the surface.

When Nusakan had first been colonized, this district had been the site of massive strip mines that laid open the earth. Those wounds had never healed and the rivers that formed the western edge of the battlefield ran brown with heavy metal poisons—staining the ice above them the color of dried blood.

She has chosen well. Verena had arrayed her troops atop a plateau that jutted out into the plain below. A river running from the western edge of that bulge slanted to the southwest, where it connected with another river running north to south. The triangle of land between them led to the only easy manner of egress to the plateau. The steepness of the edge beneath her troops prevented a direct assault, yet the way she positioned her troops, she was clearly inviting it.

Then again, they can hit the entire battlefield with long-range weapons. The idea of looping around to the east was a nonstarter because the plateau's steep edge extended for five kilometers in that direction. Stringing his troops out along that route would just allow Verena a chance to hit them hard. While forcing her to move would reveal, he hoped, a lack of coordination among the trio of units, the long trek would dilute his firepower and could embolden even the Demons.

Verena had positioned her Djinns in the center of her formation, with the Stormhammers to the east and the Demons tucked back along the western edge. For all intents and purposes that made the Demons her reserve unless Alaric tried to push up into the river valley—a dubious prospect that would bunch his troops and give the Stormhammers time to cross over to a position where they could pound on them.

Alaric had arranged his troops simply in a staggered line. His Alpha Trinary formed the northern point, with Bravo Trinary on the right. His command Star had the left, and behind it came Striker Trinary, acting as his reserve. He brought them up tight because the western route to the plateau seemed the only logical way to attack. This meant it would be well defended and he wanted a force that could hit hard deployed to deal with the defenses.

He allowed himself to chuckle. He had been outmaneuvered in the negotiations. Verena had surprised him, being far more direct than he would have imagined possible. He managed to take heart from the fact that Kennerly seemed as surprised as he was. She had gone completely off script. This newfound ability could make life difficult. She became unpredictable. If she was able to sustain that change, she would become very dangerous.

But what are the chances that her change is permanent?

Ultimately it did not matter what the chances were. He had to assume she would maintain her drive and her edge. He had to assume she would be the most determined, bloodthirsty and focused commander he had ever faced. This complicated his task, but he had always believed it would be complicated.

Alaric faced the same challenge countless warriors had faced before him. His foe had the high ground and prepared positions. While the enemy's troops were not as good as his, there simply were more of them, which promoted longevity, and the last man standing on the battlefield was the victor.

Which leaves me only one choice. He keyed his radio. "This is Alaric. Tactical plan A-Seven will go into effect. You know your parts. Make Clan Wolf proud."

That said, he brought his crosshairs up onto the ridgeline, and started forward with the other Wolves.

Verena wished for psychic powers, not so much to know what Alaric was planning, but to know why. She knew he would be thinking tactically, but she wondered at his strategic goals. Even if he defeated her forces here, he had to know that the Wolves had been broken on Skondia and that the Wolf Hunters were on their way to help her crush his Wolves.

Not that she wanted the help, or needed it, but she would get it. Likewise there were countless other units heading toward Prefecture IX to blunt the Wolf spearhead. The drive for Terra had awakened old passions and fears. Nations had begun to respond generously and the Wolves would soon find themselves up to their necks in warriors looking to stop them.

It made no sense, therefore, for them to pursue the invasion. Alaric had to see that, and that he persisted surprised her. She could imagine him agreeing to orders from the khan, but she found it easier to picture him arguing against such lunacy.

Then again, he did have his 'Mechs all arrayed for effect in the hangar, ignoring the tactical stupidity of such a thing.

Looking out at the diamond formation advancing below, Verena wished she had called the DropShip in to destroy them all. That she would have died in such an attack really mattered little to her. It would have pointed out, yet again, how vulnerable warriors and their machines were in the face of a determined enemy who felt he had nothing to lose.

And she would have done it, too, but it hardly seemed she had anything to gain by the action. The Wolves would have come to Nusakan again, and likely would have visited horrible atrocities on the civilian population. Back in the first invasion the Smoke Jaguars had done exactly that in the Draconis Combine. She harbored no illusions that the Wolves were so far removed from the Clanners who had invaded that such conduct would not happen a second time.

The radio crackled with Kennerly's voice. "It appears they have chosen to come up the throat. He sees the Demons as our weak link."

There was no question that the Demons *were* the weak link. The unit had been formed of MechWarriors who were better at running their mouths than running their 'Mechs; and the techs had barely managed to keep things stuck together. Their morale had plunged to serious depths after they watched a single Clanner take apart their command lance, and Colton, in her new role as media commentator, had been waxing eloquent about how she would miss her faithful comrades after the coming battle. Rumors even had it that bookies on far Solaris were measuring the Demons' life span in nanoseconds.

"Just stick with the plan, Captain."

"You sound sure of yourself."

"I am." Verena smiled. "Alaric thinks he is invulnerable. It is his weakness. He will pay for it."

"Roger that. Kennerly out."

Down below the Wolves came on, heading toward the valley beneath the Demon position. It took them completely out of range of anything the Stormhammers could toss at them, but her first company of Djinns started to acquire targets. She drifted her crosshairs over the incoming mass of Wolves and picked out a *Mad Cat* much like the one in which she sat. It had to be Alaric and she smiled as she covered it.

"Attention Djinns and Demons. Acquire targets by priority. Fire as they come into range."

As far as Alaric could determine, the only advantage to fighting on a dimly lit world like Nusakan was that it made it much easier to know when you were being fired upon. All along the ridge the burst of flames that marked the launching of long-range missiles lit the horizon. Green, red and blue lances of energy flashed down from the heights. Silvery gauss rifle projectiles arced down, chased by pulse laser darts and streams of depleted uranium.

Missiles sowed fire through his ranks. Several hit his *Mad Cat,* shivering armor from a leg and flank. Through the firestorm a green laser beam stabbed, carving a third of the armor from the 'Mech's right arm. Alaric stared at it as the armor peeled off the weapons pod. He shifted in his seat, correcting the 'Mech's balance, and waited for a trickle of fear to trail coldly through his guts. It didn't come, and in that, he took heart.

Somehow he knew it had been Verena who had picked him out and targeted him, for the rest of the fire had poured down on Alpha Trinary. Two 'Mechs actually went down, but had not suffered crippling injuries. They would be back up and running by the time his command Star reached them. The enemy attacks had just sanded off armor—the only real effect of which was to make his pilots more eager.

The Wolves fired back, concentrating their attacks on the Demons, and especially the heavy company on the Djinns' flank. Shooting up at them did make it more difficult to hit them, but made the shots far more telling. Missiles flew and beams flashed, searing the eyes with red and green slashes. A humanoid *Exterminator* flopped over backward, the cockpit nothing but a smoking hole, while other 'Mechs lost limbs and armor by the ton.

Another exchange and Alaric again took laser and missile damage. The missiles crushed more leg armor and nibbled away at his flank. Then the large laser's emerald beam melted armor over his left side. Again, it was not enough to put him in any jeopardy, but the attrition would tell in the long run.

But you won't get me that easily, Verena.

He picked her out from amid the defenders, marked her in his targeting computer, then shifted to one of the Demons. Both weapons pods covered a *Bombardier*, but when Alaric pulled the triggers on his joysticks, the blue ropes of synthetic lightning flashed past the squat 'Mech's shoulders.

How could I have missed? He glanced at his hands, then his diagnostics monitor, but nothing looked out of the ordinary. *This is not possible.*

Any sense of doom died immediately, however, as

Star Captain Xeno of the Alpha Trinary crowed triumphantly, "They're breaking!"

It was true. The Demons were pulling back, both companies. The path to the plateau was open. It would be slow going, tedious and dangerous. Verena had to have known the potential for the Demons' quitting battle.

And she would have planned for it.

"Be careful, but go. Go now, go fast."

Verena keyed her radio. "Now, Captain Rollins, fire at will."

From prepared bunkers on the river's far shore, Verena's armor and artillery opened up. Missiles flew in the hundreds, raining fire and shrapnel among the Wolves. Alaric's Striker Trinary had swung west along the river's edge, stringing itself out, and it caught the brunt of the assault. She would have preferred the attacks to go into the main body, but the prepared positions had been set up to oppose a run at the more gentle slope on that side of the river. Tactical maneuvering prior to the first assault would have revealed their positions.

Nusakan's dim atmosphere robbed her of any easy assessment of the damage being done, but in many ways the abstraction was far more powerful. Explosions lit the area as shock waves rippled through the snow. Ice cracked on the river, opening dark holes. 'Mechs fired back and bunkers exploded. Armor began to maneuver as artillery fired again and Clan 'Mechs plunged into the river.

But they're not supposed to do that. And down below, the command Star was breaking off and heading west, fording the river as well. *If they blow past the armor, then they come up to the west!*

Variations of strategies and tactics flew through her

mind, but she banished it all. The only thing important in that moment was killing Clanners. They attacked up the slope because they'd seen the Demons pull back. They assumed they were broken, but their retreat had been part of her plan all along.

"Kennerly, we are moving north."

"Already under way, Colonel."

"Colonel Tucker, come west."

"As ordered, Colonel." The man sounded almost elated. "You called this one right."

"I certainly hope so." She dropped her crosshairs on a *Ryoken* and fired. *Now it's just a question of how fast we can kill them. Faster, I hope, than they can kill us.*

The enfilading attack from across the river did not surprise Alaric too much. He'd expected something, and did admire how Verena had positioned her artillery at the top of the ridge to cover the armor. He and his command Star broke to the west and drove forward to the river. He hit it first and the crackling of the ice resounded like gunshots in his cockpit. The 'Mech sank deep in the river, to where sludge washed halfway up his cockpit windscreen. He forged ahead with all speed and emerged on the far shore just as Striker Trinary made landfall and advanced.

Verena's armor had pulled back toward a second line of prepared positions, but the Wolves came on too swiftly for them. The artillery didn't fire from on high for fear of hitting their own people, but it wouldn't have mattered. 'Mechs stalked among the vehicles, shooting and smashing them. Alaric's Star, hitting them from the flank, melted the turret from a *Zhukov* heavy tank and the armor formation began to scatter.

The artillery hammered the Clan 'Mechs, dropping two of the Strikers. That did not daunt them. They returned fire while the command Star skirted the plateau's edge, then cut north and started up the slope. More missiles flew from above, but Alaric didn't care. He'd be up and among the artillery, which would die even faster than the armor.

Then, Verena, I come for you.

He laughed to himself, then crested the plateau. There, beyond the artillery, he found the other surprise she had waiting for him. *Unexpected, but so be it. I will* not *be stopped.*

Kennerly's medium 'Mech company led the shift to cover the hole the Djinns had made with their departure, and Verena's heavy company held his southern flank. Her troops shot at the advancing Clanners, pouring fire into their flanks. They raked the enemy with missiles and shells, the strobing explosions revealing the Clanners clawing their way up the slope.

As they came Verena realized part of Alaric's strategy. Bravo Trinary remained below, lofting flights of missiles over their comrades, hammering the Djinns' medium 'Mechs. Missiles pummeled an *Assassin*, spinning it around and dumping it to the ground. One green laser beam cleaved through the left shoulder of Kennerly's *Clint*. In the blink of an eye the severed limb buried itself in the snow, while the other arm came up and the PPC spat blue death back at the attackers.

Verena picked out a *Man-O'-War* stalking up the slope. The massive Clan 'Mech's arms ended in muzzles, and it looked as if it wanted hands to assist in the climb. The machine hunched forward, broad flat feet digging into the earth. The pilot fired uphill, burning armor from a hapless *Cicada*, then struggled on.

Once her targeting dot blinked, Verena tugged on the triggers. She sprayed missiles over the blocky 'Mech, then lashed it with a large laser's beam. The green energy scalpel whittled armor from the 'Mech's breast, while missiles scattered armor on its left arm and leg. Despite the damage done, the machine did not waver or slow. Worse yet, the pilot paid her no mind and fired directly ahead again.

At one point she might have felt outraged at being ignored, but that part of her no longer existed. Again she picked out the *Man-O'-War* and fired. More missiles hit, crushing armor on its chest. The large lasers—she hit him with both—ablated armor from over its heart and on its left leg, but did not stop the 'Mech from climbing yet farther.

Will you never go down? Verena shivered. *If I cannot stop you soon, I will have no chance of stopping the 'Mechs you are bringing to flank us.*

The Demons, Alaric learned to his chagrin, had not broken and run. They'd pulled back and swung around. Verena's plan had been simple and quite direct. Had he not sent a force across the river in his own flanking maneuver, the Demons would simply have appeared on the far side of the ravine and been able to fire into his troops as they struggled up the other side.

But since he had flanked her, here they were, two companies. Hardly an even match for his troops, but Verena's artillery was shifting fire and blew a *Thor* from his Striker Trinary back off the edge of the plateau. Their fire would buy the Demons enough time to set up in good order and engage in a fighting retreat that could further wear his people down.

Alaric punched his communications wide open. "You are the Demons! I destroyed your command lance. Now I have come for you."

He settled his crosshairs on a *Vindicator* in the middle of the Demon formation. Even as the pilot brought the PPC in the right arm to bear, Alaric fired his pulse lasers and PPCs. Heat spiked in his cockpit, but his weapons fired hot and true.

A hail of scarlet laser darts nibbled away at armor over the 'Mech's chest, left flank and right leg. The PPCs stabbed out with twin forks of lightning that joined in one brilliant white bolt. They evaporated the armor on the 'Mech's right arm, then melted the artificial muscles and ferrotitanium bones. The limb vanished in a puff of black smoke and the *Vindicator* spun away, crashing hard to the ground.

Behind Alaric came the rest of his command Star, weapons flashing. Waves of missiles exploded over the artillery and carved through the Demons. The Strikers began to emerge onto the plateau, with one Star intact, and the other formed from remnants of Alpha and Bravo. They started along the ridge, finishing the artillery, while the command Star pushed forward.

Combat did not slow for Alaric, for there was no way to keep track of all the variables in play. Some of the pilots were overwhelmed, of this he had no doubt. He ranged toward the northwest, placing himself on the far edge of his line, then picked out targets at the enemy's flank. As he hit them, they would move toward the cover of others, exposing new targets to his wrath.

He did not advance unscathed, but the Demons mostly fired into the thick of his men where they hoped their shots would not miss. He took more missile damage and a PPC liquefied sixty percent of the armor on his left flank, but nothing got through. Nothing did him any harm—forever banishing any hints of dismay he felt at missing his first shot.

Alaric shot at a *Centurion* squaring around to engage him. The PPCs both hit, ripping up armor on the 'Mech's left leg and over its heart. Only one of his pulse lasers remained on target, delivering a flurry of energy darts that dissolved armor on the 'Mech's left flank. The damage shifted enough weight that the 'Mech staggered, but the pilot kept it upright and fired back.

The autocannon built into its right arm vomited fire and metal that savaged the armor on the *Mad Cat*'s right arm. A medium laser whipped over the Clan 'Mech's left leg, burning a dark scar across the ankle.

The *Centurion* made no effort to retreat and Alaric felt a pang of admiration for the pilot. The man was brave, and quite probably stupid, but he had accepted the burden of being a warrior. Alaric decided to honor that—which did not diminish his desire to kill the man, but increased it.

The *Mad Cat* fired again. The PPC disintegrated all but the last bits of armor from the 'Mech's right arm and right leg, but failed to breach the protection on either one. The single pulse-laser shot blazed through the last of the armor over the 'Mech's heart, but did no further damage.

Alaric could scarcely believe it. *Brave, stupid, and lucky.*

The *Centurion* returned fire. The autocannon's metal rain ground through the last of the armor on the *Mad Cat*'s right arm, then ate away at the structures from elbow to shoulder. The laser further slashed at that arm, but somehow neither assault rendered it inoperable.

Very lucky.

Even though his 'Mech's right arm hung on more by chance than anything else, Alaric continued to shoot. He laced the *Centurion* with fire one more time. This time his attack had devastating effects. The first PPC beam gutted the *Centurion*, blowing the half-melted engine out through its back. The other PPC beam took the left leg off at the knee, while the pulse lasers denuded both arms of any ferroceramics. The shower of red darts snapped actuators and weakened metal bones to the point where a stiff breeze would have carried them away.

Not that it mattered. The *Centurion*'s upper body collapsed, and then the broken remains of the 'Mech clattered to the ground. A second later the 'Mech's faceplate exploded outward and the pilot ejected.

Alaric watched him go, then glanced at the armor diagram for his *Mad Cat* on the secondary monitor. *He even scored armor with a final shot. I want him. I will make him a bondsman and raise him to glory.*

He smiled, then looked to the west. *But first, I have a battle to win.*

The Clanners came up over the lip of the plateau, and just for a moment, it appeared as if they had won the day. Their assault had blown through most of the Djinns' medium company and had eaten badly into the heavies. The Wolves began to curl south to fend off the heavies, and Verena found herself facing the *Man-O'-War* she had tried to bring down from a distance.

The *Man-O'-War*'s weapons stabbed at her. Twin PPCs in the right arm spat blue lightning at her 'Mech. One beam devoured armor on her left flank, and the green darts of a large pulse laser finished all but the last of it. The second PPC flensed armor from her 'Mech's left arm. Angry red needles from a pulse laser further nibbled away at that armor, but nothing got through.

Warning klaxons blared in her cockpit. The instant evaporation of tons of armor so shifted the 'Mech's center of gravity that she struggled to keep it on its feet. The gyros howled, but the 'Mech stood its ground and Verena, a grim smile baring her teeth, fired back.

Both of her large lasers converged on the *Man-O'-War*'s left arm, slicing through the last of the armor. Her medium laser's molten caress finished the remains of the armor over the *Man-O'-War*'s chest, leaving its heart vulnerable. The missiles she launched exploited that weakness, blowing out bits and pieces of the 'Mech's internal structures. More of them slammed into the left arm, rotting myomers, pitting bones and exploding the large pulse laser housed there. Yet more missiles chipped away at armor. Even so, despite the damage done, the *Man-O'-War* remained upright and lethal.

And would have killed Verena cleanly, but just then the Stormhammers arrived.

Missiles and beams flew so thickly that Verena could have walked her 'Mech on them and risen above the attacking Clanners. The *Man-O'-War* disappeared in a curtain of laser light. Explosions topped the rim and shrapnel ricocheted from her cockpit. The leading edge of the Stormhammers eclipsed her view of the Clanners as Tucker's troops sailed in to envelope the Clan beachhead.

Verena cut to the east and raced behind the Stormhammers' formation. She glanced at her scanners to see if her Djinns were following her. The computers showed nothing. *Can they all be gone?*

In a heartbeat she knew they were and, there to the west, she knew why. There came a lance of Clan 'Mechs, led by a battered *Mad Cat*. They were all that had made it through the Demons, and she didn't need computers to tell her that none of Colton's troops had survived.

She tight-beamed a message to her counterpart. "Shall we finish this now, you and I?"

"I will fight you, yes, Verena." Alaric paused for a moment. "But you know this will not be the finish."

It will be if I have anything to say about it.

She spitted his *Mad Cat* on her crosshairs and triggered her weapons. Missiles corkscrewed out from her shoulder-mounted launchers and pounded Alaric's 'Mech on the right leg, right flank and left arm. Only

one of her two lasers hit, and it likewise scarred the
armor on the 'Mech's right leg. *If it had only come
up, I would have taken that arm off.*

Alaric's return shots hit hard. The PPCs burrowed
into the armor over her 'Mech's chest and left leg.
The trio of pulse lasers unleashed a cyclone of energy
projectiles. They melted more armor over her *Mad
Cat*'s heart; then a flurry of them lanced through the
weakened armor on the left flank.

Multiple warning sirens sounded as the heat spiked
in her cockpit. The lasers had damaged the magnetic
containment vessel around the engine's fusion reactor,
allowing novalike heat to fill the cockpit. Worse yet,
they'd blown all the control circuitry for one of her
missile launchers.

If I don't finish him now . . .

She fought her 'Mech to keep it upright. Sweat dap-
pled her flesh. Heat sought to suffocate her. Panic
began to rise, but she choked it back down. *No!*

Verena targeted Alaric and triggered one last salvo.
Her missiles splashed around him ineffectively. One
laser flashed off into the sky, but the other only dissolved armor on his 'Mech's left breast.

Then Alaric swung his left weapons pod in line with
her 'Mech. It seemed for a moment that he did so
with the pity and disdain a man might show when
dispatching a wounded animal. *Save, in this gesture,
there is no pity.*

The Clanner's PPC carved through the left side of
her 'Mech's chest, melting every bit of ferrotitanium
skeleton. The left arm fell away and the left hip
snapped. The *Mad Cat* wavered for a moment, then
slowly fell victim to gravity's seduction.

"Now this part is done," she heard Alaric say, almost gently. Then her 'Mech slammed into the ground,
her restraining straps snapped, and Verena's world
sank into oblivion.

32

DropShip* Jaeger, *Nusakan
Former Prefecture IX, Republic of the Sphere
20 March 3137

Anastasia stood in the DropShip's holotank and smiled as Alaric's image solidified. "Greetings, Star Colonel. I hope I have not caught you at an inopportune time. With what will you be defending Nusakan?"

"Good to see you as well, Colonel." Alaric stood tall, cloaked in furs. The way his hair lay, and the red pressure marks on his forehead and cheeks, said he'd lately shucked his neurohelmet. "I will defend it with exactly nothing."

"I assure you, Star Colonel, I will be attacking with far more than nothing."

Alaric allowed himself a guarded smile. "And I would defend with something, if I had it. I could take this holocam outside and show you the ruins of the battlefield, if you so desired. You may have already seen images of it from the local media. I would even deign to give you a tour of it, but I will not be defending it."

She nodded. From the moment the Wolf Hunters had entered the system, they had been sucking up every local news feed. Anastasia had caught enough of Colonel Colton to last her a lifetime, and sincerely regretted the fact that the woman had survived her fight with the Wolves. The images of the Mudana Refuge battle had been horrific, the field littered with BattleMechs scattered, broken and burning. The news helicopter had kept a safe distance, but did manage to capture blurred images of dispossessed MechWarriors limping from 'Mech to 'Mech, looking for friends, checking for salvage—less human jackals than comrades concerned for comrades. *But the jackals, they would come, too.*

She wondered if Verena was among the survivors, or if she had died in the battle. The news media made it clear that the Wolves had won, but if the Wolves had two Stars available, it was only because those 'Mechs could limp. For all intents and purposes, the 279th Battle Cluster had ceased to exist as a fighting force. The Demons, Djinns and Stormhammers had similarly been pounded. Techs might have been able to cobble together a lance of 'Mechs from the various parts, but nothing from the defenders' force had been left standing.

You did well, Verena, but you might have done better. Anastasia looked up at Alaric's image. "You may, of course, deploy the Fourth Wolf Guards. You have that right."

"And make them feel they are garrison troops? No, Colonel, I would never dishonor them so."

"Then you are abandoning Nusakan?"

"Do not think I am shrinking from a fight with you, Colonel Kerensky. I would gladly fight you, but I am not given leave to do so. As you once did, I follow the dictates of my khan, and I have been recalled."

She raised an eyebrow. "Then the drive to Terra is finished?"

"I do not know, Colonel, but it would be folly to assume it is." Alaric shrugged. "Perhaps the khan, in his wisdom, has seen that Nusakan will not be vital to that effort."

"Of course. And I shall not commit folly."

"Nor shall I." Alaric nodded a salute to her. "I regret not being able to meet you when you arrive, but we are preparing our departure now."

"Pity. I would have given you the chance to ransom back Donovan, as he did you."

Alaric laughed. "*I* was worth a Star, but Donovan? Accountants I can find anywhere. Not one of them would be worth a single bullet in trade."

Anastasia ignored the hiss from the shadows behind her. "I bid you well, then, Star Colonel. I am certain our paths will cross again."

"I am sure they will." He smiled, but his eyes narrowed. "I look forward to repaying your hospitality. Alaric out."

His image faded and she turned slowly to where Ian and Donovan stood. "It would seem, Donovan, that you are not well liked. He called you an accountant."

The Clanner held himself stiffly. "One day, Colonel, you will give me a single bullet, and I will show Alaric how wrong his judgment was."

"I suspect it will take more than *one* bullet, Donovan, but you will get that chance." She waved him away. "Go to your quarters, plot your revenge."

She waited for him to vanish, then looked at Ian. "What do you make of the Wolf withdrawal?"

"Strategically sound. They have lost two prime front-line units and have had other forces nibbled to bits. They must know that the entire Inner Sphere is mobilizing against them. They have overextended, and while very few nations have much love left for The Republic, they would be happy to take worlds under the guise of fighting the Wolves."

"It would seem that is it, truly." Anastasia smiled. "But just in case there is something else going on, we will take possession of Nusakan and prepare to defend it against all comers."

Alaric stalked from the tent that had been set up as a temporary headquarters on the battlefield. A cold breeze had sprung up, blowing smoke and snow through the area. He liked how it obscured the ruins and hid evidence of how close he had come to losing the battle. He had gone in with insufficient strength and had attacked where he perceived weakness. The enemy still had been strong. He had grossly underestimated the depth of guile of which the other side was capable.

But I survived. These lessons are learned.

Other leaders might have seen the lessons. Based solely on the fact that they had *won,* they would conclude their strategy had been sound. Winning a battle did not confer wisdom or superiority on plans. They might vow to do better in the future, then be happy when they reduced casualties by ten percent.

But a wise commander will know what they are thinking, and destroy them.

The only bright spot in the entire affair—aside from being the victor—was that he lost very few pilots. Machines were easier to replace than people, and most all those who died had been marginal anyway. The fact that the others had survived together would build greater unit cohesion, and they had seen him in battle, so knew he was truly a war leader, not an accountant.

Alaric crunched across the snowy field to the hospital tent. Elementals opened the flap for him and he ducked his head to enter. Of the casualties, easily sixty percent were from Verena's force, and they made up the majority of those lying on the dozen cots toward the tent's rear. Alaric passed through a crowd of people with bandaged heads, bloodstained faces, and blankets clutched tightly around them.

He found Verena seated on a cot, holding a man's hand. Alaric recognized the man as her aide, Kennerly. He had numerous cuts, a bandage over his left eye, and wrappings over a chest wound. Tubes were draining out bloody fluid.

She looked up. "I would stand, but . . ."

Alaric shook his head. "Will he recover?"

"Your medical technology has an edge over ours. I hope so."

"I will see to it he has the best of care. Right now, I need to speak with you."

"I don't want to leave him in case . . ."

"I understand."

Verena half smiled, then looked down at Kennerly again. "I do not know if you do. I hated him. He constantly was after me. He would tell me I was a fool. He would tell me that I did not see things. He would refuse to tell me what it was I did not see. Then he stopped."

Alaric nodded. "After you bargained for Nusakan."

Her head came up. "Yes. How did you know?"

"You changed." He pointed to Kennerly. "Do you want to know what he saw?"

"Please."

"You always wanted to be certain you were right. You studied to make no mistakes. You can never, no matter how hard you try, be completely error-free. Kennerly knew that, and he knew the corollary to that."

"What? Tell me."

Alaric laughed and swept a hand from beneath his

cloak to point at the battlefield. "After all this, you do not know? After what happened here, you do not know?"

She shook her head for a second, then stopped. "If you cannot always be right, maybe you just have to be more right than the other guy."

"You almost have it." The Wolf lowered his arm and the cloak shrouded him again. "You have to force the other man to make more mistakes than you do. You almost did that here, and I believe you could do it again."

Verena laughed. "I will never get that chance. My career is done. I was built up to be the heroine of Nusakan, the savior of Prefecture Nine. Now I will be the woman who lost it."

Alaric nodded. "I believe Colonel Colton has already dubbed you 'Defeat's Bride.'"

"Great." Verena scrubbed her free hand over her face. "You defeat her and she becomes a star. You defeat me and I become nothing."

Alaric's cloak opened again and he tossed a loop of cord into her lap. "I can raise you up from nothing."

Shock widened Verena's eyes. "A bond cord?"

"The very same Donovan gave me."

"You would make me a bondsman, a Wolf bondsman?" She fingered the cord slowly. "You would have me fight against my own people?"

"I would have you vanquish the demons that haunt you." Alaric nodded slowly. "Join me. I will train you, and when the time comes, you will use the lessons you have learned to slay the greatest demon of all."

Verena met his stare. "Anastasia Kerensky."

"Exactly."

Lifting her arm, Verena exposed her wrist and placed the bond cord in his hands.

About the Author

Michael A. Stackpole is an award-winning author, game designer, computer game designer and podcaster. In 2006 he and Brian Pulido won the *Fade-In* magazine scriptwriting contest grand prize for their script *Gone*. At DragonCon, Mike's writing podcast, "The Secrets," took the first-ever Parsec Award for writing-related podcasts.

When not writing or podcasting, Mike enjoys indoor soccer and salsa dancing. Both are similar—it's all in the footwork—but for one you get to dress up nicely.

His Web site is www.stormwolf.com. Information about his podcasts can be found there or at www.pod castpen.com.

MECHWARRIOR: DARK AGE

A BATTLETECH® SERIES

The ShadowRun Series

Roc Science Fiction & Fantasy

THE ULTIMATE IN
SCIENCE FICTION AND FANTASY!

From magical tales of distant worlds to stories of
technological advances beyond the grasp of man, Penguin has
everything you need to stretch your imagination to its limits.

penguin.com

ACE
Get the latest information on favorites like
William Gibson, T.A. Barron, Brian Jacques,
Ursula K. LeGuin, Sharon Shinn, and Charlaine Harris,
as well as updates on the best new authors.

ROC
Escape with Harry Turtledove, Anne Bishop,
S.M. Stirling, Simon R. Green, Chris Bunch, Jim Butcher,
E.E. Knight, and many others—plus news on the
latest and hottest in science fiction and fantasy.

DAW
Mercedes Lackey, Kristen Britain, Tanya Huff,
Tad Williams, C.J. Cherryh, and many more—
DAW has something to satisfy the cravings of any
science fiction and fantasy lover.
Also visit dawbooks.com.

*Get the best of science fiction and fantasy
at your fingertips!*